Race to me

A SERIES

H.L. SWAN

COPYRIGHT

This is a work of fiction. Names, characters, businesses, places, events and incidents are either the product of the authors imagination or used in a fictious manner. Any resemblance to actual persons, living or dead, or actual events is purely coincidental.

Copyright © 2021 H.L. Swan

All rights reserved

ISBN: 9798708124173

Mom, this one's for you.

A storm was coming
but that's not what she felt.
It was adventure on the wind
and it shivered down her spine.
                           -   Atticus

FOSTER'S PLAYLIST

1. BON IVER - SKINNY LOVE
2. LORD HURON – THE NIGHT WE MET
3. THE SPILL CANVAS – SO MUCH
4. HARRY STYLES – SHE
5. ALEX & SIERRA – LITTLE DO YOU KNOW
6. SLEEPING AT LAST – TURNING PAGE
7. BRIGHT EYES – FIRST DAY OF MY LIFE
8. LANA DEL RAY – YOUNG & BEAUTIFUL
9. IRON & WINE – FLIGHTLESS BIRD
10. X AMBASSADORS – UNSTEADY
11. THE CINEMATIC ORCHESTRA – TO BUILD A HOME

ONE

Today is going to be perfect, and *nothing* will ruin it! I draw a neon pink checkmark on my calendar, marking the day I've been waiting for.

Using my palms, I smooth my freshly curled hair, making sure that no strands are out of place. I can't afford to not look my best. It's a new environment, after all. One I'm entirely unfamiliar with.

Skirt is pressed, button-up is crisp. With a light sigh, I grab my bags and head out into the warm summer morning.

Bouncing across the pavement, I make sure to give my housekeeper a peck on the cheek. "You look beautiful today, Mrs. Rita!" I gush, twirling my keyring around my manicured nail. She sends me a brilliant smile as I trot down the driveway.

The salty wind catches my hair, attempting to knot it. I pull down the sun visor, checking for any imperfections. Once satisfied, I turn the ignition of my pearl range rover. It hums to life, and I slip out through the open wrought-iron gate.

My car phone rings, breaking me away from my sing along with the radio. "You bitch! You better hurry up and get me."

It's Kate. "About to pull in!" I tell her, laughing when I see her rushing down the driveway.

"Are you nervous?" She stares at my shaking leg while she climbs into the warm leather seat. Her crimson red hair slaps me in the face when she throws her suitcase in the back.

"Ouch!" I squeal, trying not to laugh as she plants herself firmly back in her seat.

"Sorry!" Kate giggles, looking me over with worry while I tap my nails on the leather wheel. "For real, are you nervous?" she asks.

I nod. This will be my first day attending a public school. I had to beg and plead with my father for months after I loathed every minute of my first semester at an all-girls private college. Elementary through high school has always been private, but at least it was co-ed.

I may have done a little more than beg and plead, I may have given him no other choice, but I like to think that he caved. He had rules, of course. It was hard for him because he's always prided himself on keeping me in the best schools. "Education can get you far in life." he would tell me, all the time.

His rules were as follows: I couldn't live on campus, no parties, and I'd better keep my grades up. I jumped on the deal, naturally. I'd do anything to keep from going back to Crestview.

As for Kate, she lives in the dorms, but on certain special occasions, like my first day of school, she'll stay down the street at her parent's house.

"I just don't know anyone." I nervously grin.

Kate's laughter booms through the car. "Skyler, you have nothing to be nervous about. You're literally perfect. Look at you! Everyone is going to love you." She smiles, turning up the radio to drown out my worries.

I take in a deep breath as the ocean springs into view, calming me. Salty air flows through the open windows, surely ruining my hair this time. But I need to breathe in the therapeutic scent of the ocean breeze. Surprisingly, the heat is calm. Not suffocating like a typical August in Florida, but then again, it's only morning.

"You know you have me and Brett," She winks. We've all grown up together. We've just never been to the same school.

An unusual sense of freedom blankets over me as we pull into the University of Miami. Orientation with my parents was interesting but seeing it in full swing is completely different.

I drive past the front lawn in awe. Students dot the grass, soaking in the Florida sun before we all start our day stuck inside.

Diversity flows freely in public schools. Everyone is free to express themselves through fashion. My entire life, I've worn a uniform, and now I can dress how I want. My wardrobe doesn't really go past plaid skirts and dresses, though.

Girls in all black smoke cigarettes, leaning against their cars. The jocks—I'm used to them—wear their lettermen's and play fight on the courtyard. Band and Orchestra are to my left. Endless amounts of vibrant colors shine before me. Normally, it was only the jocks and cheerleaders, then just ... everyone else.

I link my arm through Kate's. "I'm not ready for this first class without you," I groan, wishing we were able to be in every class together. But I'm optimistic; this will be a good thing. I just know it.

She lets out a sweet laugh, tossing her hair over her slender shoulder. "You'll be fine! We have gym together, so that's a plus." Kate winks, bringing me in for a hug in front of the doors to my biology class.

~

The room is empty, and I take my spot at one of the front tables. In orientation, I saw large classrooms with massive pews. This, however, is more like a high school lab, which I prefer. It's much more comfortable, smaller with less distractions.

As the room fills with students, no one sits near me. My stomach aches from the feeling of rejection, but it's only the first day. Things will get better. "Welcome back, students. You're officially sophomores, so no bullshit this semester."

I snicker hearing a teacher curse. That would have

never happened at my old school. My eyes trail down the professor's accusatory finger, landing on a lean and long boy.

"That means you, Foster Jennings. I don't want any trouble." He gives the tattooed boy a pointed look, then his eyes travel the room. "From any of you." The gritty sound of chalk on the board makes me jump. In cursive he writes out, "Human Biology with Professor Dyer."

"I'm going to need you to pair up." The class groans about being given an assignment on the first day and having to immediately start on it. I don't mind, though; I love presentations. I know that's weird, but it's kind of my thing.

My eyes float around, trying to see who my partner will be. Everyone has someone at their table except for me, and—

"Foster, sit with Skyler." The professor tells him. "Welcome to UOM by the way, Ms. Johnson," he adds. I'm so thankful we don't have to go through the embarrassing tasks of telling our life stories to strangers.

I smile back politely, nervous about pairing up with someone that looks so ... edgy? Maybe I'm being judgmental. I'm sure this will be great!

The boy, Foster, rolls his eyes. Lazily sliding his books off the table, he heads towards me. I first notice his height, since he towers over the room; people either look to him or away from him when he walks.

"It's Ghost." he informs the professor, his black hair a disheveled mess that looks like he just woke up, yet also as though he spent hours designing each piece to lay where he wanted it to.

The professor shrugs. "Doesn't matter how many times you tell me that, Foster. Your birth name sticks."

Foster's legs lay languidly under my table. His attention turns to me, a toothpick sticking out from his mouth. My eyes flit to his sharp jawline and the tattoos that decorate his neck.

The black ink matches the obsidian shade of his eyes. He cocks his head, and I give a bright smile, extending my hand. "Skyler," I say. He's the first person besides Kate to acknowledge me, even if I am his forced lab partner.

He takes one look at my outreached hand and gives a crooked grin. "Freckles." he corrects me, his deep voice bleeding into my ears. I retreat my hand quickly and open my book to no particular page. I look down, letting my hair blanket my face.

The professor hands us our assignment, and my eyes graze over the sheet. We get human anatomy, which makes me blush knowing at some point me and Foster will have to discuss the makings of the male and female bodies. In length.

Foster peels the paper from my hands, mulling over the assignment we'll be working on for a month together. He smirks when he reads over the contents.

"This project will be worth thirty percent of your grade in this class, and that's why we're starting it now." Mr. Dyer announces, sitting and thumbing through a book.

I take the sheet from Foster's hands. Thirty percent is huge, and we need to get started immediately. I can't risk my grades plummeting. "So, it looks like we can break this into two par—" I'm cut off when Foster playfully snags the paper away again.

Sighing, I begin to get prepared. Foster directs his hard gaze to me, the corners of his mouth tilting as he observes me pulling out colored pens and notebooks from my bag.

He throws his elbows on the table, planting his hands under his chin. "So, you're new here." he states, taking off his leather jacket and chunking it on the table. I stare at it for a moment. How will we get work done if he's taking up so much space?

"Yup," I smile, eagerly waiting to get started. "I came from Crestview."

"Ah," He grins back, as if he's figured me out. "The posh all-girls campus?" He laughs, nodding his head. "Should have known."

A light scoff escapes me. "What does that mean?"

His tattooed finger touches my diamond bracelet. "Well, this. The matching earrings and your plaid ... skirt. You scream prep school." His condescending tone annoys me. It also intrigues me, but I'm not sure why.

I scoff, pulling my wrist away. "Are you always so judgmental of people you don't know?" I'm surprised by my tone, but that was rude.

He collapses in his chair, folding his muscled arms over his broad chest. "Oh, I know your type. But I can almost guarantee you don't know mine."

"Rude," I mutter under my breath, but he's not wrong.

Foster leans forward, grinning. "What was that,

Freckles?"

"My name is Skyler. Why do you keep calling me that?"

His demeanor shifts from playful to downright stoic in an instant. "It suits you." Foster sits back in his chair, pulling out his phone.

I inch closer, "Won't they take it?"

His expression is confused for a moment, then a grin spreads across his face. "You're not in private school anymore, Freckles."

I ignore the nickname and continue to obsess over our assignment.

TWO

The remainder of class was spent with me gathering information for our project while Foster stayed on his phone, texting. From the looks of his lack of help during class, it seems like I'll be the one handling all the work.

Once the bell rings, I pack up my things and head into the hall, keeping the project papers in my hand to go over them during my next period. I doubt another teacher will assign such an important assignment on the first day.

It's not long before Foster is beside me, his long legs taking short strides to keep pace. "Here's my number," He places a crumpled paper in my hand.

"I have a boyfriend." I lie, not wanting to be rude to him. Why would he even give me his number when he was so rude?

He stops walking, and his black boots squeak against the tile floor. "Does he want to help us with our project, or?" I'm an idiot, and his amused smirk reminds me of that.

I shake my head, a blush of embarrassment burning my cheeks. "I thought I would be the only one doing anything."

He slowly leans forward, plucking the papers from my hands and making my back press against the chilling hallway wall. I have to look straight up to see him.

Foster's neck is craned downward, and his black eyes drink me in. Such an unusual shade for someone's eyes; endless, but also intriguing. A sinister spider is tattooed on his neck, its legs creeping around his skin, seeming to suffocate him. But that's silly; it's just a tattoo. "Why would you think that?" His breath is minty, and it tingles against my skin.

"You didn't seem interested in class." Besides the mint, he smells of smoke, leather, and trouble. The kind of trouble I've never seen in person before. The kind of trouble that would have my parents carrying me back to Crestview if they saw how close we were right now.

I jump a little when he plants his palm against the wall, trapping me in, and leans closer. His gaze travels slowly from my ankles to my eyes, "It's the first day of class. We have plenty of time to get it done." For a moment, everything around us goes still as he looks down at me. I try to read him, and I notice the faintest hint of something lays in his obsidian eyes. But as quickly as it shows, it's gone.

His expression hardens, and the bustling noise of the crowded hallway returns to my mind. "Or you can just do it yourself, little miss perfect." He pushes himself off the wall, turning away from me.

I roll my eyes behind his broad back as he walks away. "Okay, Foster." I try to sound rude, but it comes out in a normal tone. I wish I was more equipped to handle angry, ridiculous people, but I've never had that ability.

His boot hits the ground with a thud. He doesn't turn to look at me when he replies, "It's Ghost." I don't have time to react as he walks off.

Brett catches me off guard, wrapping my body into a tight hug. I wince when his fingers graze my aching ribs. "You okay?" he asks in a concerned tone as I stretch my stiff body. He looks worried about me, but I don't miss the grimace he gives to Foster's back while we walk down the hall.

"Yeah! I fell during practice this weekend." The ache throbs, but nothing a little ice bath won't take care of. "I don't want to fly anymore. I'm too clumsy." I joke.

"Will you be healed enough to cheer for me this weekend?" His smile takes up his whole face, as it always does.

"I'll be good as new." I promise him. I know how excited he is for me to be on the cheer team at his school. We never got to go to each other's games before since private schools only played private, so that's something I'm looking forward to if I have to cheer.

It's something I've done my entire life, and I didn't want to join when I transferred but my mom wasn't having it. I can hear her words of wisdom in my ear even now, "It's a family tradition, honey,' along with, "You know you'll regret not making those bonds."

She's not wrong, of course. I met Kate at a summer cheer camp in elementary school, and we've been inseparable ever since. I just wish she was still into it so I wouldn't be cheering with a bunch of strangers. But I know this is the best way to make new friends, and I'm pretty good at it. I just need to be more careful; a clumsy girl that twirls in the air is a dangerous combination.

As we round a corner, I realize with absolute horror that Foster pulled the paper from my hands before he walked away. I have to get started on that project as soon as I get home. I've never had a bad grade in my life. I won't start now; I can't.

I look around for him, but he's long gone. *Shit.* How do I find him? Look for a motorcycle in the parking lot? Stereotypical, but probably true.

Brett draws me back to attention, "Where's your mind?"

"Huh?" I look up, noticing that we've stopped walking and I was staring into space. I wave my hand, "Trying to figure out how to find that Foster guy."

"Ghost?"

"Yes! Do you know his schedule?" I pull out my notes, "If I could find him before the end of the day, I can get the paper—"

Brett nods, leaning into my hair. "Stay away from him."

"Reason?" I turn to him, my brows pushing together in confusion.

He gestures between us. "People like us and him ...

we don't mix."

"We have a project." I wave the number Foster gave me between us. Brett grabs it, rips it in half, and the contents float to the floor.

"Not anymore. Trust me; he's bad news. You can do the project yourself and stay away from him. He's trouble, Skyler."

I roll my eyes, slamming my book to my forehead a little too hard. "He has the fucking paper, though."

Brett shakes his head, saying, "I can get it back for you."

"I got it, Brett."

Tossing his head back, he throws his hands up. "Don't say I didn't warn you. Let me walk you to your next class, what is it?"

I scan the paper, "Mrs. Parks, Accounting, room 208"

"I got it." He smiles, placing his hand on the small of my back and guiding me towards the glass doors that lead to the courtyard. "I had her last year. she's awesome."

I exhale in relief as we walk across the courtyard, thankful he's familiar with my new teacher. I bask in the sun for a few sweet moments before being rushed into a crowd of moving bodies while we travel the long hallway.

Brett stops at room 208, gesturing to the open door. "I'll meet you here after to bring you to lunch."

I didn't get the chance to meet Mrs. Parks; the poor lady got sick the first week of school. But our substitute didn't even give us homework, so I'm happy about that. When I exit the room, I'm greeted by Brett, and my stomach growls as we make our way to the lunchroom.

Kate soon comes into view, sinking her teeth into a Fuji apple that's as glossy and red as her hair. "I'm starving" She sighs, ushering us along.

My mind wanders off, thinking about the project and the rest of my day. I have gym left and then practice after. I wonder if I'll be able to find Foster before the end of the day.

"Earth to Skyler." I return to the real world, where Kate's hands are waving in my face.

I can't help but laugh, saying, "Sorry, just worrying about classes."

"I was telling you that tomorrow we can meet up, so we can take turns taking you to your classes."

I playfully roll my eyes. "You guys don't have to babysit me. I'll be okay."

Brett chimes in, chucking my chin. "We just want you to be comfortable."

"I'm not a lost puppy." Well, *I am*. But I don't want to bother them.

He looks to Kate, adding, "She's not a lost puppy, but within her first hour here, she's already buddy-buddy with the school shit show."

"Ghost?" Kate inquires, and Brett nods his head. Her eyes widen. Looking over my face, she snorts. "You can't be serious."

Her laugh concerns me. "What's so bad about him?" Besides him not caring about the project but still taking the paper from me, inadvertently making me go insane.

"Ghost is ... well, Ghost. I don't have an issue with him, but you found the one person here that doesn't just *adore* Brett." She fake swoons, throwing the back of her head against Brett's chest. He rolls his eyes at her dramatics.

"What?" I ask, not believing it. Even someone as ... I don't really know how to describe Foster, but everyone loves Brett.

"He doesn't give a shit about anyone or anything besides his precious motorcycle." Brett sneers.

Kate playfully hits his arm, "You're going to have to let go of your hatred for him, dude."

He scoffs, and my eyes widen in inquiry. Kate elaborates, "Freshman year, Brett backed into his bike."

I look to Brett, asking, "Why does that make you hate him?"

Kate snickers. "Ghost beat the shit out of him for it. Brett's never let it go."

My mouth forms an 'O' as we enter the lunch line. The heavenly scent of greasy, cheesy pizza fills the room.

Brett scoffs, tugging on Kate's hair. "Hello? I missed the last game of the season. Coach wouldn't let me play with a busted face. He had it worse, though."

"Yeah, you really got him good." Kate coos, pinching his cheek and turning her face to wink at me.

During gym, Kate and I both regret eating an entire

pizza. "Do you have to stay at the dorms tonight? Can't you come have a sleepover with me?" I give her my best puppy dog eyes.

She shakes her head. "I can't. I have a new roommate I have to meet. I wish I would have just stayed with you last night. Mom was all about family time before I went back to the dorms," She fake yawns. "It consisted of playing monopoly with her and Dax for three hours straight before they finally let me escape to my room.

I sigh in defeat. "Fine, maybe soon?"

"Definitely soon."

After a grueling first day of body sculpting in gym class, I head back to the locker room to throw on my new cheer uniform for practice.

Kate walks in, wiping sweat from her brow. "Why did they have to go so hard on us on the first day?" She groans, holding her stomach. "I'm never eating pizza again."

"I know, and now I have to head to practice." I sigh, unzipping my duffel bag and tugging out my uniform.

She throws her crimson hair into a bun. "Where are your keys?"

I suddenly remember needing to meet Foster. Hopefully, he's still here. "I'll go with you. Just let me get changed,"

She takes in a deep breath, scrunching her nose. "It smells in here. I'll meet you in the parking lot."

Walking into a private stall, I shudder at the

realization of my new uniform; it's a short skirt with a top that has long sleeves but is cut off, showcasing my midriff. I can't wear this.

During practice, we've always just worn whatever, but they wanted us in our uniforms today since our first game is on Friday, and we need to go through our routine. I have to find my coach immediately ... shit. Foster.

Maybe it won't be too bad? Slipping on the uniform, I groan, tugging down the tight material to reveal less skin. My old uniform was a knee-length pleated skirt with a long sleeve, full-length top. This ... is much different. I listen for signs of life in the locker room, stepping out slowly when I don't hear anyone.

I pause when I see a girl standing in front of my stall. She tilts her head to me.

She's short, with a tired-looking face. I smile at her, and she returns the gesture, but it doesn't quite reach her dull blue eyes. Her long blonde hair sweeps across her shoulders, exposing skin dotted with deep bruises that travel along each side of her ribs.

I reach out to her, and she reaches out to me.

I step back into the stall, averting my gaze from the reflection in the bathroom mirror.

Ripping off the uniform, I shove it back into my bag and change.

I can't wear this ... it shows too much.

Hey, I never said my life was perfect ...

Everyone else did.

THREE

I rush to the parking lot, meeting Kate near my car.

"Where's your uniform?" She grabs her suitcase from the back.

My eyes roam the parking lot; Foster's nowhere in sight. *Wonderful.*

Thinking quickly, I flash a smile. "It was too small! I have to find the coach to get another one."

Kate brings me in for a hug, and thankfully her arms are around my shoulders and not my waist. "I'll see you later! Have to go meet this new roommate." Her fake enthusiasm makes me chuckle.

"You better not like her more than me!" I joke as she walks away, wishing it were me who could stay on campus with her.

My sneakers squeak against the gym floor as I rush into practice. I'm the last one here, by the looks of it. "Why aren't you in uniform?" Coach Parks checks me off on her clipboard, looking unhappy.

I give my brightest smile, "I was wondering," I look away, sighing when I see my teammates glaring back at me, angry that I'm slowing practice down. "Are there any more uniforms? I don't feel comfortable with how short the top is."

I wait patiently as she takes in my request. Finally, she leans in so the other girls can't hear, saying, "I never liked those when I cheered either. Here. Medium?" She hands me a new top from a nearby cabinet.

Air releases from my lungs in waves. I didn't know what I would do if my only option was the other top. "Thank you."

I change, returning to practice and going through the routines until I can barely stand. I'm already worn out from gym, and I should have never signed up; it isn't mandatory for my major. But it was the only way me and Kate could have a class together.

After practice, I drag myself to the parking lot, not bothering to change out of my uniform. Cracking open the back hatch, I throw my cheer bag in.

"Not only does she drive a range rover, but she's also a cheerleader."

I roll my eyes before I turn towards Foster's deep baritone. Thankfully, he's still here even after school's ended for most.

He's now in a white T-Shirt, but still in dark jeans

and boots. Black splotches smother his clothes, face, and hands. "Why are you so dirty?" I ask, surprised.

With a crooked smile, he places his grimy hands on the roof of my car. "I'm here for mechanical engineering, so when someone breaks down, they call me."

"Oh," I imagine him working on cars. His muscles flexing while he sweats underneath the hood. *What?* Why am I even thinking of that? "I'm actually glad you're here. I was looking for you earlier."

Foster slides closer to me, his hand still placed on the hood. "Missed me?"

His cocky tone earns a yawn from me. "You took the assignment." In reality, him being so close makes my heart race.

"I did that on purpose so you would see it's not the end of the world."

I throw my head back, sighing loudly. How after one day of knowing him can he annoy me so much? "Can I have it back?"

"Tomorrow,"

Damnit. "Why?"

The way only half of his smile shows, crooked ... dangerous. "Because tonight, you're busy."

"With?" My heart races. Is he about to say I'm busy with him? Is Foster going to ask me to hang out? Would I be ab—

"With whatever rich people do on Monday nights," He deadpans, sliding away from me. I bite my lip, feeling foolish for my thoughts. "Relax, Freckles. We have plenty of time."

His eyes travel down the length of my body and surprisingly, I don't mind. I think he enjoys messing with me. Annoying me.

"I'll relax when it's finished. Just let me get started," I extend my hand, but he shakes his head, a boyish grin softening his hard edges.

"It—"

"Foster!" A new guy, one equally covered in grease, comes towards us. A guy like Foster, but not as strikingly tall. Tattooed and in all black, light-skinned, and holding a helmet in his hands. Quickly, Foster fumbles through his backpack and practically tosses the assignment towards me, giving up the cat-and-mouse game abruptly.

"I'll see you tomorrow, okay?" He walks away, not turning back to look at me as he greets his friend with a shake. The two walk off, but when the guy turns back to look at me, Foster slaps his large hand across his friend's shoulder, directing his attention forward.

I can't hear what they're saying when they walk towards their bikes.

As I said, stereotypical but true.

Foster's is matte black, and twisted metal wraps around the frame in a threatening manner. The only sign of color, a small speck of bright blue, lays on his gas tank, but I can't make out what the shape is. His friend's bike is a bright crimson red, reminding me of Kate's hair.

They remind me of something.

Fire and Ice.

Foster climbs on the bike after putting on his jacket and throws a black helmet over his head. He makes eye contact with me. Obsidian, unreadable eyes gaze at me for a few silent moments until they're covered by his shield.

As if summoned by the loud sound of humming bikes, two girls walk up to them. Carrying their own helmets, a brunette saddles up on the red bike.

A girl with long black hair with strips of neon green slides in behind Foster, wrapping her lanky arms around his leather-clad chest. She glances at me, tilting her head against his broad back to flash a quick smile.

I look away.

With that, they speed off.

The drive home is quick, and my stomach growls the moment I inhale the delicious aroma of a juicy pot roast that's been simmering all day, wafting through the house.

I know what roast means.

"Mrs. Rita!" I sigh, sliding onto the barstool while she makes me a plate. I'd do it myself, but she'd refuse.

Her smile brightens the already too bright kitchen, the light making her grey hair shimmer. "How was your first day, honey?"

My nails grind against the marble countertop as I hastily retrieve my fork. Roast is my favorite, so it always comes before bad news. "It was good. Practice sucked, but what can you do?"

"Quit," she states, then shakes her head. "Sorry, I know that isn't possible."

It gets quiet, and I point to my plate. "When?"

A frown lays on her normally cheerful face.

"Tomorrow."

Mrs. Rita is a devoted mother and grandmother, so I know the fact that my parents are rarely around bothers her.

Even when they're home, they're still not here.

Her only reservations about my parents are their lack of time in my life. I don't want her to know any more, and I don't want her to know the truth. But the solemn look on her face tells me she does, especially when she makes my favorite meal as a pick me up when she warns me of their impending arrival.

Luckily, everyone hides their secrets well in our glass castle. My father would never lose his temper in front of other people, even the 'help', as he calls her.

Dick.

As usual, she tries to make things easier for me, which only makes me feel guilty. "So tonight, we binge Netflix!"

Her ideas make me smile, but all I can think of is the work I need to get started on. "I wish! But my biology professor gave an assignment that's worth thirty percent of our grade."

"On your first day! That's unreasonable; too much pressure for one student so early in the semester." She plants her hands firmly on her wide hips.

I look at the countertop, grinning for whatever reason. "Well, it's not just me."

Rita can tell by my voice; I can't hide anything. "So, you have a partner?" She inquires, her smile widening. "And it's a boy."

"Why would you think that?"

Her rosy cheeks bounce with a grin. "He must be cute."

"Rita,"

She pinches my face, laughing. "What? You're blushing!"

"He's cute ... but he's also irresponsible, and impossible, and covered in grease." I ramble.

Plus, I don't know him, and I honestly don't even know why I'm talking about him.

Her brows rise. "Grease?"

I wave her off, blushing. "Long story."

"Niña Dulce!" *Sweet girl.* "You're never one to judge someone. What's gotten into you?"

I shake my head, grabbing a cookie from the jar. "I know," A sigh escapes my lips, and I add, "But he really is impossible."

Rita laughs, grabbing a cookie for herself. "I say it's a crush."

Ignoring her I stand. "Dinner was delicious. Thank you," The accusing grin doesn't leave her face. "I take it back. He's not cute." I lie, trying to make her innocent interrogation stop.

I'm so thankful for her; the one good thing my parents have done is to hire Mrs. Rita. She's like the fun aunt I never had.

I retreat to my room, looking over the assignment in my hands. Foster's fingers left black smudges, and the paper smells slightly of grease.

I set it on the desk in my room and get started,

working long into the night.

Rita peeks her head in my door around eleven. "I'm going to bed, honey. Let me know if you need anything."

"Goodnight, Mrs. Rita!" I call out, wishing for her to always stay but at the same time wanting her to leave so she can spend time with her husband.

It's people in Rita's situation who make me look around at my big house and fancy things and be thankful, even if it comes at a cost. I've thought about leaving, but where would I go?

If I didn't have her, I don't know how I would stay sane.

Keeping this facade of the perfect family up is draining, especially when it only benefits my parents.

Having the perfect daughter and two parents who are happily married living in the perfect home.

I'm the broken daughter with two parents who only married for power and status, and we live in a glass castle that's ready to shatter at a moment's notice.

Sometimes ... I want to be the one who shatters it.

FOUR

"Still mad at me?" Foster slides into his seat next to me in biology class. His ripped black jeans catch my attention. A short sleeved black T-shirt shows off his tattoo; a snake coiling on his forearm, ready to strike.

I don't look up from my work. "No,"

"Why do you look so angry?" he asks carefully, his head peeking to look past the hair that blankets my face.

My parents are coming home today. "I'm not. Want to see what I've done so far?"

A boyish smirk plays on his face when he says, "So far? I thought you'd be done by now. It's been what," He leans closer to me. "One whole night?"

I roll my eyes, secretly welcoming his sarcastic attitude. "Funny. Here."

I hand him the first part of our project, a diagram of the male and female human bodies. He shakes his head, a mischievous glint in his eye.

"So, I broke it into four parts," I point to the pink ink on my notebook. "I figured I'll handle human anatomy, and you can have ... reproduction." I ignore his smirk.

"Why can't we work on sex together?" Foster's minty breath tingles my neck. He's that close. I scoot away, swallowing the lump in my throat.

"You're impossible."

Foster leans back, relaxed. "What? It's always better with two."

My head dives into my hands. "We're never going to get this done."

Professor Dyer is busy buried in his book. Foster gives me a confused expression, asking, "Why do you need it done so fast? You *do* know we have plenty of time, right?"

"Well, if I fail anything, I'm going to be shipped back to Crestview."

He thinks about this for a moment. "Why did they send you here if they're hell-bent on getting you back there?"

I look around the room. "They didn't send me here. I gave them no choice."

Foster's eyes widen at my confession. His no doubt rule-breaking side is excited. "How did you give them no choice?"

"I withdrew when they told me no." *And I paid the price.*

He nods his head in approval, his black hair dancing above his sharp brows. "Okay, why didn't they just re-enroll you?"

I laugh, remembering. I explain to him in detail the events of that night,

"I waited until a very, *very* important dinner party to make my announcement. One of their friends was like, 'Skyler, are you excited for your sophomore year at Crestview?' and I said, 'Actually, my parents are sending me to UM this year.' Their heads snapped to attention, and my dad was fuming. 'Is that so?' their friend asked, and they were super shocked. My father told them, 'Yes. We wanted her to be more well versed with a larger school.' Obviously, he lied."

I look to the window, taking a break from the story. I'm also remembering what happened after they left. My ribs ache thinking about it. He knew he couldn't change his 'decision', or people would talk. So, he set the 'rules', and that was that. It was ridiculous to me that both of my parents attended public schools but were so hell-bent on me going private, another form of control I assume. Another thing to brag about to their friends.

Foster bites the end of his black pen. "Rebel."

"Hardly," I remember the repercussions from it. "I got in trouble."

He scoffs, "Oh no! Did they take your Range Rover away? Ban you from teatime at the golf course?"

"I don't play golf." I roll my eyes at him but laugh when he chucks my chin.

"For real, I don't mind doing this with you. Why don't I come over to your mansion this weekend?"

My eyes widen at the thought of Foster in my room, laying on my bed, talking about how sex works. My cheeks heat at the thought. "Can't this weekend," I don't know when my parents are leaving again, but it shouldn't be long. "Why don't we go to your house?"

"Can't. Off limits," He looks away, stopping that idea.

"Why?" I ask, growing curious.

He shakes his head, his gaze growing dark. "Stop the inquiry, Freckles."

Fine. "Well, I'll let you know by the end of the week what day works for me." I suggest, and he nods. I still, my lips stretching into a thin line. "Wait. How did you know I live in a mansion?" The thought alarms me.

Foster snickers, toying with the corner of our biology paper. "I didn't."

I stand in front of room 208, excited to meet my accounting teacher. This is my most important class, since Accounting is my major. *Yay.* But Brett said she was sweet, so this should be fun.

I'm the first student that arrives in the room, and the teacher sits at her desk, thumbing through a large stack of paperwork. "Mrs. Parks?"

She nods her head, not looking up. "I'm Skyler," I tell her.

"That's good." She still doesn't look up, and her brows crease while she concentrates on her papers.

"So, I guess I'll go—" I walk backward, throwing my thumbs awkwardly at the desks. "—Sit down." I finish.

"I don't know why you like her so much." I point to the door as Brett walks me away from Accounting.

He shoots me a suspicious glare, "Mrs. Parks? She's fucking amazing."

I shrug. "Maybe she's having an off day. She didn't even acknowledge me."

"Maybe," Brett looks at me wearily, asking, "Can I talk to you about something?"

"Of course!" I say immediately. He looks so serious. Unusually serious. "What's up?"

"So—"

"What's up bitches?" Kate cuts us off, slinging her arms around our necks. I look to Brett for him to continue, but he gives a faint shake of his head.

Practice ran late again, but I was thankful for the delay because when I got home *their* cars were parked in the driveway.

I open the door to find my mom sitting in her chair, sipping on a glass of white wine. "You're late." *Nice to see you too.* She flicks her manicured nail at me, ordering, "Get dressed. Guests will be here shortly."

I creep upstairs to my room, going to the formal section of my walk-in closet. My hands trail on a black, floor-length gown. After showering and getting ready, I head back downstairs. Brett sits in the living room, grinning from ear to ear. "Nice dress."

"Shut up," I snicker, "You know how they are." *Well, sort of.* I look at his black suit and fix his tie for him. "I didn't know your family was coming over tonight."

He shrugs. "Yeah, last-minute thing, I guess. Ready to go in?"

I look towards the dining room, not wanting to see my dad. The last time he was here was *that* night. "Sure," I plaster on a smile, not wanting Brett to know how scared I am to simply walk into another room of my own home.

FIVE

This dinner is already stabbing at my nerves. My mother is talking happily with Veronica, Brett's sweet mom. My father is twirling a stiff drink in his hands, the ice clinking against his glass while he discusses business with David, Brett's dad.

My father hasn't even acknowledged me since we sat at the table, except for once when the first course was served, and he cut his eyes to me because my elbows were on the table.

"What is up with you?" Brett leans over, poking my side to make me laugh. He doesn't realize the gesture sends a shooting pain through my side that radiates to my core.

I continue to aimlessly push roasted vegetables around my plate, uninterested in fake small talk and ridiculous outfits. Why can't we be like normal families that eat dinner on the couch, snuggled up watching a movie?

"Earth to Sky?"

"Sorry," I feign a smile. "Just worried about school."

His wide, all-American smile teases on his lips. "Nothing to worry about. We're a lot laxer than Crestview."

Distant chatter interrupts our conversation. "Brett here has scouts coming to the game this Saturday." David announces, looking proudly at his son with a beaming smile.

My dad nods his head, knowing full well what that could mean for Brett. "Impressive," He takes a sip of his drink, his own glory days likely mulling in his mind. "I'm sure they heard about the scouts watching when you were in high school. It's only a matter of time before you're picked up for the NFL." His tipped grin shows interest, but I know he doesn't care. As long as the dinner goes smoothly and we all look the part, that's all that matters.

And here they go, with the bragging. Brett doesn't talk about it, but I know his parents put him under a lot of pressure too; he hides the stress well behind his shiny smile. The gesture is a mirror of mine, and another reason why me and Brett get along so well, even if he doesn't know the truth.

"Yes, sir," He tips his water back, and Mrs. Rita quickly fills the glass before retreating to the kitchen. "I'm a few years away from NFL drafts, but I think they're starting the lookout now."

Mom chimes in, her speech slurred from the bottle of wine she devoured earlier, "Skyler here has just been going on and on about cheering for you at your games."

She looks between us, smiling. "You two would be quite the pair." *Seriously?* I can see the twinkle in her eyes, but it's muffled by the void of what marrying for status means, even the status of a cheerleader and football player.

Truly, Brett would be a great boyfriend, but it's not like that with us.

I'll set the scene of the twinkle behind my mother's eyes. My father was the captain of the football team in high school and valedictorian. My mom did varsity cheer since freshman year, and she was prom queen alongside my father, who was prom king. A prime example of two individuals who peaked in high school and have been holding the flame ever since, dying to not let it burn out.

They want me to recreate their perfect charade.

As they discuss drafts, work, and other meaningless things, I zone out. I nod at the parts I need to and ignore the rest.

I honestly don't know what's gotten into me lately, but I am so sick of it. Normally, I'm positive and carefree, but these past few weeks have changed me slightly.

It all started when I mentioned to my parents during summer break that I loathed my all-girls private college and wanted to go somewhere more open. Somewhere bigger.

I don't go to parties, I'm a straight-A student, and I don't hang out with boys. Simply, I've never defied my parents, and I found out quickly why I shouldn't.

When they told me no, I looked in the mirror and thought to myself, like I normally do, that I shouldn't be questioning them. I mean, look at everything I have; all these opportunities are available to me because of their wealth.

Most kids only dream of the kind of life I lead, but the moment Mom sat me down and told me the only reason that I was going to an all-girls college was to collect a meaningless degree until they married me off to Mr. and Mrs. Hollingsworth's son, I broke.

It's not that I hate Warren Hollingsworth; I'm sure he doesn't even know of their master plan. I just don't believe my parents should dictate how my life plays out. I'm an adult, and I will marry for love when I find the right man.

The next day, I called and canceled my upcoming semester for Crestview, effective immediately. I signed up for Miami State and didn't look back. When I told them, it was during one of their fancier dinners, with their most influential friends, the Hollingsworth's.

I knew they couldn't stop me if I played it off like it was their idea. I looked at everything in a different light at that point, with my unknowing future husband sitting next to me.

It was the wrong choice. When they left, Dad's immediate reaction was to yank me from the chair by my hair. I looked to Mom as I was being dragged across the hardwood floor into the living room, but she simply shook her head and walked away.

With a few quick jabs to my ribs, I was left with dark bruises on each side, and that wasn't the first time.

They couldn't deal with their perfect daughter crumbling their perfect life.

"Honey," Mom's voice snaps me from my thoughts, and my eyes trail towards her voice. The table is empty, and I hadn't even realized anyone got up. "Come to the kitchen. Veronica made apple pie."

I tip-toe across the marble floors, my heels tapping against them while my dress flows around me. Her and Mrs. Miller are chatting while Rita cuts the pie and plates it. Couldn't they have cut it themselves? David is on his phone in the living room—I can hear him—and my father is with Brett on the porch. His hand is firmly planted on his shoulder as they talk about something that surely entails football.

Rita hands me a plate, always giving me the biggest piece with a grin. I slip a bite into my mouth, saying, "It's delicious, Mrs. Miller."

"It's wonderful isn't it?" Mom gushes, then leans in so Veronica can't hear, adding, "Be careful with that or you won't fit into your uniform."

That's the longest conversation we've had in months. I place the dish back on the table, losing my appetite. "I'm not feeling too well. I'm going to go lie down."

The house goes quiet after an hour. That is, until Rita slips into my room like a secret agent, carrying a plate of warm apple pie that she surely heated in the oven with a side of cold milk. "Here's a little late-night snack." She gives me a knowing look, indicating she'd heard everything.

I give her a tearful hug, and she sits with me while I eat. "I don't know why she's like that." She moves the fallen hair from my face, cupping my cheek. "But you're every bit as perfect as a flower, Skyler." Her accent is warm like the pie, and it heals my heart.

I shrug, not wanting her to think it's a normal thing. "I'm fine. She's just looking out for me."

Rita hesitantly nods her head, patting my hair in the process. She exits, and as soon as my head hits the silk pillowcase, my phone dings.

Unknown Number: 'You up?'

Another text comes in.

'Never mind, it's nine … You probably went to sleep hours ago.'

I don't need to ask, but I do anyway.

Me: 'Who is this?'

Unknown: 'It's me, Freckles.'

For some reason, my heart flutters in my chest.

Me: 'How did you get my number?'

Foster: 'I know people.'

Me: 'Right … what's up?'

Foster: 'Did you figure out what day I can come over?' Immediately, another text comes through. 'Since we just have to have this shit done so soon.'

Me: 'Haha.'

I can't think of anything better to say.

Foster: 'Does Saturday work?'

Me: 'Can't … I have a game.'

Foster: 'Skip it.'

Me: 'I wish.' No, erase that. 'I can't. What about Sunday at your place?'

Foster: 'For the hundredth time, my place is off-limits. We'll figure this out tomorrow. Try and pencil me in your busy schedule.'

Me: 'Night, Foster.'

Foster: 'Ghost.'

Me: 'Foster.' I add a laughing emoji at the end.

Another text comes in.

Brett: 'Your dad told me to keep an eye on you. Wanted to give you a heads up since I didn't get to talk to you.'

Of course he did.

Me: 'Thanks for letting me know.'

Brett: 'I'll give him stellar performance ratings every Friday.' That makes me laugh outright.

Then, I remember something.

Me: 'What were you gonna ask me at school?'

The bubbles appear, then disappear a few times before he finally replies.

Brett: 'I forgot.'

Right before I drift off to sleep, my tired eyes read a new text.

Foster: 'Actually, plans changed. I won't be at school for a couple of days, but I'll see you in class on Friday.'

For some reason, the thought of Foster not being in class the rest of the week bothers me ... and I don't know why.

Me: 'Where will you be?'

Foster: 'Damn, gonna miss me already?'

Me: 'Definitely not. I'll have the whole desk to myself. More room to get work done without your jacket taking all the space.' I wonder if my reply is good ... Did it make him laugh? Why am I thinking about this so much?

Foster: 'Night, Sky.'

SIX

"What is it with you and your obsession with lattes?"

I sip on my creamy drink, ignoring Kate's judgmental glare. "I'll have you know that this keeps me alive." I hold up my cup while we walk onto campus.

Kate smirks, tossing her crimson hair over her shoulder. "From all that studying you do?"

"Yes," I reply, smiling. "And cheer, plus gym with you before that."

"Hm," She taps her chin, looking mischievous. "Want to do something fun this weekend?"

"Can't, I'm—"

"—Studying. Yeah, I know, but you've moved up in the world, Sky. We have this big old campus. You need your introduction to the real college experience."

"I have a game this weekend." I grip the cup tighter in my hand, inhaling the warm cinnamon and sweet vanilla. "Plus, I go to Brett's Frat parties."

"That was once, and I forced you," Kate laughs. "Doesn't count."

We pass by tall brick buildings. Students flutter around us, trying to get to class. It's so insanely busy around here, I wonder if we'll be late.

Hopefully, it's something calm. "So, where would you like to go then?"

With a calm shrug, she turns around and walks backward, facing me. "How about Bike Night?"

My eyes widen in surprise. "What's that?"

Kate chuckles, placing her hands on her hips. "You really do need to get out more. Every weekend, everyone goes to the strip and they race. It's really fun. I've only been a few times, but I think you'd like it."

My head tilts back in laughter; she knows I never go to the strip. Influential people aren't allowed there, or whatever bullshit my parents said. "Why would that be something I'd like?"

Twirling her hair, she heightens her voice. "Because Ghost is there,"

I try not to spill my coffee. "And?"

"And you like him. If I would have known you were into the whole bad boy vibe, I would have taken you years ago!"

I play off her accusation with a chuckle. "I don't even know him."

Finally, we reach the courtyard. Kate hops onto a short brick wall. Our classes don't start for another ten minutes. "You don't have to know someone to want them in bed."

"Kate," I snap, rolling my eyes. "It's not like that."

She nods, gesturing up and down my body. "If it's not like that, then why are you wearing this?"

"What?" I fake innocence, knowing full well that my outfit had been specifically chosen to impress Mr. Tattoos and Obsidian Eyes. I can't get him out of my head, and I don't know why. He's just stuck there, and I haven't seen him all week.

He's finally back today.

Kate hops off, circling around me like a flaming vulture. "Beach waves, minimal make-up, but no foundation." I didn't want to cover my freckles, but I don't tell her that. "Short summer dress, but still innocent. I guarantee you that you changed in the car, so your mom didn't see."

I sigh, growing annoyed; she was already gone shopping for the day when I left. "Are you in the CIA? It's just clothes."

Kate nods, narrowing her eyes. "Clothes specifically picked out for the mysterious bad boy on campus."

"Again, it's not like that."

She shakes her head. "I don't care; I think it's hot. Sweet innocent girl meets the dangerous, tattooed college boy. It would make a good smutty novel."

"I'm peacing out of this convo!"

As I walk away, Kate yells, "Bike Night. Don't forget!"

I raise my hand, waving her off. "Not going!"

Foster slides into his seat next to me in biology class, throwing his leather jacket onto the table. "Did you miss me?"

"Hardly," I scoff, pushing it away. "You do know we live in Miami, right? It's like a million degrees."

He shrugs, a crooked smile playing on his lips. "Better to be hot riding than risk scraping your body if you fall." He moves his jacket over the back of his chair. "Plus, girls love a man in all black." Foster winks, and I roll my eyes.

With that, we dive into work. I handle the notes, and we spend a good portion of the class period working together in sync but in silence. Which is actually nice.

Foster's eyes graze over my body, a crooked grin taking over his face. "You look pretty."

"Huh?" I ask, instantly blushing. "No joke about my clothes?"

"You're still pretty even though you hide it under your pressed shirts and skirts." His inked finger grazes the thin straps of my dress. "At least you didn't cover up your freckles."

I can't explain my immediate draw to him. Maybe I sense something in him that reminds me of myself. Maybe I'm envious of his freedom and the way he speaks his mind. Something I've never been allowed to do.

Foster takes a sip of my latte without warning. His lips curve into a smile when I glare him down. "What? I don't have cooties."

Rolling my eyes, I pull the cup away from him. "You don't want to see me without my full dose of caffeine."

"Fair enough,"

I tilt the cup, missing my lips. "Shit." The remaining contents spill all over my bright white dress. "Damnit! It's only first period. What am I going to do?"

"Clumsy," Foster chides, reaching behind him to drape his leather jacket over me. It swallows me whole. "Yup, you're so short it'll be like a second dress." He laughs, chucking my chin when I look over at him.

"Thank you," I say, flustered by the strong scent of his cologne hugging me. "You won't need it today?"

"I'll meet you in the parking lot after school." He pulls out a fresh notepad and an unopened pack of pens. "Please tell me you didn't already finish the project while I was away."

"Woah, I'm impressed you got school supplies just for this." He ignores my remark with a scrunched nose, but the gesture is playful. Far from the usual stoic demeanor I've seen from him over my first week here. "Saturday night works for me." My parent's flight leaves during my first big game. Go figure. They're going to Aruba. I could have gone, but they didn't invite me.

He shakes his head, and black shaggy hair dances above his eyes from the movement. "While I'm impressed that you're brave enough to have me alone with you in your room on a Saturday night, I'll have to pass."

"Why is that brave?" I ask.

He goes to speak but stops himself with a shake of

his head. "I'm busy that night."

Oh. "The race thingy?"

His back stiffens. As he straightens up, I'm reminded of his height. "How did you know about that?" The way he's looking down at me, it feels like an interrogation.

I gulp, my eyes going wide. "Kate,"

He relaxes, returning to doodling in his notebook. "Okay, well, it's called Bike Night, and you're not coming."

I didn't say I was, but his harsh tone bothers me. "Why not?"

"You just don't belong in that scene."

Okay? "But you do?"

Foster nods. "Yes. It's exactly where I belong."

I scoff. "It's a free country. I can go wherever I want."

He looks me dead in the eye. "If I see you there, I will personally throw you onto my bike and take you home. That's a fucking promise."

What's so bad about it that he doesn't want me to go? Or is it that he's embarrassed to be seen with the 'perfect' rich girl around his friends?

"I'm going." I argue, keeping my voice level.

"I'm not playing around, Skyler." Foster puts major annunciation on the full use of my name. It bothers me, and I don't know why. "I don't want to see you there."

"You know, I thought we were cool." I nearly laugh at my stupidity. "I thought maybe we could be friends."

"You thought wrong," His tone is void of emotion,

like he could care less that he's talking to me.

"Whatever, Foster."

He scoffs, raising his voice when he snaps, "It's fucking Ghost." Students look and hushed whispers circulate the room. I'm so heated that I don't care. Dyer is too busy on his laptop that he simply shushes the class without acknowledging anything else.

Without warning, Foster storms out of the classroom. The bell rings right then, and I gather my things slowly. Why is he so hot and cold? Why does he not want me to go? The devil on my shoulder is telling me to, but another, angrier part of myself is whispering to not waste my time.

I don't want this stupid jacket reminding me of Foster and his shit attitude all day. I throw it on his empty side of the desk, defying my own rule of no jackets on the table, and I toss my belongings into my bag.

I stand with every intention of walking out of the room and leaving his stupid jacket there ... but I'm covered in coffee and it does smell kind of nice.

―――

"So, is it official?" Brett asks me as we head towards Kate.

I give him a confused expression. "Is what official?"

"Normally, when a guy gives a girl his letterman, they're dating. I guess with delinquents they give you leather jackets instead."

I scoff, retorting, "That sounds like high school,

Brett. Also, I'm not his girl. I spilled coffee on myself." I open it up and showcase the brown sticky mess on my white cotton dress.

He stifles a laugh. "I'll never understand how you cheer. You've always been clumsy as shit."

˜

The remainder of the day drags on, and before I head to the parking lot, I change into my uniform for practice, so I don't have to sport a soiled dress after I give Foster back his jacket.

The sun blares down, making me sweat while I lean against my car and wait for him to show. After ten minutes, the girl with black and neon green streaks in her hair comes bouncing over. Her hand is out, and she doesn't say a word.

I smile at her, confused. "What's up?"

She motions with her hand again, holding it out further. "Can I have it?"

"What?" My voice rises to an unfamiliar octave, matching the contorted expression on my face.

She taps her thick leather boots against the concrete, clearly irritated that I can't read her mind. "Ghost's jacket,"

I can't help the laugh that escapes my lips. "He's a big boy. Why can't he get it himself?"

She twirls her green nails around her hair, adding, "He's busy getting dressed." The devilish smirk on her face leaves little to be desired, and the disheveled look of her cut-off shirt mixed with tangled hair tells me exactly why.

I take it off and hand it to her without a word.

She graces me with an eye roll before stomping away.

I'm not going to practice today. Fuck that.

I don't know why I'm so mad; I literally don't know him. What I *do* know is that he can't tell me what to do.

I yank out my phone.

Me: 'I'll pick you up after my game tomorrow. We're going to Bike Night.'

Kate: 'That's my girl.'

SEVEN

The stadium lights beam onto the lush green football field. Illuminating the crowded grandstands. I didn't think I would be this nervous, but everything is just so much bigger than my old school. The bleachers are packed, and the crowd is already roaring, excited for the game.

The players rush out from behind the sign, ripping open the hours me and the other cheerleaders spent painting the school's mascot on the giant banner. Our pom poms rustle in our hands when they run through the field.

Brett gives me his all-American smile as he runs by. A few of the girls giggle when he waves.

We start our routine, and the crowd goes wild while the guys make play after play. I find myself searching the stands for Foster, but it's wishful thinking. I don't think he would be caught dead here. Besides, his rude girlfriend made it very clear that he's taken, and the longer I think about my wonderful encounter with her, the more my blood boils.

Lifting my mood is Kate, who's sitting in the front row. She mocks me playfully as I belt out cheer after cheer; she knows I don't want to be here, but she also hears me talk about how much I love cheering in front of other people. It's exhausting to always have a smile on your face. To always cheer for someone else when you wish, for once, someone would cheer for you.

I robotically repeat the spirited chants that I memorized during practice and before I know it, the game is over. Brett comes rushing to me, wrapping me in his arms after a big win. "You're my good luck charm."

With his helmet in his hands, he places a sweaty kiss on my cheek. "Ew!" I laugh, pushing him off me. "Good game, Brett."

"Picture!" Kate yells, rushing onto the field. "We need to document this."

Brett slings his arm over me, his helmet slack in his hands. I stand on my tip toes and plaster on a smile big enough to match his. She snaps a few pics, one in which he kisses my cheek again.

Kate checks the time and slides her phone back into her pocket. "Okay, we've got to go."

Brett throws his arms over each of our shoulders. His uniform is hard and hurts against my side. "You ladies coming to the frat to celebrate?" he asks, obviously surprised.

I grin, completely forgetting about his parties after a winning game. "Uh—"

"Nope, honorary girls' night." Kate chimes in, saving the day. I have an inkling suspicion that Brett knows Foster is at Bike Night, and he would literally force us not to go if he found out.

With a shrug, he gives me one final glance. "Your loss," As he runs away, he yells out, "I'll see you guys Monday!"

"Locker room?" I suggest, and Kate nods.

Luckily, the girls clear from the locker rooms quickly to head to the after party. "I brought you a change of clothes." Kate tells me from the other side of the shower. It's going to be tricky getting out and her not seeing my ribs.

I quickly lather the shampoo on my scalp. "It's fine; I've got my own clothes."

Her laugh booms through the desolate locker room. "No, you've got preppy Crestview clothes."

I throw my head back, letting the water drench my hair. "That doesn't even make sense Kate. We wore uniforms."

My freshly-ironed cardigan and skirt magically fly over the shower curtain, landing in a heap at my feet and quickly turning into a soaked mess. "Whoopsies!" Kate giggles.

"You bitch!" I yell, but I laugh too. I guess a change of pace will be good. Hopefully, it's not something too revealing.

―――

"Nope. I'm not wearing this."

Kate hunches her shoulders over as I look at my reflection in the all too familiar bathroom mirror.

"You are fucking hot," she argues. "Own it."

The tight black dress stops mid-thigh, and the boots rise to my knees. "I look like a prostitute version of Ariana Grande."

She flips her hair, saying, "Well, you like Ariana."

"True," I agree, studying myself some more. I don't want to risk going to my house for another change of clothes. My parent's flight left about an hour ago, but it's the opposite way of the strip. "Screw it. What's it gonna hurt?"

"That's the spirit." Kate retouches her makeup while I start mine, being careful to not get anything on the dress.

My phone chimes, and a text comes through.

Foster: 'You and your boyfriend looked cute tonight.'

Boyfriend? Does he mean Brett? Was he here? I don't reply. Instead, I put mascara on. Another message comes through.

Foster: 'Gonna leave me on read? Okay, Sky.'

I sigh, tossing my phone into my bag. Kate whistles, saying, "What's got you worked up?"

Shaking my head, I spritz on some perfume. "Nothing, I'm ready. So, what's this like?"

We head down the empty hallway. The school is so different at night, it's peaceful. Absent of the chaotic noises of hundreds of students shuffling to get to class on time. "I've only been a couple of times, but it's pretty straightforward. They race, we drink, then the cops break it up." She shrugs.

I stiffen. "I don't want any trouble, Kate."

With a laugh, she twirls her crimson hair. "We don't get in trouble, they do. Unless," A mischievous grin spreads across her lips. "They outrun them."

I try to imagine myself running from cops, and my heart thumps in my chest at the idea of something so dangerous. I could never.

I pull out my phone once more on the way to my car. There are no more texts, but I see where Foster saw me and Brett looking cute: Instagram. We look like the popular couple in high school, and stadium lights beam behind us as Brett kisses my cheek. My palm is flat against his chest, and a manufactured smile sparkles on my face.

Could Foster perhaps be a little jealous? I double tap the photo and leave a heart emoji for good measure.

We soon pull up to Bike Night. Cars and motorcycles are scattered around, and people flood the strip. Warm Miami summer heat sweeps across my face when I open my car door.

As soon as my heels hit the dark pavement, I cut my head to the mechanical sound of roaring thunder to my left.

With every intention of making my presence known to Foster that I'm here, I scope the area for him. He damn sure can't tell me I'm not allowed to come to Bike Night when he doesn't even have enough respect for me to get his jacket back on his own.

    Kate fixes her dress, checking her red lipstick out in the mirror. "You look beautiful." I remind her, taking a lock of her hair in my finger and twirling it to help the bounce of her curls.

    She smiles, leaning close to me. "I'm so excited you came out with me. You never do this."

    I nod, intertwining my arm through hers. "Well, I'm looking for some change in my life." I admit.

    She looks to the ground, replying, "I also have something to tell you," When my brow raises, she continues, "It's still a girl's night, okay? So, don't get mad."

    I shake my head, confused. "I won't."

    "Promise?" she begs, her lip puckering out.

    I roll my head back. "Jesus, Kate. What is it?"

    "I've kind of been talking to someone, and he's here tonight." She blushes.

    I laugh and ask, "Is that all? Another hook-up?"

    A bike speeds past us, and I jump back from the sudden sound. "No, I've gotten to know him … Like actually know him. His name's Ryder."

    I've never known her to get serious with anyone, and the smile on her face tells me she's not fooling around. "I'm happy for you! Why would I be mad about that?"

    "I don't know," Kate admits, shrugging. "I didn't want you to think I was bringing you out here to be the third wheel—like, that's not what's happening. I may not even talk to him. I ju—"

    I give her a 'breathe in, breathe out' motion with my hands. "Oh you're very serious about this guy." I laugh.

"You're rambling! I don't care if he wants to hang with us all night. It's whatever you want." My eyes don't stop looking for Foster, even when I try to ignore him being here.

From the distance, I spot a girl walk onto the dark street, holding her hand high in the air. "Oh! The race is about to start. Hurry!" Kate yells. She grabs my hand, and we rush to the edge of the dark street.

Bikes are lined in a row, with some still pulling up to the starting line. "Cash your bets with me!" A guy walks around, a stack of bills in his raised hand. He stops every so often to write names down and exchange money.

When he gets closer, he stops in front of us. "You girls want to place any bets?"

I shake my head; I'm already here at an illegal race, and I don't want to add to the crimes. "I do!" Kate exclaims, waving a five in his face, grinning. My heart rate picks up. Maybe I should?

"Who on?" he asks, turning to his notebook.

She winks to me. "Ghost,"

"A popular one. He's never lost." Of course he hasn't.

The crowd around us buzzes with music, talking, and cheering. Such a dark contrast to the game I was just at; like night and day. A crimson red motorcycle pulls up to the starting line, alongside another familiar matte black bike. Fire and Ice.

Foster.

Everything happens so quickly. The girl, who I now realize is Foster's little green girlfriend, stands in the center of the street, wearing a short leather skirt and a green bandana for a top, to match her hair. The farther she raises her arms up, the louder the engines growl.

Greeny brings her hand straight in front of her, and I'm assuming it's to let them know it's about to be go-time. Before she brings it all the way down, I look back to Foster—and find that he's already glaring me down.

Icy black eyes peek through his open visor where his tattooed hand sits, about to pull it down, but he never does. He looks pissed yet incredibly sexy.

She lowers her hand, and everyone takes off—except for Foster. Cutting off a few people with precise movements, his bike screeches to a halt directly in front of me. "What in the fuck, Skyler?"

EIGHT

"Just came out to enjoy the festivities." I smile when he throws his head back in annoyance. Kate watches on with interested eyes.

The other racers are long gone, and Foster doesn't seem very happy about it when he lets down the foot peg of his bike with more force than necessary and rips off his helmet. "I told you not to come here."

I look around, at everyone else that's here, narrowing my eyes. "It's a free country." I repeat.

Kate whistles, biting her lip. "Feisty,"

Foster turns his rage to her, but his tone is calm. "Hey, Kate. Do you mind taking her home? I'm missing my race."

I laugh at the thought, retorting, "You'd never catch up, they're all gone!" I point to the desolate street and try to ignore his cocky grin.

One hand is slack over the handlebars while the

other rests on his helmet that's sitting on his leg. "You've never seen me race."

I throw my hands up, exasperated. "You're impossible. I'm not going anywhere." I turn away from him, trying to pay attention to anything other than Foster Jennings.

His boots hit the ground as he steps off, towering over me. "And I promised you, that if you came here, I would throw you over my bike and make you leave."

I scoff, giving him a dismissive wave of my hand. "You wouldn't dare." He looks to my outfit, his dark eyes gliding from head to toe.

"I'll go slow since you decided to wear nothing tonight." He smirks, clearly enjoying himself.

Kate looks between me, Foster, and her phone. I sigh, saying, "Kate, I can handle him. Go find Ryder."

Foster grins. "Ryder Parsons?"

Of course he knows everyone. Kate looks nervous, blushing. "Yup,"

"Should have known." He stands closer to me, "At home he wouldn't shut up about some red headed girl." So, they live together? "He's near the taco truck at the end." Foster points down the road, but Kate hesitates. I nudge her arm, and she heads down the street.

I don't want Foster ruining her night too, even though he seems fine that she's here. Is it just me he hates?

As soon as she's gone, Foster's cool demeanor melts away. "I told you not to come here."

"I can go wherever I want." I challenge him.

He gestures into the darkness. "You made me lose

my race."

I cross my arms, "Thought you could catch up. Go ahead."

He points to his bike, growling, "Get on."

"No freaking way."

He takes in a deep breath, glancing around uneasily. "Please, let's get out of here. Just us, okay?"

Butterflies zip around in my stomach at the thought. "What about Kate?" Why am I even considering this?

He gestures down the road. Kate and Ryder are already enjoying tacos next to that food truck. "She's fine."

I shake my head. "Girl code. We don't leave unless we get the okay."

His nose scrunches. "She legit just said it's fine."

"You don't understand. I need the second okay."

He stares at me in confusion, and I'm not even sure why I'm explaining this to him. I'm not getting on that bike, and I'm not going anywhere. My phone dings, and I look down to read the message.

Kate: I'm fine. Go with the angry guy on his bike. Lol. Live a little, Sky.

"See, she's fine. Your little second okay says so." He's peeking over my shoulder smirking at her text.

I step away, nearly tripping over my heels. "Invasion of privacy much?"

Just then, Foster looks to his left, and while he's irritated with me for some reason, that doesn't explain the paleness of his face when two large, tattooed men start heading towards us.

He looks at me so seriously that I can't help but feel sorry for him for some reason. "Get on my bike, Skyler."

"Foster—"

Gently, he grabs my wrist and pulls me closer. "I don't have time for this."

He slides his helmet over my head, and his scent is everywhere. A shampoo that smells of cedar and spices tingles my nose. I dangle my keys in front of him.

"What about my car?" I ask when he fastens the strap under my chin. He snatches the keys and saddles the bike, then puts my hand on his shoulder and twists his body to help me get on.

I can't help but slide my fingers through his hair. "You gave me your helmet."

With a shake of his head, we start moving. We pass by Kate who giggles seeing me on the bike. She mouths, 'You okay?' I nod, sighing. I am okay, but he doesn't need to ride without a helmet.

Without warning, Foster tosses her my car keys and speeds off. Only when the dark city streets zip by behind us do his tense muscles soften.

Warm wind sweeps over my bare shoulders, encasing me. It feels so free to be whizzing past the dark city streets, like everyone is asleep but us.

I thought I would be more scared, but with my arms wrapped around his waist I feel … safe.

Finally, he slows down. His hand goes back to rest on my bare knee, and his head turns to the side. I lift the plastic visor of my helmet, admiring his sharp profile that's illuminated by the moonlight. The further we get from the city; the more stars twinkle overhead. "I wish you had proper clothes on." he yells over the rumble of his bike, nodding his head up to the dark sky. Through my lifted visor, a trickle of water hits my nose.

I shout back, "Well, I wish you had a helmet on!"

With a shrug, he picks up pace again. The light sprinkles turn into drops, and the black pavement becomes glossy in no time. The drops turn into a downpour until finally, he pulls over on the side of the street.

The desolate road offers no indication of where we are, and when his headlights go out, the surroundings match his eyes.

I step off the bike, pulling the helmet over my head.

Rain patters down overhead as my eyes adjust to the midnight around us. I look to everything except his obsidian eyes, which stare back at me with anger and worry as he gazes towards the wet road. "I can't risk it."

I huff, irritated with him. "Of course you can't! You weren't even wearing a helmet."

He shakes his head, a crooked smile playing on his face as he puts down the foot peg and steps off his bike. "I don't care about that. It's legal here. I'm more worried about the roads being slick with you in that outfit."

I ignore the way his fingers brush against my bare shoulder, then my upper thigh. "I don't care that it's legal; it's stupid." I start to walk away from him, but I'm too heated. From him telling me I can't go and him sweeping me away.

But I can't ignore the pounding in my heart over

the fact that I'm with Foster on a dark street, alone. He's so inviting yet closed off. So warm yet freezing cold. I want to unwrap his layers; to find out the real him. And for some unexplainable reason, I want him to find out mine too.

We're completely drenched at this point, standing on the side of the road, and no cars have passed by since we parked. "Why did you even care if I went?" I have to holler over the beating rain.

He steps closer to me, tilting his head downward. I cross my arms when his eyes dart further down. I'm only wearing a wet dress which now has suctioned itself to my skin. *Wonderful.* "Because I told you not to come."

For the sake of me not sounding like a child, I step closer to him, planting my feet firmly on the ground. "And you can't tell me what to do." I shake my head. "You don't even know me."

His knuckles tilt my chin up, and I look into his endless eyes. "Why aren't you with your boyfriend?" Foster questions.

"My boyfriend?" My brows furrow in confusion.

He sighs, biting his lip. "Yeah, remember? You told me you had a boyfriend. Then tonight ... You, Brett ... kissing pictures."

I can't help but smile. "Why does it matter if I have a boyfriend?" My voice is low, and I'm not sure if he hears me over the pouring rain.

Foster shakes his head, bringing his hands through his soaked hair. He looks around, scoping out a different location. It looks like the weather isn't about to clear up. "It doesn't matter." His tone oozes boredom, and the way the words roll from his tongue bothers me, reminding me of why I was angry with him in the first place.

"What about your little green girlfriend?" I spit the words out, and for once, I don't hold back my thoughts. I'm sick of people being mean to me.

"Envy," He mutters under his breath. He guides me to cover under a large tree.

I scoff, turning away from him. "I am not envious of her."

With a laugh, he spins me around, whirling me to face him. "It's her name. Her nickname," I nod at the realization. The green hair. "And what the fuck did she say to you?"

I shrug, feeling less angry at him since he didn't know. "I waited for you after school to give you back your jacket." I retort, my cheeks flushing a bit.

"I wanted you to keep it for the weekend." he tells me. My heart jumps at his reply. "She must have seen you in it and got jealous."

"Oh," is all I say, feeling foolish.

He steps closer, hesitating. "I'm not the type of guy you should be around, Freckles."

I tilt my chin up. "I don't care."

The rain continues to pour, and trickles escape through the thick, twisted branches of our clearing overhead.

I try to speak to mask the rapid beat of my heart, but the thud of water hitting the ground is enough to cover any sound. "We're going to have to wait the storm out."

With a glint in his eyes, he asks, "Are you scared to

be alone with me, Skyler?"

I shake my head, and he pushes me back against a tree, trapping me. "No." *I'm scared because I like you, and things I like normally turn on me.*

His hand comes to my hip as he presses his body against mine. I try not to wince from the sudden pain in my side. "You really should be."

Out of breath, I try to speak, try to let him know how much he doesn't faze me, even though the butterflies say otherwise. "Why?"

"Because," his neck cranes down to get a better view, "Girls like you normally steer clear of guys like me." Well, he's not wrong.

Foster's hands travel the length of my dress, which doesn't take long. "I want to rip this fucking dress off." He mutters between ragged breaths. "Too short,"

I want to tell him to do it.

His black eyes bore into me, and I can't help but look away. "I thought you would like this look."

He smirks, saying, "You look hot, but it's not you."

I gesture to my body, but his hand holds my face. "You normally make fun of my sweaters and skirts." I reply simply.

He comes closer, his lips a feather away. "That's not you either." *How does he know?*

A warm breeze rustles in the air, making the dry parts of my hair blanket my face. As if Foster can't stand the sight of me not looking at him anymore, his large hand gently slides across my cheek, his fingers moving the hair from his view.

"I should step away," he tells me, his chest rising and falling fast, but there's no conviction in his tone. I continue to look up, and he continues to glare down, not moving an inch. "Fuck it." he growls.

In an instant, his lips collide with mine.

NINE

The moment our lips touch, I feel that spark; the kind that lets me know that it's the real deal and I should run like hell. But the more his hands trap my face and the more my fingers feel through his soft hair, I can't find the strength to care.

Foster's silky mouth doesn't match the feel of his palms; his firm grip is calloused and rough. His tongue parts my lips, and I gasp when he pins both of my wrists above my head with one hand. His other one travels down my curves.

When his attention travels to my neck, I worry about my inexperience. I've kissed guys before, but never like this. So, why does it feel so natural? Why when his neck cranes to pepper kisses on my skin does he fit so perfectly?

Through open lips, he mutters so quietly that I almost can't hear him, "I knew it would be fucking perfect."

The rain calms when his mouth leaves mine, as if us touching caused a cosmic effect that transcends weather. Why am I like this right now?

The ache from his absence bothers me more than it should. In perfect silence, his eyes, which match the sky, look to me in the most 'I want you now' kind of way.

I realize in that moment, in the dark near his motorcycle, in the pouring Florida rain, that Foster Jennings kissed me and took my breath away.

I steady myself, having to ask him a question that's lingering between us. "You do realize I never answered your question about Brett being my boyfriend, right?"

Foster shrugs, trailing his fingertips up my arm. "Wouldn't have stopped me." I don't miss his smirk at the new information. He looks towards the damp road. "Maybe you should call Kate?"

I lean firmer against the damp tree, my clothes already drenched. "Why?"

He gestures to the road, saying, "Too slick,"

"What about you?" I ask, shaking my head.

"I'm not worried about me." We continue to stand under the tree. Our tree.

I look away, not wanting to say it out loud. "I am,"

"You don't have to lie." Foster laughs. I shake my head, and water drips down my face.

"I'm not lying."

He looks at me like he's never heard those words before, and a crooked grin spreads on his face—but only for a moment. "My place isn't far from here ... want to go?"

The breath squeezes from my lungs. He wants me

to go to his house? Does he want me to stay the night? "I thought I wasn't allowed."

Foster chuckles, pushing my hair out my face again. The wind is picking up. "You're not. We're just getting my car and then I'll take you home."

～

During the ride to his house, the only thing I can think of is the way he kissed me, the way he touched me, and the way it made me feel.

I hardly realize we've stopped until he shuts off the roaring bike. "I'll only be a sec," He helps me off, and I stand on the wet ground, looking at his home. Cars and bikes riddle the driveway, and music booms from inside.

"Is this a frat house?"

He smirks at my question, saying, "Fuck no. Me and my racing guys live here." His hand interlaces with mine, and he takes me to his garage. I'm surprised by the two cars that sit inside with covers over them.

"Which one is yours?" I ask, gesturing to them.

He takes the cover off the one closest to me, unveiling a shiny muscle car. "They both are."

"What is it?" I raise my voice; the pounding rain has returned.

He pats the hood, replying simply, "A 1970 Chevelle SS."

I nod my head, and he opens the passenger door. "So, you race this too?"

"No, this is my everyday car. I race the Cuda."

I giggle at the name, and he tells me he'll be back.

As I slide into the seat, a familiar hint of cedar and leather whirls around me. With a black interior and trimmings, this car fits him perfectly.

My fingers glide over the glove box, and I'm about to open it when Foster's door swings open. He climbs in with the leather jacket in his hands before handing it to me with a grin. I smile back, but then I realize she had to come over for her to give it back. "It was on my bed," he replies, as if reading my mind. "I'll talk with her tomorrow."

I frown. She was in his room and is obviously allowed to be at his house. "So, does she go on your bed often?" I wring my hands as I ask.

He grips the steering wheel tighter. "Do you really want me to answer that?"

Quickly, I decide I'd rather not know, and I shake my head. He hits a button, the garage door opens, then he turns the ignition. His car roars to life beneath us.

"Why is everything you own so loud?" I exclaim, wrinkling my nose.

Foster grabs the shifter and changes gears. "Sorry we can't all have Range Rovers." He gives me a smile.

"You call me rich, but you have all this."

"Your kind of rich and mine are different. I race ... that's why I have these." He winks.

During the ride, whenever he's not changing gears, his fingertips lay dangerously close to my exposed thigh. I don't know what to say to him; the tension between us seems to grow the closer we get to my house.

Do I invite him in? My parents aren't home, so no one would know ... but would he even want to?

Finally, we reach my side of town and pull up to the gate. "The code's 9812."

Foster feigns innocence. "Not good with numbers." he lies, giving me a sweet smile. "Guess you'll need to enter that info yourself."

Rolling my eyes, I slide my body over his and extend my arm out. His warm hand slides up the back of my thigh, and I forget the code for a moment, lost in the way his hands feel on me. "Are you not good with numbers either?" he breathes, his voice low and rugged, reminding me of the deep tremble of his motor.

I slide back down, but this time, he holds me flush, making me sit in the middle seat. His wrist rests against my leg while his hands work the shifter. My breathing grows heavier when he shifts down and his thumb grazes my inner thigh.

I try to steady my breathing to speak; I look to him and can see his lips curve into a smile. He knows what he's doing to me, and he likes it. "This one." I point when my house comes into view, and he pulls in the drive.

"Shit," He whistles, "You're richer than I thought."

I want to tell him it's not all it's cracked up to be when you live in this family. "Do you want to come in?"

He shakes his head, "Your parents are cool with me coming in?"

I bite my lip, and he looks towards it longingly. "They're not here."

He grips the leather steering wheel harder, fighting with himself. With me in the middle, our faces are not far apart, and his hand lingers on my thigh. "Are you sure you can handle me?" he asks, his eyes slicing through me.

When I nod, he helps me out of the car while I fumble to grip the keys.

Foster presses me against the door, similar to the tree, and I feel the heat rising in my core. In a frenzy, he takes the keys from my hands and slides it into the lock. Without hesitation, his tongue goes down my throat after his lips crash into mine.

"Fuck, Sky. I won't be able to control myself once we walk through this door. Are you sure?" He looks to my eyes for permission, and I don't hesitate.

"Yes,"

With strong arms, he grips the back of my thighs and I wrap my legs around him. He turns the knob, and we step inside the dark foyer. He maneuvers through a home he's never been too, knocking down a vase on the way. I laugh when he apologizes, asking, "Where's your room?"

I nod my head upward, but it's too dark for him to see. "Upstairs,"

Then, the light clicks on.

"Skyler Johnson!" my mother's voice screams.

Shit.

TEN

Foster takes his time setting me down on the marble flooring. The butterflies that once lived happily in my stomach are replaced with wasps that swarm in fury.

I fumble from his grip once my feet land on the ground, and my heart pounds from the look of my mother unexpectedly standing in a robe on the living room carpet. "Mom, I um—"

She points an accusatory finger at Foster, not waiting for me to explain. "Is this why you wanted to leave your school so badly?" She scoffs, scowling. "So, you could whore around with some—" Her cheeks redden as she takes in his tattoos. He crosses his arms and glares her down as I step closer to her. "Some low-life?" she finishes.

I shake my head, in shock that she would be this way in front of him. "Don't talk about him that way!" I yell at her, not knowing where that came from; I never, ever yell. I look back to Foster and he shakes his head, not wanting me to defend him.

She runs a hand through her perfectly styled hair. Even at night, she looks ready for company. "You were supposed to be at Kate's!"

The fact that Foster hasn't budged or left gives me strength. "You were supposed to be on a flight." I deadpan, which only makes her angrier.

Lightning cracks outside, and she gestures to the window with a wild hand. She hardly takes her eyes off of Foster and refuses to let me forget the disgust she feels by the look of her scrunched-up nose. "Delayed." She spits.

I turn to Foster, "I'm sorry," I mouth, nodding my head to the door.

"Warren will never want you now!" She huffs, and I cringe when Foster seems to deflate. Why did she have to bring that up? Embarrassment courses through me, from such a heated moment to now this, and when my father walks in, I step back towards Foster.

"What is all the yelling for?" he asks, remnants of sleep still etched on his face from the pillow. His eyes widen at the sight of the three of us. Mom boiling with rage. Me, embarrassed. Foster, walking up to shake my father's hand. *Shit, shit, shit.*

"Get out of my house." He sneers, gesturing to the door and refusing to touch Foster's hand.

Foster just nods, sensing the tension, and as he walks past me his fingertips brush my shoulder.

Mom steps closer to me when Foster walks away, she opens her mouth to speak but shuts it for a moment.

"Go to bed, young lady!"

I take in a deep breath as the front door clicks shut. "Talk to me however you want, but don't speak to him that way again."

Dad takes a threatening step forward, and I stay put, waiting. He tries his hand at talking, "Don't embarrass the family name, Skyler. You can't be friends with people like that."

I'm in shock, but I shouldn't be. They've always been this way: judgmental. "People like that? He tried shaking your hand."

Mom chimes in, interrupting whatever he was going to say. "She busted through the door with her legs wrapped around him!"

My cheeks redden, both in anger and embarrassment. "I'm an adult!"

"Enough!" Dad booms. "You're grounded. We're leaving tomorrow, and I'll make sure the maid is here to watch you." *Her name is Rita.*

Mom grabs a glass, pouring herself some liquor from a nearby decanter to cool down. "Thank God our flight got delayed or you would be making a terrible mistake right now."

When the room goes silent, I ask, "When will you be back?"

Mom looks to Dad, thinking. "We were going to be gone until Friday morning, but now coming back Sunday sounds better, right honey?" She looks to him, he agrees. *Seriously?*

"You're really going to miss my birthday, again?"

"Cut the attitude. You don't deserve to have us here. What were you thinking bringing that into our home? What if someone saw?"

The way he called Foster 'that' does something inside of me, and rage boils through my blood. "Oh! What if someone saw us not being picture perfect?" I'm screaming now, and my throat burns.

Dad's finger flies in front of my face. "Don't push your fucking luck, Skyler."

"You wouldn't have cared if it was Warren."

The way that they stare at me with no response answers that question for me. They leave, and I run to my room, slamming the door.

Things didn't escalate, and I think that's because for the first time in my life, I raised my voice.

⁂

I dive onto my bed, and my face landing on the sleek silk pillowcase does nothing to comfort me as tears stream down my cheeks.

Until a sound breaks my angry, saddened tears.

A tick, then another—no, a ping.

I walk to my window and push the curtains open to find Foster standing below, chucking pebbles at my window.

I smile brightly as I open it up. "How did you know this was my room?"

He points towards me. "Pink curtains," Then, he looks serious. "Who's Warren?"

I laugh, wiping away a tear. I don't need to be too

quiet, but I'm scared to risk it. My parents controlled their hostility with me tonight, but I don't want them to catch us again. Their wing is the opposite of my room, though, so we should be fine. "All of that and you're worried about some guy?"

He looks so boyish, standing near the garden below me with his hands in his pockets. "Should I be worried?"

"Warren Hollingsworth, my parent's dream guy for me." I shrug.

Foster laughs, doubling over. "What kind of fucking name is Hollingsworth?"

The name always makes me laugh, too. "His family owns the country club on Willow." He starts to speak, but I already know what he's going to say. "And no, I don't have teatime with him."

He places a hand over his heart, feigning shock. "Not even on Sundays?"

This moment with him has cooled down every bit of anger I felt for my parents. I understand it was an awkward situation for them to see, but we're all adults, and they should have been nicer to him. So quietly that I almost didn't catch it he asks, "Is he your dream guy?"

I shake my head slowly. Foster nods, a smile creeping up his face.

I try to keep the hair from blanketing my face as I lean over the edge. "I'm really sorry about my parents. They're dicks."

"Don't worry about it. You're lucky they care about you so much."

I hate that he's sticking up for them; he deserves

better. "She should have never called you a low-life."

He shrugs, saying, "They want what's best for you." He gestures to the mansion in front of him and then to himself, adding, "I'm not really the kind of guy you bring home to mom."

"Yes, you are." *A normal mom would love you.*

Foster flashes a smile, but I can hardly see him in the black of night. "I'm going home. Text me if you need anything."

When I sniffle from my crying session before, he grabs the wooden lattice underneath my window and pulls on it. When it doesn't give, he begins to climb. "What the hell are you doing!"

"Coming to kiss you."

"You can't sneak in here. My parents will kill you!" My heart races the closer he gets, imagining his lips near mine again. He continues his climb. "I'm not Rapunzel!" I remind him, but I don't mention that I do need saving.

I lean out of my window when he gets close, and the sudden wave of nausea I feel from seeing him dangling on the lattice and vines from two stories up scares me more than my dad killing him. "Get in. You can leave through the back door." I plead, but he shakes his head and wraps his fingers around the ledge of my window.

"Like I said," He leans forward, and so do I. "I just came up here to kiss you."

Our lips touch, not wild like earlier, but calm. Like they've known each other for years. No tongue involved, just a slow, delicious kiss on the mouth. My eyes are still closed when I feel the warm breeze brush across where his lips once were.

He looks at me as he climbs down, and my heart lurches when one of his hands slips from the wood. "Foster!" I half whisper, half shriek, hoping not to wake my parents.

Foster only laughs, waving it in the air. "I'm kidding, Sky."

He jumps when he's about three feet from the ground, and when his boots collide with the pavement, I release the breath that I was holding.

"I'm really sorry about tonight!" I call down as he walks away, not caring if I'm quiet anymore. He's almost away from here; almost away from them.

He waves it off, walking away. "Goodnight, Freckles."

"Goodnight, Foster." I smile when he doesn't correct me.

ELEVEN

"Ryder is amazing!" Kate flops down on my bed, wearing the same clothes from the night before.

I smile through sleepy eyes. "Who let you in?" I can't help but notice that I'm waking up with a smile as big as Kate's. I'm still reeling from my moment with Foster last night but hurt by my parents' words. I heard them leave this morning without saying a word.

"Rita," She grins, holding a muffin and handing me my keys.

"You stayed the night together?" My inner enthusiasm doesn't match the tone of my voice, and she notices.

"What happened?"

"I don't want to talk about it," I say quietly.

Kate sits up, scrunching her nose. "What did Ghost do?"

"Nothing," I sit up too, my cheeks instantly

heating. "Foster's ... different than I thought he would be." I admit. "He's so sweet, Kate. I know he hides it, but there's more to him."

She listens intently, grinning. Kate's never heard me talk about a guy like this. "I'm so happy for you!" Then, she frowns. "So why does it look like you cried all night?"

I avert my eyes towards the window. "Just a bad night ..."

She grabs my hands when I don't respond, her crimson hair so long that it brushes my fingers. "Come stay with me at the dorm tonight."

With a sigh, I rub the sleep from my eyes. "I can't."
"Why?"
"Grounded."

She laughs, thinking I'm joking. That is, until I don't return her laughter. "For what?" Her eyes go wide.

"Me and Foster left the race, and it started raining so we pulled over." I can't help the ridiculous smile that spreads on my face at the memory.

"He kissed you in the freaking rain, didn't he?" she demands, sitting up on her knees. "Oh my God! He did!"

The night replays in my mind, making me giddy. "And things got a little heated but then the night was ruined." She quirks a brow, and I continue, "We got his car and came here. I thought my parents were gone, but the storm stopped them. You can imagine what happened next."

"Oh, shit!" She whistles. "Well, where are they now?"

"Their flight was delayed until this morning. They

already left." I shrug, knowing they won't be here for my birthday Friday.

Kate quirks a brow. "So, come with me then."

"Kate, I just said I was grounded."

"Oh, Rita!" she yells out.

Mrs. Rita comes to the door moments later, peeking her head in. "Yes, dear?"

"Can Sky come stay with me tonight?"

I hit her leg, "Sorry Rit—"

Rita gives me a mischievous grin, like she's been waiting for this small act of rebellion from me for years. "Yes, just don't tell your parents."

Oh. That was easy. "Thank you!" Why did I think she would say no? She's always been so nice to me.

She smiles, adding, "You girls be careful. Grab breakfast before you go."

I get up and take a quick shower, making sure to dab on a little make up just in case I see Foster today.

I want to text him as I grab a muffin off the kitchen table, but I refrain.

Kate grabs a bottle of water and sits down at the bar top. "Can we swing by Midtown? I need a new dress."

I think for a moment about Foster's words last night. He said that outfit wasn't me, and when I questioned him about why, he made fun of me and my sweaters saying that wasn't me either. So, who do I want to be? Who am I? Even the simple decision of choosing clothes that aren't solely meant to make me look presentable and perfect excite me.

I smile from ear to ear. "Yeah, I want to grab a few

things too."

※

The Miami heat is sweltering as we walk through the parking lot towards the mall. I worry the soles of my shoes will melt if we stand still for too long.

Once inside Kate's favorite store, her eyes linger on a familiar dress. "Don't you have that exact one?" I ask, chuckling.

She rolls her eyes, retorting, "It got ... ruined."

I start to respond, but my eyes are transfixed on a mannequin wearing light blue denim jeans, ones that are both distressed and shredded on top of being jaw-droppingly beautiful. I love the top too; a simple white shirt that ties in the middle. But until my bruises heal—and unless I don't get anymore—I can't wear it.

I find my size on the rack, not bothering to try it on. "That's going to look so cute on you!" Kate touches the fabric of the jeans, then she flips through the top sizes, handing me one in a small.

"That's a little too much for me." I lie, desperately wanting it.

She shakes her head. "You'll wear it, and it'll look perfect on you! Trust me." I scrunch my nose, worried. But I cave, grabbing it and hoping that the marks will be gone soon.

"I'm ready. You?" Kate asks. I quickly grab a similar white shirt to wear for now that hangs off the shoulder but doesn't tie.

I look in the mirror for a moment, taking in my

reflection. I left the house in a mid-length khaki skirt, my hair tied slick on my head, and a light pink collared shirt. I still love pink, but I desperately need different options. My eyes pan down to my practical dress shoes.

"I need some new shoes too."

She nods eagerly, knowing that typically when we go shopping it's for her since my mom usually buys the 'uniforms' I'm supposed to wear to fit into the family. "Who are you doing all of this for?" she asks.

I smile, knowing full well who it's for. "Me." I need to do more for me.

We mull through the wall of shoes, with Kate trying to convince me into buying heels and me shaking my head numerous times. "You don't want heels, you don't want boots." she complains, letting out a dramatic sigh.

"Nope. Heels aren't my thing unless it's for something like a dress up occasion. Boots are too hot. I shouldn't have even bought jeans with how freaking hot it is." I snicker.

"They're ripped, so that won't be a problem. We need to get a tan going though. Maybe the beach soon?" I freeze up at the idea, but I can always wear a one-piece.

"There!" I point up, thankful for Kate's height when she grabs the pink Vans with ease. "Perfect."

After paying, we step out of the store. I have the urge to get out of the dress flats, and I do. Slipping them off and throwing the new Vans on, I love how relaxed they feel. The responsibility of dress shoes may sound funny to some, but the casualness of the comfy, cute shoes is freeing.

I want to throw them out, but they were three-hundred-dollar Ferragamo's. "Do you want them?"

Kate smiles, immediately taking them from me and tossing them into her bag. "We have to do business dress during presentations, so you just saved me from having to wear my mom's."

"Okay," I snicker, dusting off my khaki skirt, looking ridiculous in this outfit with my new shoes. "Let's go to the dorms."

Pulling up onto campus feels relaxing, I know that's unusual for some, but this has become my escape. "I'm starving!" Kate exclaims, clutching her stomach and breaking me from my thoughts.

"Should we order in Chinese and watch sappy love movies?" I suggest.

She nods, grinning. "Definitely."

We grab our bags and link arms, laughing as we walk down the hallway. I have to admit, I'm a little jealous of Kate and how she gets to live here. The freedom she has is what I crave.

"So, tell me about Ryder," I ask, admiring the hallway. The walls are lined with posters of events happening around campus. As we pass the open doors of her hallway, you can tell different personalities from the way the rooms are split into two and decorated.

"He's so sweet! I followed him back to his place in your car and we stayed the night together." I don't want to mention that I'm apparently not allowed there. "Maybe we could set up a double date!" she suggests much too eagerly.

I nervously laugh, checking my phone. "Yeah, he hasn't even texted me back, so I wouldn't be planning any dates." Worry creeps in. "But I'm happy for you!"

We turn one last corner and walk into Kate's room. Her side is decorated in white and peach hues. It's sort of a boho theme; live plants cascade down from shelves and a little meditation mat lays on the floor. I already know the plants are from her mom who loves to garden.

To my right, her roommate's' side is decorated in—

"What is she doing here?" an all too familiar voice snaps.

Kate rolls her eyes, but I can't speak. She says, "Hello, sunshine. Meet my best friend, Sky—"

Envy, who I still prefer to call Greeny, scrunches her nose in disgust. "I know who she is. I asked why she was in *my* room." She sneers.

I almost can't take anymore of her attitude. "It's not just your room."

"Whatever," Envy rolls her eyes, slipping on her thick boots that match the aesthetic of her side of the room. Black and neon green. "I'm out. Don't touch my shit."

Kate waves goodbye sarcastically, and when Envy is gone, she turns to me. "How do you know that wretched bitch?"

I plop down on her bed, glaring at the other side of the room. "She thinks she's Foster's girlfriend."

"Of course she does! She's a total psycho!" Kate

throws her head back, reeling. "I haven't been able to tell you how awful she is. I didn't want to bother you."

"Don't ever feel like you're bothering me. What happened?"

"So, miss chia pet thought it would be okay to borrow my purple dress. You know, my favorite one." Kate begins. I remember that's the one she just bought a replica of. "Well, it wasn't short enough for her, so she *cut* it." I roll my eyes angrily as Kate digs the shredded piece of fabric from the trash. "And the bitch just threw it back into my closet when she was through." She chunks it back into the bin.

"That's so ..." I can't find the words. "Shitty! Did you say anything?"

"Very," Kate nods eagerly. "I talked to the school board, so we'll see what they say after the review. I didn't even want to start drama until she did something else that really pissed me off."

"What did she do?" The idea of Envy being mean to me is annoying and frustrating, but she's jealous of me. For her to be a bitch to Kate for no reason infuriates me more.

"She stole my earrings! The ones my grandma gave me! But I can't prove it. The only thing I could show them was my dress."

Without hesitating, I walk over to Greeny's side of the room and begin my search. I turn over her mattress and open up all her bags. Rage for my friend overtakes me as I tear open every drawer and turn them over, chunking the contents onto the ground.

I do have to admit that the new, rebellious side of me roars to life a little bit.

That purple dressed can be replaced, and it was. But the earrings her grandmother wore as a teenager and in turn gave to Kate for her sixteenth birthday are something that can't be replaced. They're one of Kate's only items of hers, since she passed away last year.

A pile of dark clothing sits on a nearby black rug, but a sparkle shines through. "Here," I hand Kate one earring and ruffle through the rest of the clothing until I find the other. She almost cries when I place it in her palm.

"I searched a little, but damn, Sky! You're like the FBI." Kate thanks me with a tight hug.

We settle in, slipping into pajamas and spending the day watching a mix of sappy love movies and B-rated horror films.

"I'm so full." I let out a long sigh, setting down the empty carton that was once full of chow mein. Nightfall has crept onto campus, and the halls are quiet apart from the distant laughter of girls hanging out on a Sunday night.

Kate's phone dings, and her grin spreads further when she reads the text. "Ryder?" I ask, checking my own phone. Nothing. I should just text him, but what if it's too soon? I'm way overthinking this.

"Yup!" She squeals, adding, "He wants me to come over."

"Will the alien be back tonight?"

Kate looks at me in confusion. "Probably not. She always stays out. Why?"

"So, you can go, and I'll stay here. I brought my

stuff for school tomorrow."

"Yeah, right!" Grabbing my arm playfully, she pulls me up. "If I'm going, so are you!"

I blush, my heart racing. "He's so weird about me going over there."

"He'll be excited. You can wear your new outfit!" She says, trying to lure me in, but Foster still hasn't texted. What if he doesn't want to see me? "Seriously, let's go have some fun."

Screw it. "Let's get ready."

TWELVE

Changing into my new outfit feels empowering; more like me. And as we head towards Foster's place, I find a sense of clarity and self-confidence that I haven't felt in a very, very long time.

"Turn that up!" Kate yells over the wind, our windows letting in a warm breeze while we ride down the busy Miami streets.

She puts her phone in front of my face. "Jesus! Kate, I'm trying to get us there in one piece. What does it say?" I ask.

She gives me a cheeky grin, and it doesn't fade. "Ryder asked me to stay the night."

"Did you bring anything to sleep in?"

We stop at a red light, and she gives me a 'come on, Sky' look. "I would sleep in his shirt."

"Would?"

She nods, and the light turns green. "Yeah, I'm not

staying the night... We're having girl time. We'll just chill for a while and then head back to the dorms."

I sigh. "You don't have to worry about me, I don't mind staying at the dorm alone."

She nudges my elbow as we zip down the road. "You won't have to stay at the dorm if you just stay with Ghost."

I laugh nervously, glancing at her before turning back to the steering wheel. "He hasn't texted me all day. He might not even want to see me."

"After what you told me, I bet he's dying to see you. Maybe he's asleep?" she suggests, which doesn't help my nerves at all. But it's college, and this is a party, so it's not like you need an invitation.

Beer cans litter the front yard when we step out of my car. I try to avoid getting my brand-new shoes dirty, and luckily, we hit the sidewalk right before a rush of black hair speeds by and tumbles into a puddle.

"Do you need help?" I ask, trying to extend my hand. She giggles, shaking her head but thanking me anyway. Everyone here is shit-faced.

I pan the yard for Foster or Ryder, but I don't see them.

The front door is wide open, and from the moment we enter, red solo cups are pushed in our faces by strangers. We know better, and instead, I walk with Kate to the fridge to get her a can of beer.

I opt out of drinking unless by some miracle Foster

wants me to stay the night. I really want to, but I'm also unnerved that I want him so badly.

It may be confusing to some, but I'm drawn to him. Magnetic, pulled, fucking cosmic alignment ... I don't know. Maybe it's the fact that I know he's as messed up as I am.

"Where is he?" I gesture to the mass amount of bodies dancing through the house. Now that I can take a moment to take it all in, it doesn't really remind me of a frat house. There's a keg, but that's about the only similarity.

I'm so used to that kind of scene—not that I go to the parties—but just the football lifestyle in general. If I were to have been the frat party type, this is how I could explain the differences.

Instead of jerseys, leather jackets.

In exchange for painted faces, inked bodies.

In lieu of beer pong, it's ... what the hell is that?

I nod my head to Kate, and she grins. "If you had to!" She says excitedly. I quirk my brow, and before she can explain, Ryder swoops in and slings his arm over her shoulder.

I can get a better look at him now that it's not dark and I'm not whizzing past on a motorcycle. He's handsome. Tall too, which is good considering Kate's height. He has a friendly smile. "You're Ghost's girl, right?" Ryder asks.

He extends his hand, and I can't shake the stupid smile on my face. "Sky, and no."

"She wishes she was." Kate tells him, which earns

a playful slap from me.

Ryder throws up his hands, signaling innocence. "Your secret's safe with me." He pretends to zip his lips and throw away the key before kissing Kate on the cheek, which makes me happy. I check my phone once more before finally shoving it into my back pocket and asking what I really want to know. "Do you know where Foster is?"

Ryder looks around. "Haven't seen him all day." When I frown, he changes his pace. "He may be in his room?"

I nod, not knowing where to go and feeling foolish that I even thought of walking in his room, at night, during a party.

"Go find him!" Kate says with a wink, lightly pushing me. "Where does she have to go?"

Ryder points up the stairs, and before I can change my mind, I steel myself to move forward. "Black door!" he yells over the thumping music while I ascend the staircase. People are everywhere, and cups riddle the ground.

I pass a couple of closed doors, a bathroom and a washer and dryer that's tucked into the wall as I walk down the hall. It's so loud that I can barely hear myself think.

I find the one black door on the entire floor and turn the knob. It's dark, but I'm instantly hit with the comforting scent of Foster when I step inside. I feel for the switch, but something soft is in the way.

When I find the light, my eyes adjust to the scene around me, and I look straight to his bed, finding it empty. I take in a deep breath, thankful he isn't here. Partly because I don't want him thinking I'm a creep, and also because I was worried about a girl being in here with him.

It's a standard guy's room. Unmade bed, white sheets that desperately need to be bleached from the random black grease stains, and navy comforter. One pillow lies on the floor, coupled with a few black t-shirts. Dirty clothes fill the nearby hamper.

There's a bookshelf, but it's empty aside from a few textbooks. There's mostly notepads laying everywhere with scribbled, ineligible writing on them.

Two acoustic guitars sit on a display rack against the wall, and I finally realize what the soft padding was on the wall: absorption panels. We had them in my music room so I wouldn't bother dad during piano lessons growing up. The room is drastically different volume-wise when I shut the door behind me.

I look to the ground, impulsively wanting to tidy up but telling myself it's not my room. I bite my lip, thinking. But it *would* look so much better if I just made up the bed.

Okay, the bed is made, but the sheets need to be washed *desperately*.

I remember the washer that's right next to the door in the hall. Quickly, I pull them from the mattress and rush outside. Thankfully, no one sees me put them in, and I'm lucky they have all of the softener and bleach I'd ever need.

I go back in and am once again hit with the strong scent of leather. I imagine us in his room. I wonder if he can play the guitar. Would he play for me? 'Stop, you sound insane! He hasn't texted you all day.' my inner voice screams at me. *Stop cleaning. What are you doing?*

But before I know it, his room is spotless, and I'm heading back downstairs like nothing happened. I stress clean. What can I say?

Back at the party, everyone's having a great time. The energy is so high, and I want to be in a good mood too. I dance with Kate, which is something we do together on girls' night, but it's usually just us in our pajamas.

I was so worried I wouldn't fit in, but everyone seems to be really nice. One guy even noticed Kate was drinking from cans, so he went to the store and got her a twelve pack while I was cleaning.

An hour later, I switch the sheets to the dryer and head back downstairs.

"Do you want to play the game?" Kate grins as she leans in to talk to me.

I look at the table of people laughing. "The 'if you want to' thing?"

She giggles, saying, "You mean, 'if you had to'?"

"What do you do?"

"It's a drinking game." she tells me. "But you don't have to drink alcohol or anything!"

Ryder chimes in, "Wait, why aren't you drinking?"

I pull the keys from my pocket and dangle them. "I'm DD."

He shows me his empty hands, adding, "I'll drive y'all home." I notice his southern drawl from and raise a surprised brow. "I haven't drank a drop."

I think for a moment; I want to loosen up. "Maybe

later. Let's just see how the night goes—"

"What the fuck happened to you?" I hear an unfamiliar voice as a herd of people gather around the front door.

I see Foster, his busted lip, and his black eye. I gasp at the sight of him being hurt, and I almost rush to his side until his eyes lock on mine and he shakes his head in disapproval.

He looks a little tipsy, with his arm slung over Envy. A few friends had arrived with him. The sight of him with her… it hurts.

He walks to the keg and pours a cup, looking at me, then looking away.

Kate grins at me, whispering, "There's your man." She's too tipsy to realize he's ignoring me. "Go talk to him."

"I'm okay." I'll wait to see if he comes to me instead. I thought after our moment that things would be different. I wait and wait …

But he never comes, and thirty minutes later, I take Ryder up on his offer to drive us home. I crack the crisp can of apple beer and let the alcohol slide down my throat, trying desperately to not feel unwelcome by attempting to feel nothing.

I continue to dance, ignoring the pain in my chest from Foster passing by me about five times and acting like I'm not there.

What did I do wrong?

Envy is hanging on some random leather-clad man, and I'm trying to ignore Foster's beat-up face as he talks to a group of guys in the far side of the room.

I remember the dryer. He may be being a dick, but I also don't want him to be searching everywhere for his sheets since I cleaned his stupid room. Plus, I have to pee really bad.

After successfully escaping from Kate's drunken clutches, I head to the bathroom, then I grab the warm sheets.

"What are you doing here?" Fosters venomous tone frightens me, and I whirl around with his freshly cleaned sheets in my hand.

"Um, so—" I didn't think this would be his reaction to me being here. Or the first thing he said to me all night. I feel extremely foolish for this. He looks down at my hands, and I wonder why I even started cleaning his room in the first place.

"Are those my sheets?"

Since he's close to me, I can really see the deep bruises adorning his cheekbone and eye. "Holy shit, Foster. Your face," I deflect, but I'm also concerned.

Even through his anger, he can't help but be charming. "That's not the normal reaction I get, but okay."

"The bruises ... what happened?"

"Fight," he states, as if it isn't obvious.

I search through the dim hallway lighting to get a better look. "With who?"

He stiffens. "Doesn't matter."

I bring my fingertip to touch his face, momentarily forgetting that I'm upset that he's ignored me all night. "You're hurt."

"You should see the other guy."

"Haha," I say, rolling my eyes.

"No, seriously, he's in the hospital." He doesn't grin for long. Foster's strong jaw clenches, but I can tell it causes him pain.

I can't help myself; I need to understand. "Why do you treat me good when we're alone, but not in front of anyone else?"

"It's all bad timing, Sky. You can't get wrapped up in this." He sighs. "You can't get wrapped up in me. I'm not trying to be a dick."

Foster almost continues, but a guy walks down the hallway. When he gets closer, I realize it's the one with the red bike. Foster's demeanor shifts; I can tell even in the dimly lit hallway. "This must be Freckles."

"Skyler." That isn't me correcting him. It's Foster.

"Nice to meet you." I say, extending my hand to him. Without warning, he brings my knuckles to his lips.

"Callum," he replies, and I can't help but giggle at the way that Foster seems to be boiling over with anger.

Foster shakes his head and steps closer to me, towering over me as usual. "She's busy." His tone isn't friendly, but his friend doesn't seem to care.

"I wouldn't call her Freckles," Callum walks backward, retreating with his hands up. "Blue suits her better." He looks to me and winks. "Your eyes are like the sky, Sky."

Foster chucks a box of dryer sheets at him. "That's fucking lame, dude." But they laugh, and Callum disappears from sight. Foster leans his long body against mine, taking the now cool sheets from my hand.

"It's time for you to go."

I look around, scoffing. "I'm already here. Can't you just enjoy that?" He smirks at my words but doesn't budge.

"As I've told you before, it isn't safe here."

"Everyone's been nice to me. What about your friend?" I gesture down the hallway.

His palm presses against the wall behind me, and our lips are a mere feather away. I'm reminded of the bridge, the smell of rain, our tree. His cold tone draws me from the warm memory. "Especially stay away from him."

"You ride with him."

"He's worse than me." Foster whispers, but I can't quite decipher the reason behind the venom in his tone.

"Okay," I grin. "So, I'll stay away from him. Let's go downstairs."

He grabs my wrist, not my hand, and leads me down to Kate. "I think it's time for you two to head home." he tells her when we find her.

"Huh?" Kate sips from her drink, dancing against Ryder. She caresses my face with her hands when I get closer. "Why are you so pretty?" she asks me, slurring her words.

"You're prettier." I say, helping her steady herself. "And you need water." I do too; I don't normally drink, so the few cans I've had have made me a little too tipsy.

Ryder is still sober; he kept his promise. And I'm ready to get far away from here. "The girls can stay here." he suggests.

"She's not staying with me." Foster spits, and I try to ignore his hateful tone, but the frown that lays on my face shows exactly how I feel... sad.

I grab my keys from my pocket and Foster grips my wrist softly and hisses, "You're not fucking driving. You drank. Ryder will take you home."

I honestly don't know how to handle him. "And why do you fucking care? For your information, that was already the plan." Before he can respond, Kate hunches over and dry heaves. The bathroom is occupied, and the stairs are covered with people.

"Outside?" I gesture, but I soon realize Ryder is already helping her out the front door. I follow behind, and so does Foster.

"Does she have everything? I checked her purse. She's got her phone and wallet." Ryder asks, momentarily turning his head to me before glancing back down at Kate. I'm really beginning to like him.

"Yeah, that's all she brought."

I look to Foster, hoping he'll say something—anything to make up for how he treated me. He doesn't.

Ryder senses the tension, but I can tell he's in a rush to help Kate. "You good to go then?"

I check my pockets and sigh. "No. Shit. Go ahead and take her. I don't know where my phone went."

"Nooo," Kate slurs, drawing the word out. "You come home with me. Witchy bitchy will kill me in my sleeeep." The guys quirk their brows in sync, and I shake my head.

"I'll be right behind you, okay?" I'm lying. I'll have

to wait for an Uber once I find my phone. Foster's drunk too, and he's the last person I'd ask for help right now.

Once Kate is safely in the car and they pull off, I turn to Foster, hoping he'll move out of the way.

"I'll go inside and find it for you." he offers.

I scoff. "Are you really so embarrassed of me that I can't look for my phone on my own?" That, and the solid hour of Foster ignoring my existence, puts me over the edge. "Why did you act like you didn't see me?" I yell, not worried about who hears. "You looked straight at me and acted like I didn't exist."

"Why were you doing fucking laundry?"

I won't let him deflect. "Answer my question." I order.

He taps a few buttons on his phone and stares back at me with a blank expression. "Your Uber will be here in seven minutes, red suburban, already paid for. I'll give your phone to Ryder tomorrow, but you need to leave."

"You're impossible!" I shout, infuriated. "I'm not leaving this house until I have my phone."

"You really want to see impossible, Skyler?" He pronounces my name in full when I walk past him to go in.

I stop and nod, ready for whatever mean words he's going to spit at me.

But when his legs travel about five feet past me, and his hand dips behind Envy's neck and pulls her in for a kiss, I find myself praying for his hateful words instead of ... this.

When he turns back to me and smirks with a drunken, boyish grin, I can feel my heart crack inside my chest. He wraps her hand in his and goes to guide her inside. Bile rises in my throat when she flashes a cocky smile my way.

When he's close enough, the only words I can mutter are, "Did my kiss mean nothing?" And I know he hears me because a frown forms on his lips as a result of his selfish bullshit.

I can't help but turn and watch them go in. It makes me sick and hurts my heart, but I need to see with my own eyes how much of a jerk he is and why I'm never going to speak to him again.

A newly familiar voice breaks me from my hate glare. "Hey, Blue!" Callum calls out, racing from the front door and running between the two love birds. I laugh through tears when their hands disconnect.

Foster's head spins around so quickly that I'm sure he hurt himself. He's seething, and it fuels me.

"I found this. There was a picture of you and your red-headed friend as the screensaver." He hands me my phone, and I almost hug him.

"Thank you!" I say with a smile, even though my eyes are red. "You just saved my ass." Everything is on my phone. My schedule, my notes, and my life.

Envy tugs on Foster's arm, but he stands like a statue and watches us.

Something about Callum being near me bothers Foster, and there's nothing more that I want to do right now than bother him.

Carefully, I slide my hand around the back of Callum's tattooed neck and turn us both sideways so Foster can see my lips pressing against the lips of another man.

THIRTEEN

When my mouth leaves Callum's, it isn't because I pulled away. It's because Foster drunkenly stumbled in between us.

He sizes Callum up; Foster has a good five inches over him. He's at least six-three, and I'm mentally kicking myself in the ass for making friends argue.

"Let's just go to bed." Envy whines, twirling a piece of chewed, stringy gum around her fingers as she stands on the porch. "Little miss perfect will be fine."

"Don't fucking call her that." Foster points an accusatory finger at Envy, but he doesn't take his eyes off of Callum.

Envy sighs, annoyed. "Why not? You do." *He does?*

Ignoring her, he keeps his threatening stance next to Callum. Indistinct words stumble from the two of them, but I catch one part.

"I'm not fucking around here, Smoke. You're not to fuck with her. She's too good for you." Foster's words are slurred, and his footing is off. Callum shakes his head and retreats inside, then Foster turns his attention to me.

His current intoxicated state is more notable as his long legs stumble closer to me. It doesn't make up for anything he did, but he's not in his right mind. "Your rides almost here. Please, Freckles. None of this is okay. You can't," He brushes my cheek gently, and I retreat in disgust.

Shaking my head, I look into his dark-as-night eyes. "Yesterday, I would have listened to you. I thought we had something; I've never felt like this before." He smiles but frowns when I continue, "You ruined that. Because of her."

I turn to walk away, seeing the headlights of the Uber pull up, but he gently grabs my arm. "Sky ... I'm so fucking sorry." He nearly falls from just standing in place.

I just want to get far, far away from this place and never return. Before I can take one more step towards the Uber, Callum rushes outside with two helmets. Foster tries to stop him, but he can barely hold himself up.

I can't help that I'm worried about him; I am. I'm drawn to him. To what I know he is. Not what he's acting like.

Callum hands me the helmet and walks over to the Uber to tell him to leave. Foster stumbles over, not speaking. Instead, he puts on my helmet and tightens the strap.

"You didn't drink a drop, correct?" he asks Callum. All anger in his expression is gone and replaced with worry instead.

Callum shakes his head and helps me onto the bike. Without another word to Foster, we speed away onto the dark street. I look back to see Foster with his head in his hands and Envy making her way towards him.

I swallow my sadness and hold on tightly to Callum. It isn't like with Foster, though; my hands are trembling with fear. I just don't feel safe with Callum on the bike, and I hate that.

At a red light, he pulls up his visor to talk to me. "Where should we go?" he asks with what I'm sure is a wide grin. The streets are bare, and we could go anywhere, but I don't want to go on an adventure. Tonight was too much for me. "Can you drop me at the dorms?" I ask, and he grunts but heads towards the campus when the light goes green.

We pull into the quiet campus, parking next to my car. Ryder is sitting on the hood with a curious look on his face as to why I'm on Callum's bike. "She's passed out. I didn't want to get her in trouble being here this late, so just make sure she takes some medicine when she wakes up."

I smile appreciatively. The only thing good to come out of this night is knowing just how good Ryder is to my best friend. Callum helps me off the bike as I thank Ryder with a hug. "Take my car home. Just bring it back to campus tomorrow, if you don't mind."

"Sure thing," He wipes his tired eyes and pulls away, leaving me to deal with Callum who is looking at me with an expression that says he wants more. We stand there awkwardly for a few minutes.

I run a hand through my hair. "Callum, listen,"

He laughs, stepping towards me. "No, don't sit here and say some bullshit." He moves a piece of hair out of my face. "We both know that kiss wasn't a mistake." Callum slips on his helmet before I can say anything else. "See you tomorrow, Blue."

With my head whirling, I walk into the quiet dorm. Well, semi-quiet. Kate's snoring so loudly that I can barely hear my disturbing thoughts. I look to the dark side of the room, thankful that Envy isn't here, but my stomach churns when I know where she is. In Foster's bed.

With Kate sprawled out on her bed and me not wanting to disturb her, I grab a blanket and crawl on the floor. There's no way in hell I'm going to sleep in Envy's.

I pull my phone from my pocket, terrified when I see fourteen missed calls and six texts.

It was on silent.

But it wasn't my parents, and I roll my eyes when I open the drunken texts from Foster. Some are almost illegible.

'Please ... pleasego straiight home.'
'Freckless ...'
'And byy go s traight home Imean ALONE.'
'Or come back to me baby.'
'I'm sorry for the last text. I'm sooo fucked up right now. I don't want to scare you away.'
'Please text me backk. I'm fucking sorry.'

I turn my alarm on and put the volume on high, hoping that Foster has fallen asleep, so I don't get any more texts from him. No matter how much my heart jumps when I see his name on my phone, he hurt me.

I lay my head on the pillow, trying to get comfortable on the hard floor. Twenty minutes later, I'm almost asleep when the phone loudly rings. I fumble it in my hands, not paying attention or looking at the caller ID as I answer.

"Hello?" I whisper, worried I'll wake up Kate, but she's out.

Foster's voice is small and slurred. "Why are you whispering? Are you with him?" He doesn't sound angry, more so tired and sad.

"Are you serious right now, Ghost?" I try to disconnect myself from him; whispering with a stern tone is hard.

He grunts, asking, "What's wrong, Sky?"

"You kissed her right in front of me!"

"What are you talking about?" He's muffled.

"Envy! You stuck your tongue down her throat in front of me." I remind him, not understanding how he's forgotten already. The line goes quiet, so I continue, "I just can't believe our kiss meant absolutely nothing to you."

I should just hang up. I should ... but his desperate reply makes me think twice.

"It meant everything." Foster says, his tone different. Sterner.

I scoff. "Then why did you do it?"

"I don't know ..."

"Where are you?" I ask, pushing my brows together.

He groans. "I got sick, so I'm sitting in the tub."

I can't help that I'm worried and also pissed. "Get Envy to help you."

"Listen to me, Sky," It takes him a long time to get his words out. "I don't fucking want her. Please, just listen." I don't respond; I wait. "You *are* with him, aren't you?" Foster sighs, sounding upset. "I can hear him."

I try not to snicker. What he hears is Kate's loud ass snoring. "It doesn't matter who I'm with." I retort.

"It does to me. None of us deserve you. I don't know why you can't see that. We'll only bring you down—and Callum? He's not the prince charming you think he is." I laugh, wondering why he's assumed I'm thinking that. "I'm just a fucking idiot." he finishes.

"Glad we can agree on something." I tell him, then I hang up.

༺༻

I wake to Kate yelling at me while she holds her aching head in her hands. "Why are you on the floor?"

I wipe my tired eyes, checking the time frantically. Class doesn't start for another hour, so I'm good. "I didn't want to wake you up." I explain with a yawn.

"Skyler!" she huffs, then grips her head from the loud noise. "You could have just shoved me off the bed." She groans, "I drank way too much last night. I probably scared off Ryder." Kate's faces scrunches in embarrassment as she recalls bits and pieces of how she acted the night before.

Her budding relationship makes me smile. It's

much better than thinking of my own ridiculous feelings. "You didn't mess up anything; he's crazy about you."

She grins but shakes her head. "I don't even know how I got home."

"He took you in my car." I explain.

With a quirked brow, she takes some Motrin. "You weren't there?"

I sigh, knowing this is going to be confusing. "I rode with Callum."

Her eyes widen in shock. "Wait, what about Foster?"

I stand, grabbing a brush and pulling it through my hair. "I don't want to talk about him anymore." I respond quietly, and she nods. Then, she pulls out a really cute outfit for me to wear. Her grin reminds me that in a short forty-five minutes, I'll have to be in front of Foster again.

"Ignore him then, but at least make sure you look your best doing it." She gives a really bad wink because she's too hungover, and with a flop, she's back under the covers. "I'm not going to class today." she states, and I almost want to join her. But I need to work on this project, and I don't want Foster messing up any more of my day.

I grab a latte, trying to perk up for my dreary Monday morning. I get to class, but Foster doesn't show.

On Tuesday, there's no sign of him either.

FOURTEEN

Wednesday rolls around and when I walk into class, I see the newly familiar sight of an empty seat at the table. I try to push down my worry from Foster not showing up all week.

I sit down, pulling out my colored pens and binders, not understanding why I'm so discouraged that he hasn't been here. I don't know what I expected. That he would have called by now, maybe? At least sent an apology text, I guess. I'm not sure. He's been absent before, so he'll be back, but it won't change the fact that I'm upset.

Upset that he would be so sweet and then so cruel.

Kissing me in the rain, climbing up to kiss me at my window, and then ignoring me in front of his friends and locking lips with someone who has been awful to me right in front of my face.

But he warned me not to come to his place; I should have listened. I should have seen that he was embarrassed by me.

"Okay, class, the deadline is quickly approaching for your group project." Professor Dyer takes a seat, distracting me from my spiraling thoughts. "Two weeks. That's all you have left."

I breathe out a sigh. I've broken the project into four parts, with each of us taking care of two.

I've finished my portion. The internal organs, along with the diagrams of the male and female bodies. Naturally, I did that with the assumption that Foster would do the other two: reproduction and the short essay on human anatomy. I'd text him, but I don't want to engage first. I don't even know if I want to talk to him at all.

But my mind keeps floating back to him, which isn't a surprise since he's been completely dominating my thoughts ever since the moment my eyes landed on him. But now, instead of his dimpled smile or the way his hair looks when he pulls his helmet off, all I can see is his hand cupping her face and her lips touching his.

I can't close my eyes without seeing it.

To distract myself, I work for the majority of the class, focusing on perfecting my part of the project. I'll finish the other parts over the weekend.

"Glad you could join us," the professor announces.

I go rigid when I see Foster walking towards me, the vivid memories playing in my mind again. I'm embarrassed about that entire night, and I regret kissing Callum. I should never have done it out of spite, but he kissed Envy first for some reason I can't explain. Why did he do that to me?

Foster sits in the empty chair beside me and crosses his arms atop the desk. He looks to me once, then looks down. The way his mouth opens and closes tells me he's trying to collect his thoughts.

Under the harsh fluorescent lighting above, his healing bruises make my stomach hurt. They were bad. There's a thin scar running along his right brow.

"Sky ..." he finally begins, and then the bell rings.

I stand up and walk out.

○○○

Mrs. Parks, Accounting. The class that feels like it lasts for hours as I mull over everything I should have said to Foster. I mean, why did he show up with only a few minutes left in class?

"Ms. Johnson," Mrs. Parks places my Entrance to Accounting test in front of me. "Very good job. You've got the highest grade in the class." I see a smile form on her face, but it's quickly gone.

What I've realized about my accounting teacher is that she's very straightforward, only using few words at a time. Professor Dyer is similar; I swear he gave us the anatomy project so he could sit on his phone all class and not talk to us.

"Thank you," I say with a grin, taking the paper and looking at the perfect one hundred on it. Accounting is my major, so this is my most important class.

○○○

On Thursday, I walk into Biology with tired eyes. I

was so exhausted after practice that I couldn't focus on what should be Foster's portion of our assignment.

I thought he was going to be a no show again but surprisingly, he got here before me. He's sitting languidly in his chair, and a dimpled grin attempts to melt my anger. I can't explain why whenever I see him my heart races like crazy.

I want to smile back and try to forget what happened, but there's more going on in my life; it's not just Foster. My birthday is tomorrow, and I haven't even heard a word from my parents.

I sit down next to him, trying not to show any sense of happiness with the way he's looking at me. And when I pull out all of my work, he continues to stare at me with a boyish grin. "What?" I finally ask, my voice light-hearted even though I didn't intend for it to be.

"Nothing," Foster says. "You look beautiful today."

I pull on my pink sweater, rolling my eyes. "You're lying, and I can't handle your mood swings today." I focus on the empty sheet of paper in front of me.

He leans back in his chair, appearing unfazed. "Not lying. Also, I won't be here tomorrow, but I'm going to come over when you get out of school."

"No, you're not." I reply, looking at him in disbelief.

He shoots me a smirk. "We need to finish the project, and you're not doing it all on your own."

"I ..." When I stumble on my words, he tilts his head and nibbles his lip. Shit.

"So, I'll be there tomorrow at five. Cool?"

I shake my head again. "No. I'm busy."

Foster leans forward, intrigued. "With what?"

I want to say with Callum, just to give him a taste of his own medicine. But I already did that, and I regret it. "Practice." Not a lie.

"Well, I'll be waiting for you at home."

Shit. "I won't let you in." My tone is a little playful, but stern. I can't help myself; it's hard when he's right in front of me. His curled black hair above his brow, the way his eyes drink me in. But he hurt me. I'm so tired of being hurt.

Then, the bell rings.

"I'll break the door down." he tells me with a wink before walking out of class and disappearing into the mass of bodies.

⁓

"I'm not letting him in, Kate. I'm not kidding." She gives me a look that tells me she doesn't believe me.

"Screw him. Lock the doors." Kate stands in front of her mirror, holding up different dresses in front of her tall body. "So, since you won't be spending your birthday tomorrow sitting in your room working on a project with mister tall, tan, and tattooed, what do you want to do?"

I laugh, but it's small. I *do* want to hang out with Foster, but again, I've been hurt enough in my life. This entire college experience was all about a sliver of freedom, and I'm free to decide who I want in my life. Right? But the heart is a tricky thing, and I know Foster is more than what he lets on.

"We could get Chinese food, binge some Netflix?" I suggest.

"Uh, no." Kate shakes her head. "You're coming out with me."

This smells like trouble. "Where?"

"Brett's throwing a party. It'll be fun!"

I tilt my head to the side, trying to weigh my options. "Maybe,"

"It starts at ten, and you better be there!" She smiles brightly at a pressed, white bodycon dress, and I'm just imagining all the ways that it's going to get stained after a few rounds of beer pong. The door creaks open, earning my attention. "Oh, wonderful. Barbie is here."

"Oh, the wicked witch of the east is here." Kate sneers at Envy as she walks into the room. She's dragging loads of suitcases inside, struggling to do so.

Finally, she lets out an exhausted breath and plops onto her bed. "Fuck you."

"No thanks," Kate retorts.

Using her neon nails, she twirls her hair. "Whatever. Just keep a leash on your lost puppy. She seems to wander around."

I want to scream that I'm right here and she shouldn't talk about me like I don't exist, but I refrain. My singular focus is on Foster's leather jacket that's draped around her shoulders. It's not the one he normally lets me wear, but I distinctly remember this being in his room when I cleaned it.

Envy notices me staring. "What?"

"Nothing. It just seems crowded in here now." I gesture to her things, not sure where this sense of self-confidence came from to talk back to Satan herself.

Kate chimes in, "Yeah, your closet is already full. Why are you bringing more stuff?"

"Normally, I stay at Ghost's place, but he kicked me out."

Kate and I laugh in unison.

"Don't find too much humor in it. He always lets me back," She winks and lays down on her bed.

I know she wasn't staying in his room because none of these bags or clothes were in there. "What did you do?" The question comes out before I have time to think. I want to know, but I'm not normally this intrusive.

"It's just some bullshit." She shrugs. "After the fight, he was so riled up. Kept going on and on about how things need to change and that he needed to be better."

I scoff. "There's nothing wrong with being better."

"Look, I don't want a lecture from you. What happened that night wasn't his fault and you know it. He doesn't need to change." I want to say he needs to change certain people he hangs around, but that's not my business.

"Care to elaborate? Because I have no fucking idea what you're talking about." Our voices keep rising in octaves as we go back and forth, but I can't help it.

She leans forward, slumping over as if the conversation with me is literally boring her to death. "I gave him something to calm him down."

Even Kate is listening intently at this point.

"And by gave him something you mean?" I ask, my

voice low.

"Some pills," When I gasp, she laughs at me. "Chill dude. Everyone does it." Envy replies, now playing with her nails. Can this girl not have a direct eye-to-eye conversation?

I stand up, unable to sit any longer. "Does Foster?"

"No, but it's not like he got hurt." Envy laughs, adding, "He just needed to chill after all of that adrenaline."

I'm furious she would do that to him and then take advantage of the situation. "So, Foster unknowingly took drugs?"

"Chill out. It was obviously fine."

I slam my hand down on the desk, "He drank alcohol, Envy! Do you have any idea what kind of effect drugs and alcohol have on each other? You could have fucking killed him."

She rolls her head back, laughing like a maniacal villain. "Oh my God, do you have to be so fucking dramatic? It's none of your fucking business, anyway." Envy stands up, getting in my face.

"It is my business. *He* is my business." I reply, rage boiling inside of me.

She crosses her slender arms over her chest. "You're trouble. I see past your bullshit, Skyler. Stay away from my crew. I'm not joking."

"I don't have any idea what you're talking about!" I scream, and Kate pulls me back a bit when I lunge forward.

"Oh! He didn't tell you?" She cackles again, doubling over. "Of course he didn't. Why would he ever want to burden perfect little Skyler with anything." She rolls her eyes, and my first instinct is to rip the green from her hair, but I'm not a violent person. Not yet.

With a swift motion, she rips her phone from the comforter. "I'm out of here. I'll come back when she's fucking gone." Envy remarks, her black boots heavy against the ground as she stalks out and slams the door shut behind her.

"What was that about?" I look to Kate in utter confusion, and she shrugs. I can't help but pace the room, "She drugged him! What kind of friend does that and acts like it's no big deal?" I'm hurt for Foster, and my anger drips away in puddles beneath me.

After hours of Kate calming me down and funneling Chinese food into my mouth, I pull out my phone and text him. I'm not going to blame him for the actions he did under the influence of something he didn't want.

Me: 'Okay, so I MAY not lock my doors tomorrow.'

He sends a little 'hmm' emoji.

Foster: 'What about practice?'

Me: 'I'd rather see you.'

Foster: 'See you then, Freckles.'

I can't help but smile at my phone like an idiot at the thought of us being alone together. But we're definitely going to have a talk.

FIFTEEN

'You're not stupid, Skyler. You just need to figure out what's really going on.'

I sigh, pulling a brush through my blonde hair and picking myself apart as I try to decide what outfit to wear.

"You also need to quit talking to yourself in the mirror," I suggest to myself one last time before deciding on a pink skirt with a tight-fitting black t-shirt, one that I have in my closet from years ago.

Foster hurt me, he did, but how can I ignore the butterflies that swarm through me when I see him? Shit. If anyone mentions his name, they create a storm inside of me.

I know there's more to him; I don't care what anyone says. It's the truth. I can see it in his eyes, and I can't explain how powerfully I'm drawn to him. We've both seen darkness, but I just hide mine with diamonds and pearls.

He hides his with a shitty attitude and a matte black helmet.

My phone rings. Kate's calling.

"*Happy birthday to you!*" she sings off-key, making me laugh. "What are you doing?" she asks, clearing her throat.

"Nothing, you?" I lie as I try to apply a little more blush to my cheeks, not that I need it. Every time Foster utters a single word, it makes my cheeks redden.

Kate chuckles into the phone, and I can imagine her grin as she shakes her head. "I told you at school, it's all going to be fine." Our entire gym class was spent with me explaining everything that happened at the party while she was a bit ... hammered. Minus him kissing Envy in front of me and then me kissing Callum.

I need to understand his side of things before I get outside opinions on the situation.

Finding out that Envy had drugged him infuriated me. He obviously knows because he kicked her out. So why didn't he tell me? Both of our actions were stupid, obviously. But can I fault him for warning me not to go around his house when the people he hangs around do shit like that?

I'm hurt by what he did, but I don't blame him. Anyone that blames someone who's been drugged is part of the problem, and I'm not down for that. I just want him to open up to me.

Honesty.

Just to put the flirtation aside slightly... so we can

open up to each other. But his dimples make that hard, and I know I want to kiss him again.

I hear his bike before he pulls in the drive, and my heart jumps at the sound.

"There's a motorcycle pulling up the driveway." Mrs. Rita announces as she passes my room with a wide grin on her face.

"Remember not to mention my birthday!" I beg her, not wanting to make Foster feel awkward or anything.

I rush out and fix my hair while I glide down the stairs, slowing when I get closer to the door so he doesn't see how eager I am to see him. He comes to a stop just as I step out onto the porch.

I move to stand in the driveway while he kicks the stand down and takes his helmet off. He whistles while shaking his hair into a mess of tousled perfection. "Looks different in the daylight." Foster says with a smirk. "This place is ridiculously big. Do you ever get lost in it?"

I shake my head with a tight smile. "Yeah, I'm always lost."

Anyone who looks at my life would say it's perfect, but that's how it's always been. I can't blame him for not knowing; I hide things well.

"I called Kate," Foster tells me, and I bite my lip nervously. "I wanted to give you something as a peace offering, and she said you're obsessed with lattes," He gestures to the bike, and I notice a ruffling sound in his jacket along with a sliver of clear plastic. "I couldn't get you one on here, so this was the next best thing."

Unzipping his jacket, he reveals more of the plastic.

It was encasing a bouquet of tulips. No one's ever gotten me flowers before, and the gesture melts me instantly. I almost feel like my legs will give out from my inner swooning.

They're half broken and sad looking, but that's why I love them.

Under his signature leather jacket, he's wearing a black hoodie, one that I already plan on stealing if we figure out whatever this ... is.

We walk through the large front door, and I point to his riding boots. "Off, or Mrs. Rita will have your head."

"Mrs. Rita?"

"My housekeeper," I say quietly, already knowing he's going to make some sort of quick-witted joke. But I have to admit, he does always make me laugh.

He playfully scoffs while we walk towards the kitchen, "You have a housekeeper?"

I shrug, grabbing a Coke from the fridge and tossing it to him. "She's more than a housekeeper; she's family." To me, anyway. And I think the only reason she puts up with my parents' crap is for me too.

He nods, cracking the can open and taking a sip of the fizzy liquid as I place my beautifully broken flowers in a vase.

I show him to my room, my heart racing hard in my chest.

"Looks different from the inside, instead of through the window." Foster observes.

We both grow quiet, simultaneously thinking about our shared kiss in the moonlight. His feet bring him to the place of our moment, and his hand grazes the fabric of my curtains. As his eyes trail around, he can't help but crack a smile.

"Everything is so ... pink." He looks out of place, black mixing with cream and pastel pink.

I set the vase on my desk. "I like pink." I shrug, unable to stop the giggle that escapes my lips when he throws himself on my bed.

I point to the desk, where I already have everything set up for us. "We're working over there." I say, but he shakes his head while patting the comforter.

"We're working here." Foster winks, and I have to roll my eyes.

"Keep the door open!" Rita chimes in, peeking her head in through doorway to wave. Foster quickly stumbles off the bed, greeting her with a charming smile and a handshake.

"It's very nice to meet you." he tells her, his body going rigid with nerves. Mrs. Rita draws him in for one of her signature hugs, the kind that squeezes your ribs so hard you almost cry out in agony, but you can't. That'd be rude.

When she walks out, he turns to me with a wry smile. "She likes me better than your parents do."

"She's my favorite." I nod.

"So, are they coming home soon? I didn't make the best impression last time." Foster says, his tone full of something I can't quite place.

"Are you joking? That was so embarrassing." I shove my head in my hands. "You were fine. It's them."

He throws his hands up innocently, adding, "Look,

I get it. I'm not the normal guy that a girl from this neighborhood would bring home. They're just looking out for you."

I'm so sick of hearing that.

I change the subject, "Anyways, let's get started. It's already, like, six."

"Have somewhere to be?" he wonders, biting his lip.

I brush my palms against my skirt. "Brett's party," I reply absentmindedly.

"Oh," Foster grabs the notebook from his backpack. "Am I keeping you? I can do the project at home. I just didn't want you home alone on a Friday night working on it."

Seeing his hesitation, I grin. "I wasn't going to go, so it's fine."

"Are you sure?" I can tell he's fighting to say this; he doesn't want me to go anywhere. His eyes tell me everything I need to know, and the way we've kept slowly walking towards each other through this conversation also tells me where my mind is.

Foster steps away, but not before glancing at my lips and sitting on the edge of the bed. "Did you already finish it?" he asks, swallowing.

"Nope!" I grab out my color-coordinated notebook and hand him the assignment papers before sitting beside him on the bed, not caring that I set two chairs up at the desk already.

There's about thirty minutes of us going over everything, mapping out the assignment, and staring into each other's eyes before Ms. Rita announces she's running to the store.

My heart races when we're alone; just me and Foster. His hair is a disheveled mess after running his hands through it about a thousand times. I can tell he's never been nervous before—it just doesn't fit his extremely confident personality—but something about me has an effect on him.

I reach out my hand to touch his leg as he tells a joke, and soon, the serious work turns into a fun flirtation.

Then, it turns into something else ...

"Human anatomy and reproduction go hand in hand." Foster says, smirking. "Do you know how it works, Skyler?" His eyes bore into mine, and I gulp.

"Of course, I do." I reply, knowing the basics.

"From personal experience?" he wonders, a dimpled grin on his face.

Instantly, I'm putty in his hands. Mesmerized by his obsidian eyes and the way they always trail around my entire face, the way he looks at me like he's trying to find something.

I try to hide my blushed cheeks with a blanket of blonde hair, but he moves it out of the way with his inked fingers. The moment his hand rests on my leg, my body tingles with pleasure.

"The human body is designed for sex, and even the slightest touch from someone you're attracted to can send your nerve endings into a frenzy."

You don't say, Foster? "Mhmm," I reply with a heady breath.

His fingertips glide above my knee, right under the bottom of my skirt. I can't help but bite my lip. "Our bodies react, kind of like you right now."

Our lips are a breath from touching, but he brings his to my cheek and plants the softest kiss. It doesn't match the way his left hand is gripping the comforter like he's about to rip it to shreds.

He climbs on top of me, placing himself between my legs. I can't help but be turned on by the way he looks hovering over me. The way his hair falls over his face, how his silver chain dangles from his neck. "And as for reproduction," He smirks again. I go to move, but he laughs, adding, "I'm just playing with you."

My hand slides up the back of his shirt, and he lowers himself back down on me a little bit.

With a grin, he looks over my face. "But if I *was* going to explain it to you." He repositions himself, and I feel his hard, thick length against my leg.

We're being playful, but I know we both want it.

"Explain it to me then." I breathe, trying to control my rapid heart.

Foster's eyes sparkle with desire that so intimately matches my own when he says, "I would prefer to do a demonstration." He brings his body forward, and my exposed inner thigh can feel his thick manhood through his jeans as he inches it forward. Not touching me there, but close.

"Is this how we're going to present it in class?" I joke, trying to hide how much I want him. But I can't get lost with him right now—or found? I think that's a better way to describe it. I always feel lost until he's near.

"Fuck no," Foster's hand grips the back of my neck. "I wouldn't want anyone to see you in this position," He kisses just below my ear. "So," His fingertips glide along the side of my body, and I get pleasurable chills from his gentle touch. "Vulnerable."

I feel so comfortable with him. So fucking comfortable. But I need to talk to him. I look to the window; it's not quite dark yet, but the sky has a pink hue to it that's inviting to me.

I give him a nervous smile and ask, "Can we talk?" He immediately moves off of me, adjusting himself and looking intently into my eyes. "Not here." I stand, opening the window opposite of the one he kissed me at. "On the rooftop."

"Are you allowed to climb onto the rooftop, Ms. Johnson?' he asks after a moment of … calming down.

"No," I let out a little laugh, but the sexual tension between us is so thick that I can taste it.

It tastes like sweet longing with hints of desire and bad decisions.

He grins. "My little rule-breaker." With a wink, he climbs out before I do, extending his hand to help me do the same.

Once we're sitting side by side, our bodies touching, he looks to me. "What do you want to talk about?"

I've been dreading this portion of the night, but it needs to happen, and I can't wait to find out everything. From certain parts of his life, to Envy, and finally to his feelings for me.

"Can you be honest with me?" I ask, my voice quivering with nerves.

SIXTEEN

With a shrug, Foster replies, "Sure."

"I mean really honest... like no holding back." I sigh.

He thinks for a moment and finally nods.

I look up to the sky and take in a deep breath, knowing this conversation will either break my heart or heal it. "Are you embarrassed by me?"

"No," he answers, the question making him uncomfortable. I can tell. "Aren't you the one who is embarrassed by me?"

I can't help but scoff. "Why would I be?"

He looks down at the lush lawn and bubbling fountain below. "You have all these posh friends and a fancy life." Foster says quietly.

"I don't care for any of that." I reply, furrowing my brows.

He laughs, placing his palms behind him on the rooftop for support. "It's because you've had it at your disposal your whole life."

I instantly feel like a hypocrite for asking him to be honest with me when I won't explain the façade he's believing about my life.

"Moving on," I grit my teeth. "Why didn't you tell me you were drugged?"

He sends me a pointed glare. "Who told you?"

"Envy," I say, shrugging. "I was at the dorm when you kicked her out."

Foster looks away, avoiding my gaze. "I didn't tell you because it doesn't excuse my actions."

I touch my hand to his knee. "It could have helped me to understand better, maybe?"

"Treating you that way was inexcusable, and I didn't even fucking remember half of it. I woke up to a clean room, minus the puke on the bathroom floor, and everyone else filled in the blanks with stories that made my stomach turn."

I can see the sadness in his eyes. "You still could have told me what she did to you." I say quietly.

"What I did was inexcusable, Sky. Apologies are bullshit, actions are necessary, and I'm trying to show you in my way that I'm sorry."

I nod my head, agreeing. Actions always speak louder than words. "So, are you going to keep hiding me from your life?"

There's a long pause as he processes my question, and his palms rub the rough grit of the rooftop panels.

"The fight happened," He pauses for a moment and looks at me. "I had been thinking about you non-stop all day, and I wanted to see you. Then I saw my reflection ... blood pouring from my lip. Black eyes, scuffed knuckles. I decided then and there that my life was never meant for you."

I gesture to where we sit. "Then why are you here?"

"I can't stop thinking about you." he admits, grinning. "I just want you in my life, whichever way you'll allow it."

"You can't just decide when and where you want to talk to me. You know that, right? I mean, you're driving me crazy Foster."

We sit in stark silence for a moment and finally, he speaks. "I mean, just look at this beautiful home—and you have two parents who love you and a rich, Ivy League boyfriend who your parents want you to marry. What do I have to offer you?"

I can't help but laugh out loud. "Foster, you are worth so much more than you let yourself believe." When he grows quiet, I can tell I've struck a nerve. With a sigh, I lay it all on the line. "Do you like me?"

With the most heart-melting, dimpled grin, he takes my hand in his and nods once. My stomach does flips as the butterflies flutter to life at an exuberant pace inside me.

"Anything else you want to know, Sky?"

I nod, knowing this was the last question I wanted to ask. Ever since Envy said it was all my fault, I haven't been able to get it out of my mind. "What was the fight about?"

Foster deadpans. "Don't worry about that."

"Full honesty or we can't be ... friends." I state, hesitating. He deflates, but I don't know what he wants this to be.

He doesn't want to tell me, but I keep pushing until finally, he does. "Well, you made me lose ten grand that night."

My eyes widen. "What? How?"

"It was a huge race, and winner got ten grand." Foster shrugs.

I chuckle. "That's assuming you would have won." How could he blame me?

"Freckles, I always win." He grins, adding, "but it's not your fault; other people are involved. If I don't race, I owe people."

"I didn't stop you, though. You stopped yourself."

Foster gently pushes a strand of hair behind my ear. "You were in that outfit," He licks his lips as he recalls the memory. "I was more concerned with bending you over that bike than running away from you on it."

I audibly gasp, the bluntness making my cheeks redden.

"When you do that, it makes your freckles more prominent." His thumb lightly grazes my cheekbone, sending a shiver down my spine.

"When I do what?" I ask, confused.

"Blush whenever I say anything remotely sexual."

"That wasn't remotely sexual, Foster. That was as obvious as a neon sign on your forehead." I reply, laughing when he shrugs.

"Anything else you want to ask me?" Just like that, he can change the subject, and I'm still blushing.

"No, that's all." I reply, admiring the way his dark eyes are staring hungrily at my lips.

His fingers curl under my chin. "Good."

His lips press against mine, and I lose myself to his touch. The way his fingertips trail my exposed thigh. The brilliant way the warm, summer breeze flows through my hair, and how my stomach growls, breaking the perfect moment.

He stops, I groan.

"You're hungry?" Foster worries.

"No," I lie, remembering the one text I received from my mom while we were working on the project. 'Remember to fast for the next 48 hours. Family pictures are happening this week when we get back.'

No 'happy birthday', no 'I'm sorry we weren't there' ... just reminding me to watch my figure. I'm already small, but words like that make me question the way I see myself. Shaking off that heavy weight for a moment, I look into Foster's eyes to forget.

My stomach growls again, betraying me. He helps me up and makes sure I get through the window safely.

Foster takes off his hoodie and hands it to me. I smile while putting it on, inhaling his delicious scent. "Want me to drive your car?" he asks, pointing to my skirt.

"Where are we going?"

He fixes his shirt, but I didn't miss the little show of tanned abs as he does. "This bomb ass place for burgers," He pauses. "You like burgers?"

"Yup!" With the way your eyes keep drinking me in, I like anything you do right now.

After we get into my Range Rover, I smirk when I see Foster, with his edgy appearance and tattoos, holding onto my pink steering wheel.

Foster grins, his pearly whites gleaming against his tan skin. "Don't even say it."

"You look cute."

The butterflies race more as we drive away, his hand clasping mine the entire time. I text Rita to let her know, but I don't think she minds if we leave, anyway. She seems to like Foster.

We get to an unfamiliar area, and I get a little nervous. "Wait, where are we?"

"Liberty City." he replies, and I internally cringe. I'm not allowed here; this is a rough part of town.

We park the Range Rover and step into the parking lot of Foster's favorite burger place, an old sign lights up the name 'Jack's Burger Joint'. Underneath, it says 'Burgers-Shakes-Fries'. As we step inside, the delicious aroma of steaming sandwiches and fries hits my nose, making my mouth water. We walk up to the counter, and Foster turns to me. "What do you want?" he asks, waiting patiently as I look at the menu.

A big cheeseburger with fries and a large chocolate shake sounds amazing, but Mom's text is replaying in my mind. "A salad with light vinaigrette dressing."

He chuckles and looks to the guy at the counter. "Two number threes, please. Two cokes and one chocolate shake. Two straws," Foster sends me a wink, taking our table number from the cashier after he pays.

I can't help but laugh as we walk away. He can be so sweet when he wants to be. "What's number three? Because I'm pretty sure you didn't order a salad just now."

He holds his hands up. "Look, I'm not taking you to my favorite burger place and letting you order a salad. That's almost cruel." Foster jokes, helping me into the seat at an outdoor table. The breeze is perfect, and I'm so happy to be here with him.

But I still can't get my parents' warning out of my head that this is a very rough part of town. It's on the news every night for a different violent crime. "Shake is here," a waitress announces, plopping down a tall glass that has two candy apple red straws inserted.

I involuntarily moan as I take a sip, "It's good right?" Foster smiles, "Just wait until you get your food."

A handful of stolen glances lay between us as we sip on the shake, waiting for our food to arrive. And when it does, I sink my teeth into the juicy burger, wondering how anything could taste so delicious.

Melted cheese, fresh veggies, perfectly grilled patty, all closed in a buttery set of buns.

"I told you." He slinks his hand to my plate, stealing a fry.

"You have a whole plate!" I laugh.

I set half the burger down, desperately wanting to devour the entire thing, but I've already gone well past my allotted seven-hundred calories for the day. I'm so hungry though... I look at the plate once more and take a fry, pushing the plate away so I don't take anymore.

Foster looks up, rolling his eyes. "Finish your plate." He orders me as he scraps down his food.

I shrug, "But I'm full."

"You sure?" Foster asks, finishing his fries. When I nod, he takes my plate and finishes it for me.

I smile. "I don't know how you do that." He quirks his brow, and I add, "Like, eat so much."

He leans back in his chair, and the golden hue that was around his face from the sunset is gone as night creeps in. "Sky, I know you won't understand this, but have you ever been hungry before?"

"Of course," I reply, a little confused by the question.

He laughs, but there's no humor in it. "Hungry, Sky. Not just from you skipping lunch. I'm talking starving. Like it's Friday night and you won't get your free school meal until Monday at lunch kind of hungry."

I shake my head. "No."

"Okay. Well, that's why."

My phone rings and I feel guilty about answering it but it's Mom. "Hey," I say quietly. Screams immediately start.

Foster luckily can't hear her cruel words. "Warren stopped by, but you were too busy to notice while you allowed that fucking misfit to drive your Range Rover—that we spent a hundred thousand dollars on, mind you, and you—" I discreetly tap the volume button down a little further, just in case.

She keeps rambling, not taking a moment to

breathe. I cut her off; I hate the way she speaks about Foster. "Mom, listen. I wasn't trying to be rude. I didn't even know." I try to speak quietly, but Foster perks up. I hate that my parents think I'm just going to live happily ever after with some dude just because he's rich. Don't they care, even the slightest bit, about love?

"You are forbidden! Do you hear me, Skyler? *Forbidden* from ever seeing that boy again! And when we get home, you're going back to your old school!" she screams.

"No, wait!" I try to stop her. "That wasn't a part of the agreement."

She scoffs into the phone. "Agreement? You don't have a say."

I'm about to cry, scream—anything to make her stop, but then she crosses the line. "You are better than him, Skyler. I don't know why you want to entertain trash. You're from a nice, prestigious family, and I will not allow you to mess up my life by whoring yourself out to the closest degenerate just because you want to get your rocks off. What if you get pregnant?" she cries. It feels like I'm breathing in pure, boiling fire. Even a sip of the cold milkshake can't cool me down. "It's not like he would take care of you! Do you get that? He just wants you for your money, Skyler. You ignorant—"

"Fuck you, Mom."

The moment the words leave my trembling lips, I cup my hand over my mouth. Foster looks so disappointed, shaking his head. I've never stood up for myself before, and it feels empowering.

I hang up just as she continues her screaming rampage. Foster pushes himself away from the table, walking back to the car without me.

I chase after him, noticing his agitation when we reach the Rover. "What's wrong?" I ask cautiously, keeping my voice low.

"It's just," He shakes his head. I've said something wrong. "I don't understand you."

"What do you mean?" I wonder, on the verge of tears for how angry she's just made me.

"Is there anything you've ever done without?" Foster asks.

'Love' is what I want to say, but I refrain. He's been through worse. Much worse. I don't know the full extent yet, but my life is roses compared to everyone's around me.

I shake my head, "No," I lie. "I have everything I could ever dream of."

My eyes glisten when I lie, I hope he can't tell.

He places his hand on the hood. "And the way you spoke to your Mom on the phone?"

"Yes?"

With a shake of his head, he leans against the car. "Is that how you normally speak to her?" No, not at all but you give me confidence. I stay silent. He scoffs, running a hand through his hair. "Do you have any idea how lucky you are?"

"Enlighten me, Foster." I challenge, trying to keep my voice level. I want to scream, but I don't.

His jaw tightens, a tell-tale sign that he's holding in what he truly wants to say, but as his black eyes cut to me, they tell me everything he thinks.

Then, the dam breaks. "You're nothing but a spoiled brat, Skyler." He says my full name, but it doesn't have its' usual velvet ring. He's disgusted.

I gesture to the door. "Just get in. Let's go back to my place."

"Fuck that." He shakes his head. "I'll walk." He hands me my keys, and I can feel something breaking inside of me.

I look around the now dark Liberty City, worried about him. "Your bike is at my house! Please, just ride back with me." I beg.

His slams his hand on the frame of my car, his eyes dark and sinister. "I'll get my fucking bike later."

I try to reason with him. Opening my car door, I say quietly, "Do you even know where you are? This is a horrible part of town, Foster. You shouldn't be here at night."

"I'll be fine. Worry about yourself." He sneers.

Lights and sirens zoom by, and then I hear a gunshot in the distance. I'm not leaving him here. "This place is a shithole, Foster. Come back with me ... please."

Foster whips around to face me. "I know this is hard for you to believe, but I grew up here, Sky." He gestures to the dangerous city surrounding us. "This place you call a shithole raised me, so you must think I'm garbage too." I cup my hand over my mouth again. I didn't know, but I never should have said that, anyway.

I sounded like Mom just now, judgmental and awful. "I'm sorry."

"No need to apologize," He waves me off, "we're too different, and this showcases just how much. The sky is the fucking limit for you, and I'm so fucking happy that it is, Skyler. I really am. You deserve to have a beautiful life, but my limit is here." He gestures to the paint chipped buildings on either side of the street. "I can't offer you anything."

When he walks away, I follow him. "Foster, please."

He stops walking but doesn't turn to face me. "Stop calling me that." he snaps. Then, Foster begins his trek away from me again. He turns his head to the side, but he doesn't stop himself from walking. "Just go, Sky."

I don't know what else to do, but the moment I crawl back into my car, the tears flow freely down my cheeks.

I find myself calling Kate, telling her I'm coming to Brett's party. I feel like shit, and I need to do something before I break.

Get drunk, forget everything.

I mean, it is my birthday after all.

SEVENTEEN

When I walk into Brett's house and see the massive group of partygoers all dressed up and having the time of their lives, I'm extremely grateful that I swung by Kate's dorm to change so I could fit in a little better. She wasn't home, so I quickly grabbed the first thing that caught my eye: a small black dress and a pair of gray velvet heels.

I'm not sure why that's what I chose, but I feel good about it. Plus, it's my twentieth birthday, so I wanted to dress up.

So, now I'm here, in a dress that barely covers anything, fueled by sadness and anger for so many things. The only bright spot of my night so far was that Envy wasn't at the dorm.

"Skyler!" Kate rushes towards me, a bright smile plastered on her face. "Happy Birthday!" she exclaims, tossing her crimson hair over her shoulder. I've always been so jealous of her vibrant locks. To be honest, I've always hated my hair; the way I get compared to a barbie doll, further projecting a ridiculous sense of perfection on myself. Barbie's not even that cool, and my hair turns green whenever I go swimming.

"Kate!" I grin when I see a little homemade banister equipped with my name written in cursive with the words, 'Happy Birthday!' Tears threaten to spill at the gesture, but instead, I bring Kate in for a hug.

A surprise party during a normal party. I don't even care; I have the *best* best friend in the world.

Her arms wrap around me tightly, but her eyes pan behind me. "Where's Ghost?"

My heart sinks, and curiosity takes over. "Well, he's not coming. Did he help plan this?" I begin to feel more guilty, but I don't think that could be possible.

"What? No!" Kate laughs, gripping my dress. "Oh, I love this on you! And I don't trust Ghost enough to know about your surprise party. I just figured since you were with him earlier," She winks, most certainly wanting to know all the details of our little study session.

Football jerseys rush by us, giving a much-needed distraction for Kate's eyes. "What were you going to do if I didn't show up?" I ask.

"I would have kidnapped you." She giggles, clutching my arm. "Do you like your party?" She gestures out to the hundreds of unfamiliar faces with a proud gleam.

"It' so sweet that I don't even care that I don't know ninety percent of these people." I joke, walking through the crowded room.

"Minor details," Kate says, grabbing my hand. "Let's party!"

We walk past a keg, surrounded by the football team chanting some mantra over and over. "Birthday girl is here!" Kate screams, and they rush over and grab me. I recognize a few from the team, but the others are unfamiliar to me. I laugh when Brett comes up, throwing me over his shoulder and proceeding to hold my dress down so no one can see my ass when they drag me to the keg.

"You thirsty?" Brett asks. I can barely hear him over the thumping music and cheers of those around.

My eyes widen as a guy is lifted from the keg, he wipes the foam from his mouth and beats his chest twice before moving out of the way. Immediately, I'm squeezing Brett's arm. "No freaking way!" I protest out of embarrassment, but they aren't having it.

I worry about my dress and the fact that I have no idea how to do a keg stand, but Brett pulls my dress down tight as two other guys help to flip me over. I would usually complain about their hands on my ribs. It hurts, but I'm numb. Kate snaps a photo, and I get about three seconds in before I spit beer everywhere.

I wipe the spilled beer from my chin and catch my footing. Being upside down made the blood rush to my head. I can't help but laugh as Kate follows behind me, doing the keg stand like a pro.

One game of beer pong later, and me and Kate are on the dance floor.

The alcohol hits me a little harder than usual, considering I've barely eaten. Not that my usual party is spent drinking, or that I'm a heavy drinker in general but I'm positive that out of the handfuls of times that me and Kate have snagged a bottle of wine from her parents and drank while watching rom-coms that I've never got this tipsy, this fast.

But normally, we've eaten copious amounts of junk food, something to quell the alcohol.

I stumble to the crowded staircase where people and empty cups fill the sticky, carpeted steps. Against my better judgment, I unlock my phone. The first thing I do is check my texts. There's one.

Foster: 'Did you make it home okay?'

I snicker at his words. He sends me away, then texts me to make sure I'm okay? I'm so sick of this back and forth, but even I have to admit it's refreshing being able to not just take it. I can also dish it back out at him.

Me: 'I'm not home.'

Three dots show up and then disappear. I decide I shouldn't be sulking in the corner, so I slide my phone back into my bra, the only place I had to put it in this tiny dress.

My body moves with every exciting beat from the catchy music. I've done it; completely lost myself to the hum of the lyrics and the dance moves that Kate and I attempt to make. I would say I feel complete, but there's a stinging pain in my chest that I can't seem to shake.

A Taylor Swift song comes on, and me and Kate sing along without a care in the world.

"My boobs are vibrating." I slur, practically falling

to the floor with laughter.

Kate responds, "You're getting a call."

"Hey there, Ghost." I slur his name as I step out of the make-shift dance floor and answer.

Foster grunts out, "What do you mean you're not home? Did your fancy car break down?" I can fully imagine the grin on his face, the deep dimples, the tan skin against a bright smile ... Shit.

"Um, why does it matter where I am?" I slur, pouring another red cup of flat, warm beer and guzzling it down before I have time to think about it.

He chuckles, then his tone becomes serious. "Wait, are you drunk?"

"You were in my bra." I giggle, not sure why I said that.

Brett walks over, clutching a water bottle. He tries to hand it to me before he looks down and pulls me to his chest. "Fuck, Skyler! Your dress is practically falling off." His hands clamp down on the top of my dress and he pulls it up, checking to make sure it's covering everything.

I should be embarrassed, but I just laugh. Then, I hear yelling in my hand. Oh shit, that's my phone. It's Foster.

"*Freckles!*" He's not yelling, just talking really loudly.

I cup my forehead with my hand. "Hiiii!"

Foster sighs into the phone and Brett steps away. I travel to the front porch so I can hear him better. "Where are you?" he barks.

I'm lost, I want to say, but I don't. "Out," I

respond.

"Obviously," I can hear the sarcasm through the phone. He adds, "You know, your smart mouth is going to get you in trouble one day."

"What kind of trouble?" My voice is high pitched, and I bring my bottom lip between my teeth.

"The kind you won't be able to handle. Listen, I'm going to pretend like I didn't just hear someone helping you get dressed. Let me come see you."

"I'm busy, and you'll ruin all the fun." Everything is a little blurry, and the warm Florida breeze is not helping the mix of cheap beer and even cheaper shots that are fighting in my stomach.

"Sky," Foster breathes, taking a moment. "My question wasn't optional. Where are you? I need to make sure you're safe."

"Oh, don't try being all protective of me. Everything's perfect. I'm perfect. My life is perfect. Remember?" I hang up, not giving him a chance to respond.

I return to Kate's side, dancing and funneling drinks into my system as the night carries on.

Our heels are off, and we're dancing on a table when I decide the sweet shots aren't doing it for me anymore. "I want another keg stand!" I shout, stumbling to the edge of the table where Brett's been standing, waiting with a nervous grin for one of us to fall off.

When I collapse into his arms, he brushes the rogue hairs from my forehead. "You sure, birthday girl? You seem like you've had enough for one night."

I give a drunken nod. "Positiveee!" I sing. My fingers gesture to the only thing I want right now.

The blood rushes to my head as a few guys from the football team, including Brett, hold me upside down to do the keg stand once more. The beer from the metal cylinder is a lot colder than the ones in the cups, and I gulp it down. I'm not even finished when I'm slung over Brett's shoulder and moved quickly.

"I could go longer!" I shout, and the guys behind me cheer.

"That's enough for tonight, Freckles."

My stomach drops at the sound of the nickname, and the further I'm taken away from the keg, the more I realize who is carrying me. It's not Brett.

Foster sets me down near the steps, the ones littered with plastic cups and people making out. I look at him nervously, remembering that I spoke to him earlier but not what I said.

My back hits the wooden banister as Foster leans down and waits for me to talk. "How did you find me?" I ask, trying to keep my words from slurring.

He tilts his head to get a better look at me. "I will always find you, Sky."

My eyes pan down his long body, taking in his leather jacket and riding boots. Dark jeans and a black t-shirt. "You raced."

"Had to," Foster looks over me too, his jawline sharp. His eyes connect with the banister Kate made. "It's your birthday?" When I nod, he frowns. "I'm sorry." he tells me, capturing my hand in his.

"Don't be," I look away, "Just go." *Please don't.*

He runs a hand through his dark hair. "You sure you want me to?"

I shake my head no, and I don't let myself tell him otherwise. He looks familiar, like me, tonight. Is he sad? "Are you okay?"

"I am now." I don't find his usual sarcastic tone; it's more of a statement. Like a breath of relief. "I was worried about you."

"I'm okay," I stammer, and he catches me when I sway.

"Two options, Skyler. It's two in the morning and you're shitfaced. Either we go now, or I'll throw you over my shoulder."

I roll my eyes, poking his chest. "Whatever, Ghost. Always with the 'I'll throw you over my shoulder' thing."

He grunts, capturing my hand in his. He leads me back to Kate and Brett and tells them something. Everything is moving quickly but slow at the same time. I hear a little of their conversation.

Kate frowns. "She can stay here."

Foster shakes his head. "It's too loud. She won't be able to sleep."

A little time passes as I focus on not falling over, and before I know it, we're outside. I laugh when I see Foster's bike in front of the steps. "I'm going to fall off." I joke.

"Yeah, that's definitely not happening. We're

taking your car." He dangles my keys in front of me. "Shouldn't leave them in the ignition."

He helps me in and closes the door behind me. It's quiet until he slides into the driver's seat, but my head is ringing. Going from the loudest night I've ever had to complete silence is messing with me.

I lay my head against the headrest, trying to enjoy the cold leather, but it's so hot. Everything is hot, and sticky. "I don't feel too great."

Foster's hand moves from the shifter to my forehead. "Fuck, Sky, you're burning up. We'll be at your place soon." he announces, turning his signal on.

The words almost sober me up. Almost. "No! You can't take me home."

"Why?" He quirks his brow, and I slide further into the seat.

"My parents are there." I lie. They'll be there tomorrow, and I don't want to see them in the morning.

"So? You're in college. At least you have a designated driver." He winks, backing out into the street and turning in the direction of home.

I breathe in relief for a moment when we pull into a gas station. Foster exits and returns with a tall, cold bottle of water. I sip it slowly and hold the cool plastic to my forehead.

"Better?" he asks, looking me over.

I shrug. "I don't know."

I welcome the rushing air on my cheeks as he directs the crisp vent to my face, but I feel like the longer I stay awake the drunker I feel. Way too much alcohol. "We can chill here for a bit before I take you home."

"I seriously don't want to go home." My tone is sterner, and I hope through the slurs he understands that's not what my plan is for tonight. "I could have just stayed at the frat house if all you were doing was picking me up to take me home."

Foster chuckles. "Okay, you've got a point."

"Take me to your place." The words stumble out, and I instantly realize how bad it sounds.

He laughs, throwing his long arm behind my seat. "I'm not so hard up I need to take a drunk girl to bed, Sky. I wouldn't do that."

I roll my eyes. "Why are you so cocky? What makes you think I want to sleep with you?"

"You're a living, breathing female." he replies simply. I want to say he's joking, but his shrug tells me differently.

"You are impossible." I bury my face in my hands. The fear of him taking me home makes me sweat. The cheap beer wants to work its way up, so I push down the awful taste.

I relax when he turns the radio up a little and turns left out of the gas station, heading for his place.

―※―

We step out of the car, and I can barely get my footing together. Foster leans against the frame, and I take a moment to try and collect my breathing, allowing the warm breeze to overtake me for a moment.

The moment I try to relax is the instant the world

begins to spin. I turn towards him to get some help walking, but I drunkenly stumble into his chest. "You smell so good." I groan. I would clamp my hand over my mouth, but I honestly don't care what I say right now.

He throws his head back, sighing. "Why did they let you get this drunk?"

"It's my freaking birthday!" I cry out, trying not to think about how much crap I consumed tonight. I grip his face in my hand, losing all filters for words. "Why do I feel this way about you." I ask him, trying to search his midnight eyes for an answer. "I don't understand."

"Well, I don't understand what you do to me either." Foster responds before securing his arm around my back to help me walk inside.

It isn't five minutes later that I'm throwing up all over his freshly cleaned bathroom. And myself.

Awful, painful dry heaves make my body tremble as I hug the porcelain throne. I barely have enough to time to apologize let alone clean myself up before I blackout.

I'm unable to tell him not to help me get undressed after I threw up on myself, and unable to warn him of what he's about to see.

EIGHTEEN

FOSTER POV

Skyler is completely wasted, and I feel a sudden urge to rip Brett's vocal cords out for having her turned upside down on a keg stand when she was already beyond fucked up.

At this point, I don't even think she's coherent enough to realize she's thrown up all over herself.

She heaves over the toilet, trying to apologize for throwing up all over the bathroom and my shoes. I hold her sunshine hair in a makeshift ponytail and reassure her, but she won't stop apologizing.

Skyler's jumping between laughter to sadness in a frantic manner, and as tears trickle down her cheeks I start to worry. "Can I ask you something?" she slurs, lifting her finger up and pointing past my shoulder.

She's undeniably the most adorable fucking thing I've ever seen, even when she's drunk as shit. I would be more concerned, but she'll be fine after she gets it out and gets something solid in her system.

"Yes," I respond, intrigued to hear what she has to say.

She drunkenly lifts her finger for a second attempt, and this time, she points to the ceiling instead of me. "Yooou!" Skyler exclaims. "Why did you yell at me on my birthday?" Her voice is so sad, and although I didn't know, guilt pangs inside of me.

I place my hand dramatically against my chest, making her laugh. "Well, no one told me it was your birthday, Sky. I'm not psychic." I remind her.

She nods, but it seems like her head feels heavy. I would get her changed now, but it doesn't look like she's over her newfound relationship of hugging the toilet.

"Why do you care how I talk to my parents?" she asks, the words barely stringing together. Only Skyler would want to have a serious talk at a moment like this.

I consider changing the topic like I normally do, but she won't remember this conversation in the morning. "Because mine are dead." I respond. Normally, I don't tell my secrets, and I'm not sure why the truth muttered from my lips.

Her only response is sticking her head back into the toilet. Once she's steady, I prop her against the wall and quickly rush to retrieve one of my t-shirts and a pair of basketball shorts, but I have a feeling they're going to fall off of her.

After a quick dash to the kitchen, I'm hauling ass back up the steps to her. When I return, she's mumbling something to herself, incoherent and upset.

I grab a washcloth from under the sink and turn the knob, running it under cool water until it's drenched. I place it on her forehead to cool her off and once she holds it on her own, I grip the bottom of her dress. "No, don't dooo that. You can't." she quietly pleads, trying to move my hands away.

I raise my hands to show her that I'm not going to do anything. I would never without her consent, but she flinches from the movement.

When I tilt her chin, she attempts to shuffle away but her back's already against the wall. She pulls her hands in front of her face to shield herself from ... me?

"Skyler, babe?" I move away slightly, letting her get more comfortable. "It's okay. I'm not going to do anything to you. I would never." I promise.

She's too drunk to understand, but I can't leave her in that dress. It's covered in regurgitated beer.

I try and make my tone as calm as possible, and my movements are slow and calculated as I inch towards her. "I'm just changing your clothes, nothing else. Okay?" I suddenly wish that Envy wasn't such a raging bitch so she could help. Maybe a girl around would make Sky more comfortable. Fuck, I wish Kate was here.

My fingers curl underneath the soft fabric, and I lift it over her head. I look away, shutting my eyes so she knows I'm not going to check her out while she's like this.

But when I place my shirt over her head and pull it down, I grip her waist to lift her and she cries out in agony. Concerned, I ask if she's okay, but she doesn't respond. I examine where my hands were on her, lifting up the shirt to reveal her delicate skin that's peppered with healing, large purple bruises along both sides of her ribcage.

A harsh reality hits me when I fall to the ground beside her, my back against the wall as I try to imagine what happened to her.

Could it be cheer? No, it was on both sides and much too sporadic to be from a simple injury. Fuck.

I don't want to upset her, but my hands are trembling angrily at my sides. "Who hurt you?" I dare to ask, even though I already have an idea.

She shakes her head, coming to a little bit. She bobs her head in my direction, her eyes like heavyweights as they open and close with obvious determination. "No one. Everyone ..." Skyler replies with a slur. I hope she doesn't notice the rage that's radiating from me as I gently clean her off with the washcloth.

I decide there's no point in trying to solve a mystery when my girl just needs to feel better and get some sleep. The rest can be dealt with later.

I hand her the bottle of Gatorade I grabbed earlier and half of Callum's sandwich that I swiped from him as I dashed through the house.

She takes a few bites and drinks about half the Gatorade.

I carefully help her to my bed and pull the covers over her. When I grab my pillow to lay on the floor beside her, I feel her fingers trap my wrist. "Ghost," she mutters.

"Don't call me that." I tell her, only wanting to admit to her when she's drunk that I love when she calls me by my real name.

Skyler turns on her side, flopping one of her legs out from the heavy comforter. "Hoooold me." she slurs, and I do exactly as she asks. I climb in behind her and wrap my arms around her gently.

"Why do you like me?" I ask quietly, hoping she'll answer because this girl has flipped my world upside down in a matter of weeks. And while it's selfish to ask, I desperately need to know.

I realize with utter certainty that I will do anything to protect her. I mean, fuck, I'm happily taking care of this girl on a Friday night instead of partying. When I ran downstairs, I threatened everyone in the house that if they make a sound, I'd beat the shit out of them.

She mumbles something, and I tilt my head forward to hear her better. "What was that?" I ask. I sound so desperate, just waiting for her to say something, any fucking thing to indicate I'm really something to her.

I can't think about the bruises right now. If I do, I'll kill everyone who comes in my path, and nothing is more important than making her feel comfortable right now.

"Why do you like me, Sky?" I ask once more.

"Butterflies," she whispers to me, just before light snores escape her lips.

I don't sleep. I can't.

But I don't mind, because right here in my arms, I

know she's safe from him.

NINETEEN

SKYLER POV

Morning light filters in through the bedroom, making my head spin, and the more I try to open my eyes, the more it hurts. I search for my phone, coming up empty-handed. "Kate. What the fuck happened last night?" I groan.

"Hey there, sleeping beauty." Foster's slightly amused tone makes my eyes shoot open. It wasn't sunlight filtering in, it was the lamp.

My eyes pan to the window, and the sun is actually setting. Foster sits with his back against the headboard, wearing black sweatpants and no shirt. He's looking at me intently.

"How long was I out?" I ask, thankful that it's Saturday so I didn't miss any classes.

He laughs. "All damn day."

I can't help but grin nervously. "What happened last night?"

"Well, birthday girl," Foster hands me a bottle of water and two Motrins. "You got a bit shitfaced."

My cheeks burn as I take the medicine, imagining what I did last night. I only remember keg stands and dancing with Kate. My hands grip on the comforter and when I peel it down, I notice that I'm not wearing Kate's dress anymore. "Are these your boxers?" I ask, rubbing my sore head. He nods, and fear courses through me. "Oh my God, did we?"

"What?"

I lean up a little. "Have sex?" I whisper, trying to recall bits and pieces of the night before but coming up empty.

"What the fuck?" Foster scoffs. "Sky, I wouldn't do that to you." Then, a grin crosses his face. "Not that you didn't try."

"That's what you think," I mutter, but I also don't know if he's messing with me. I have never blacked out like that before.

Foster pushes a stray piece of hair behind my ear. "Oh, you wanted it." He grins. His eyes hold a softness to them, like a dark night sky filled with falling fog.

I fall back onto the soft pillow, groaning. "I don't even want to know."

He lays on his side, facing me. "So, there is something I wanted to talk to you about."

"What's up?" I turn towards him, thankful to not

be blinded by the lamp anymore. Foster is a much better view.

He looks to my hands, then to my face. "What happened to you?"

When I don't respond, he thinks it's because I didn't hear him. But really, my stomach is in knots. Typically, this would be a normal question, like 'Why did you drink so much?' or something along those lines.

But the way his tone is calm and slow and the way his tattooed hand is sliding underneath my shirt tells me exactly why he's asking. I rip the blanket off of me, standing up in a hurry.

"Oh, the bruises?" I squeak, frantically trying to control my breathing. "It's nothing, I'm a flyer."

Foster stands up and stalks toward me. "I don't believe you."

"It's the truth." I stutter, looking around for my clothes. "Speaking of cheer, what time is it? I have a game tonight!" I roll my eyes. "I'm such a ditz!"

He crosses his inked arms against his broad chest, not looking amused. "Don't ignore this, Freckles." He looks at me so intently that his black eyes are glossed over. "I can protect you from him."

Shit! Did I say something about my dad last night? Evidently, I was wasted. This is not good. "I'm fine, Foster. You're overreacting."

He shakes his head, not believing me. "Let me rephrase, you won't have to worry about him anymore."

I shrug off everything and replace my worried tone with confusion. "I don't know what you're talking about

Foster, I've got to go. Coach will kill me if I'm late."

"Stop deflecting."

"I'm not." I playfully scoff, sending him the brightest smile I can. "I'll just wear this out." I decide, knowing my clothes and uniform are in Kate's dorm.

"I've got your keys." Foster tells me.

"Did I drive here?" I wonder, shaking my head, knowing I would never drive drunk. I take a moment to breathe, knowing the only way to piece together anything is to ask. "What exactly happened last night?" I make it known that this conversation won't last long as my feet slowly step backward to the door.

He steps forward. "You called me, and I found you." His fists are in angry balls, but his tone is calm. He isn't angry with me. "I brought you here, and you didn't feel good, so I chilled in the bathroom with you. You threw up, so I put my clothes on you." Foster towers above me, looking down. His palm caresses my face, and I do everything I can not to lean into his embrace because I know if I do, my life will never be the same. I've been keeping this lie for so long, and the thought of telling him makes my chest nearly collapse.

"Someone hurt you." He sneers, and I shake my head. "You flinched at me, and you have bruises. I didn't need any more information."

I turn my head away fast to avoid his accusing eyes, jolted by the sudden movement, and realize just how intoxicated I must have been last night to feel this way. "You do need more information, Foster. You're jumping to conclusions. I've got to go."

For a split second, I imagine telling him. I imagine how my life could change and what it would mean to me to feel safe every single day. Not having to be a shell of a person. A ghost.

Foster's exquisitely broken like me. I can tell because of the way we're drawn to each other, and I can't bear to break him more.

He saw me when I was hiding, and he found me when I wanted to be a ghost myself.

The tragedy of it all is that I can never tell him the truth.

It could put him in danger.

Without another word, I rush out of his house.

On the way to the dorm, I get a text from Kate. The car radio reads it for me. 'I'm all dressed up for your game. Where are you?'

My biggest cheerleader. I smile, but tears trickle down. There's nothing more terrifying to me than my father, and he's hurt me so much that I can't imagine what he would do to Foster.

"Do you want to grab food before we go?" Kate asks as she dots more powder on her nose.

I throw her a grin, my stomach craving something but not having the time. "No, I ate at Foster's." I lie. Luckily, I had a few minutes to shower at the dorm.

"Ohh," she coos. "You really like him, don't you? He came up in there last night like a caveman getting his woman!" She shakes her shoulders, laughing.

I shrug. "It's nothing serious." I lie again, knowing she can see right through me. I tug down my uniform, noticing just how dressed up Kate is for the football game. "Who is that for?" I gesture to her outfit.

She smiles from ear to ear. "Ryder is coming tonight!" She squeals.

Grabbing our things, we exit the dorms and head over to the lively stadium. My palms are sweating from the events of the last twenty-four hours, and the thrumming music and cheers of classmates are making me dizzy.

I fall into my rotation with ease. It's kind of nice to be surrounded by girls in the same uniform as me, blending in and hiding. Cheering like robots as the guys rush out onto the lawn.

As usual, Brett makes his way towards me. Through the slits in his helmet, I look to his blue eyes, and with horror, I notice the deep black that surrounds them. With a jaw-dropping realization, I just know deep in my soul that Foster is the cause of his black eye. He grips the metal barricade of his helmet and pulls it down so I can see his mouth. A busted lip is all I can focus on.

"We need to talk later." he states before rushing away.

The stadium lights get brighter, making my body feel heavier.

As I look up, Foster stands directly in front of me, but behind the gate. I don't look away. I'm much too tired of running. My eyes lock on his and his on mine as I go through the motions, the fake smiles, the loud yelling that is normally my only form of escape.

It seems like everything around us melts away. A tear trickles down my cheek, and I don't bother to wipe it away. I don't try to stop him when his tattooed hands grip the gate and he jumps over it, pushing down one of the male coaches who tries to stop him from rushing towards me on the field.

This is it; I needed to be found, and there he is. I'm not holding on anymore.

I sigh as my eyelids flutter, then groan when my body slams onto the lush grass below.

My eyelids flutter slowly. Things are happening similar to an old-fashioned picture show. Kate rushes to the same gate Foster was at, yelling. The girls on my team surround me.

But I'm not scared.

I know who is saving me.

A broken, sad boy that covers himself in tattoos and leather, who races from life, speeding like a bullet. A guy who comes from the wrong side of the tracks and is the best fucking thing that has ever happened to me.

Foster lifts me from the grass and carries me off the field. He looks worried, and I close my eyes for a second, only to open them again to be blinded by a bright light.

His room again?

No. Long fluorescent lighting that sits flush against a speckled ceiling.

A hospital.

TWENTY

Foster is so focused on what the doctor is telling him that he doesn't notice I've woken up. His arms are crossed while she goes over her clipboard, telling him this and that as he nods and listens with intent. I don't speak, too afraid of what this night will bring me when I get home.

I scan the room for any sign of my parents, but even as I lie in a hospital bed, they're not here. "She's suffering from malnutrition. That's why she blacked out." the doctor tells him. I know he's irritated; I can tell by the way his inked hand covers the back of his neck. The doctor gives him a soft smile, adding, "We've given her fluids. She's going to be just fine."

"Okay," Foster seems to breathe for the first time in a while.

She looks over her paperwork. "She's not a minor,

so we don't have to contact anyone, but did you need to call her family? Her parents?" she inquires.

"No," I cough through chapped lips, my throat feeling as dry as the desert.

Foster rushes to my side, and I nod absentmindedly when the doctor, who tells me her name is Jane, explains what happened. "You're going to be fine, but you need to have a proper diet." She looks down for a moment, then to Foster. "Can I speak to Ms. Johnson for a moment?"

I can tell he doesn't want to leave, and with his hands stuffed in his pockets, he weighs his options until I tell him it'll be just a minute.

When he steps out, Jane gives me a look of pity as she pulls a chair beside my bed. "Skyler, I'm going to ask you something, okay?"

I nod, and she sends me a barely evident smile. "Your boyfriend, Foster?" she asks. "Does he hurt you?"

I want to bury my face in my hands, but I don't have the strength. "No." I say through clenched teeth, irritation swirling inside me.

She nods, not believing me. "Then who does? Because those bruises aren't from flying."

I quirk my brow. "How did you know I cheer?"

"He told me." She gestures her head to the closed door. "I wasn't going to mention the bruises to him, but he brought them up. Normally, that's an admission of guilt or concern for your safety."

I shake my head. "He's never hurt me."

"Who did?" she asks. My sleepy eyes roam around,

looking for him. He stands outside the door, speaking with a nurse. His hands are wild, flying up as the older nurse attempts to calm him down. No wonder they think he has anger issues, but he's angry because someone's been hurting me, not because he has.

I inhale a sharp intake of breath. "No one," *Please don't take him away.* A hot tear stings as it trickles down my cheek.

She nods once, seemingly used to conversations like this. "Okay, you're an adult, so until you want to speak, I can't speak for you. But here's my personal number. Call me if you need anything." She hands me a small business card and still wearing my cheer uniform, I tuck it into my bra.

When the doctor steps out, she gives me one last solemn look while she lets him back in. Foster rushes to my side and touches my face gently. "Why haven't you been eating, Freckles?"

"It's a long story." I croak, placing my palm against my forehead, trying to decide how to explain everything to him.

He peels my fingers from my face. "You can tell me anything. You know that, right?"

"Yeah," A twinge of guilt hits me when flashes of tonight's memories replay. Particularly one where my best friend had a busted lip and black eye for no reason. "About Brett—"

He cuts me off, his features sharp. "You never have to worry about him hurting you again." Foster seethes, his brows furrowing. "I'll protect you from him.

Is he why you haven't been eating? Did he say something to you?"

"Foster ... You don't un—"

"Skyler!" My mother rushes in, and Foster steps away from me to let her by my side. A powerful urge to scream washes over me as I watch her forehead wrinkle in feigned worry.

"Who called you?" I ask quietly.

She gestures behind her where a mess of red curly hair leans against the doorframe.

Kate's worry is real, and a frown envelops her face when she says, "You okay, Sky?" I barely nod.

Dad walks in behind her, tapping on his cellphone. I wonder if anyone notices his lack of concern, but everyone else's eyes are just on me.

Never close enough, though, but Foster is catching on.

I can feel it.

I barely get a word in with Foster before my parents steal me away from the hospital, rushing the typical discharge process to get me home.

***

As I'm lying in bed, soaked in tears and completely drained from the events of the day, I begin to doze off. Dreaming of Foster, his leather scent still lingers around me. The thrumming rumble of his motorcycle winding down rings in my ears.

Then, the doorbell chimes throughout the house.

I tip-toe down the stairs, curious.

My father is standing at the door, his back to me. A familiar voice is on the other side., "I wanted to check on Sky." Foster tells him.

"It's two in the morning. Go home," Dad retorts, irritated.

Foster sighs. "She isn't answering her phone. I just need to make sure she's okay." I don't even know where my phone is.

Dad repositions the way he's standing, taking a step back and gripping the edge of the door. "Just go."

"What's your problem with me?" Foster demands.

"To be quite honest, I don't want my daughter galivanting around town with someone like you." he tells him, no hint of anything in his tone. Just like a normal conversation. My heart sinks at how that must make Foster feel.

Dad begins to close the door, but Foster doesn't let him. His palm slams against the wood, and my father jolts back. "With all due respect, who she hangs out with is none of your business." Foster spits, his calm resolve faltering.

I just want to curl up into a small ball and hide from everything around me while simultaneously breaking free and shattering my shell.

Dad scoffs, raising his tone. "I'm going to give you some advice because from the looks of it, no one ever did. Stop getting tattoos, get a job, and go after someone in your class range." He sneers, sounding like an arrogant prick. "Skyler might be running around with you to piss us off. I don't know. But the truth is that you're a passing phase; someone she'll have some fun stories about in college. She will marry wealth, and she will leave you behind."

"Stop!" I scream, and the motion feels as if it rips my vocal cords. I'm unable to allow this to continue any further. I walk down the stairs carefully, still weak. Foster doesn't look at me; he's still looking at my father. His eyes are narrowed, and if my father's words hurt him in any way, he doesn't show it.

"Sky," Foster says my name sweetly, still not looking at me. "You okay?"

"Yes," I lie, but I really want him to take me away.

Dad cuts his harsh gaze to me, sneering. "Go to your room."

I step forward a little. "Go to bed, Dad. Let me talk to him." My tone is calm and respectful. By no means does it constitute the snide reply I get from him.

"Don't fucking talk back to me, Skyler." he snaps.

With every passing second, the rhythmic movement of Foster's chest speeds up.

This is the first-time Dad's ever spoken to me that way in front of anyone; he's always been in fear of what his influential friends may think. What makes my blood boil is that he's doing this because he thinks Foster isn't important enough to censor himself.

Foster walks in the house, directly in front of my father, realization dawning on his face. "It wasn't fucking Brett. It was you!" Before I can stop him, his fist collides on my father's jaw.

Crack.

An all too familiar sound that makes me hug my body.

He staggers back, clenching onto his face. "You think you can get away with that?" Dad's voice booms through the house. "I'm sure you don't want the police called on you!"

"Do it. Call an ambulance while you're at it," Foster threatens, his bark venomous. "Or better yet, dial the fucking coroner." With that, I tug on his hand, unable to control the tremble that overpowers my body. He cuts his sharp jaw towards me and his eyes instantly soften.

Mom rushes in the living room, wrapping a silk robe around herself.

Foster leans down, not talking in a whisper. "Go upstairs and get your things."

My mother scoffs, throwing her hair over her shoulder. "She will most certainly not get anything! You need to leave." she states, completely unaware of the conversation and immediately siding with my father.

Foster shakes his head, a smile creeping up his face. He looks sinister. "Either the two of you step out of our way, or everyone in this fucked up neighborhood will know how you beat the fuck out of your daughter. Do you understand?"

They look to each other, wanting to tell him off but also noticing the obvious rage that's building inside of him. Foster's hand gently holds mine when they part, and he guides me up the stairs to my wing of the house.

The moment he shuts my door, he turns to me and holds my shoulders. "I'm very sorry if I freaked you out, okay?" Everything is happening so quickly; I almost feel as though I'm in shock. I nod, and he continues with a smooth, melodic voice. "Sit on the bed, and I'll gather your things."

I obey and curl my hands underneath my legs trying to figure out what went so wrong and how.

Then, my father's voice echoes through the hall. I guess they don't care about Foster's threats. "I don't give a shit! Who will the police believe? Me!" he yells to my mother.

Foster's long legs stop in front of me, and I look up to him. He peels my fingers from the side of my face and the chaotic sounds grow louder. I didn't even know I was clamping my hands over my ears to drown them out.

He bends down and places his headphones in my ears and presses a button on his phone. Music starts playing, but it isn't loud enough.

"I'm sorry." I tell him, unsure what else to say.

Even with everything crashing around us, the moment his eyes lock into mine, the world shifts into a safer place. *A better place.*

He plucks the headphones out, his obsidian eyes boring into me in every direction.

Down every dark corner I hide in.

He searches.

Ignoring the madness that surrounds us.

He looks around me, to me, through me.

He sees me.

He finds me.

And tears trickle down my cheeks when the palms of his hands grip each side of my face, not allowing me to look down anymore.

"Your chaos is mine, Sky." Foster says, taking that weight off of me and dividing it between us.

TWENTY-ONE

With a lingering kiss to my forehead, Foster returns the headphones to my ears. Turning the volume all the way up, he effectively drowns out every single sound besides the music.

His hands move quickly to grab my things. I focus on him and the soft yet loud music that's thrumming through the headphones. I'm instantly calmed by his playlist and the way he turns to me during all of the madness and makes a silly face to cheer me up.

Foster reaches my underwear drawer and stuffs a few things into a duffel bag wildly. His long legs guide him to my desk, where he gets my schoolwork together. I want to help him, but I'm shattered. Everything is crumbling around me.

It's weird, though, this feeling of my world-changing in an instant. I welcome it, but I'm afraid, and I don't know why.

Foster pulls the headphones out and chaos ensues. I jolt back at the sudden blaring noise that's outside my room. My father's fist pounds on the door. Foster tells him to fuck off, and he angrily stomps away.

"Put these on," he suggests in a velvet, calm tone, handing me his hoodie and a pair of jeans. I slowly slip off my pajamas. He helps me put on a pair of tennis shoes, since my hands are shaking too badly to tie the laces.

Two duffel bags, one book bag. That's all that's left of what once was my life. I already know they won't want me anymore when I walk out that door.

I'm okay with that, but I'm also terrified of the unknown. Foster grips my hand, and he stalks towards the door. I almost tell him I'd rather crawl out the window. I can't control the trembling of my hands or the tears that steadily trail down my cheeks.

At the bottom of the winding staircase, we're met with an eerie silence. Mom is clutching a wine glass while Dad stands near the door with his arms crossed. Foster continues to hold my hand and walk me outside, dropping the duffel bags on the driveway and going back in, never letting me go.

I cast a glance at my father while we grab the rest of my things. His face is red, and I can tell everyone is at their breaking point. Finally, Dad spits out, "If you take her with you, I'll have you arrested."

Foster calmly closes the front door, shutting us in the foyer with them. I don't understand why. He places my bookbag on my back and pulls the straps tight. "You can say all the veiled threats you want to. The harsh reality is you're never going to see her again." he informs them, his tone seeping finality.

My father laughs, stepping in front of the door and blocking our way. "Oh, she'll come crawling back." He turns his attention to me. "I won't tell Warren about this, for the sake of your future."

"Her future isn't defined by who she fucking marries!" Foster fumes, disgusted by their words.

My parents ignore him, and Dad plucks my keys from their hook. "Good luck getting your shit on his bike. You don't get to take your Range Rover."

Headlights whirl in front of the house, and I worry it's the cops. When I say my father is powerful, I'm not lying. He's a top-notch accountant who works for the Miami Government, and he can get away with most things. I worry Foster doesn't have that kind of pull.

Foster sends him a cheeky grin. "I assumed you were the type to cut your daughter off when she didn't follow your every command." He scoffs, turning to me. "I texted Ryder when we were upstairs. He's picking your bags up."

"I don't want anyone else to see this." I mutter to him. I then realize that I haven't spoken to my parents, but truthfully, I have nothing else to say to them.

He places his tattooed hands gently on my shoulders. "They won't. I promise."

Mom steps forward, blocking the door along with my father, holding her robe tightly against herself. "Skyler," she pleads. "Don't throw your life away. Don't throw all of this way." Her gaze roams around the glass castle we live in.

When I don't respond, Foster does. "You've got a beautiful home, but the guts are damaged as fuck." he snaps.

She ignores him. "Honey, I just want the best life for you. I know your father can have a ... temper. But look at all he provides." She's speaking quietly, and the tears slowly trickle down my face.

"You've always been obsessed with wanting everything, Mom. All I want is a good life, and our definition of good is vastly different." I choke. "I don't want to be hurt by him anymore."

Dad rolls his eyes. "Don't act like you're a broken bird, Skyler. You're a spoiled brat and nothing more!" He sneers.

Foster takes a threatening step forward, blocking their view of me. "Don't diminish what you've put her through. She's not acting like anything; she *is* hurt." He looks between them. "You hurt her, and it's taking every ounce of control I have to not beat the fuck out of you right now. I suggest you get out of our fucking way."

Dad peeks his head around to get a good look at me. "You leave this house, you're cut off." His tone is drenched in finality.

"Good!" I retort, feeling powerful for the first time in my life.

"Phone," he barks, holding his hand out. Foster takes it from my pocket, holding it directly in front of his face. He must have slipped it in there after I changed. He imitates dropping a mic, but it's my phone, and it travels six feet from Foster's eyes, colliding with the marble flooring below. The glass phone shatters, and I can't help but laugh at the rebellious look on Foster's face as he bends his head back to crack a mischievous smile to me.

I grip his hand, having trouble pulling the sleeves of his hoodie up; it's completely smothering me in the best way. Mom looks desperate as we begin to head towards the back door. They can't hold us here. "Guys like him won't help you raise a baby." she chimes, and I turn my attention to her, my jaw practically on the floor.

Foster's maniacal laugh bounces off every sharp edge of the house like a knife. He looks both of them dead in the eye, daring either of them to say another word. "Don't worry, I wear a condom every single time I fuck her."

My mouth forms an 'o', and a collective gasp fills the entryway at his words, but I can't deny the joy I receive at their shocked faces as they both turn their noses in disgust and step out of our way.

I've walked out of these oversized doors for twenty years and for the first time in my life, I'm free.

―――⁂―――

No words are spoken as Foster places the helmet on my head, nor as we get on his bike and race down the driveway. There's nothing to say—no words that can describe that experience. I'm just glad I didn't have to go through it alone.

We ride off into the night, my hands wrapped firmly around him. We're like ghosts in the night; lost and no one looking for us. We twist down the dark, winding streets where each sharp bend is different from the last, not knowing if we'll be leaning left or right in the next few seconds. That's me now, living in the unknown. Keyword: *living.*

I allow the warm wind to envelop me. Foster lifts his visor and turns his head to the side. "Scream!" he yells over the wind. I'm too nervous, and I shake my head even though he can't see me. "Scream, Sky. Let it all out!"

I get over it, the fear and anxiety, and I let go. Screaming and cursing at everything that was as we fly past the palm trees and zip down the flat roads under the night sky until we arrive at our tree.

Everything in my life feels different except for this random area on the side of the road where we had to pull over because of the rain on the night we had our first kiss. He purposefully drove here, and it melts my heart. The thundering roar of falling rain is replaced by quiet night, and the soft ocean tide laps in the distance.

I catch something in Foster's gaze when he rips his helmet off. Even in the matching midnight of the sky, his dark eyes give so much away to me. "What is it?" I ask.

"It's nothing," His tone is clipped. He shakes his head, not wanting to lie to me. "It's just something your dad said. It doesn't matter. I just—" He covers my hand with his, leading me to the base of tree.

"You can talk to me about anything." I assure him.

He leans his back against the bark, with me standing in front of him. He's so incredibly tall that when he looks straight, I'm nowhere near his line of sight.

"You've been through enough tonight." Foster tells me, shaking his head to move the falling hair from his eyes.

I grip his chin and tilt it down. "Talk to me." I gently order him.

"It's stupid, but girls like you," I can tell he hates saying this. "I'm scared of you. And what your dad said, I just—" His palm smacks the rough bark of the tree, airing out his frustrations.

"I don't understand," I admit. "Is it Warren?"

Foster pushes a stray piece of hair behind my ear, laughing. "Fuck no. I'm not worried about him." His jaw clenches. "Maybe I am," He admits, peering down at me. "I just worry that I won't be enough for you. That's why I've pushed you away so much." He pauses. "Like you'll race to something better if it comes along."

"I'm not going anywhere." I tell him truthfully, and when his shoulders relax at my words, I take a moment to breathe in his impossibly dark eyes, letting myself get lost in him.

"I don't let anyone in." Foster whispers into the night. His typically hard exterior softens for me as he grants me permission to step through his barrier.

I nod in agreement. "Neither do I." I admit.

He pulls me tight into his chest, his arms wrapping around my body. After a beat of comfortable silence, I have to wonder what I'm doing next, but tonight all I want is him near me. "Are you taking me to Kate's?" I ask.

"No, you're staying with me tonight." he tells me, a crooked grin on his face. *Just tonight.* "I don't want to hear it." Foster playfully warns, but my head is already tilted in his direction.

"I thought I wasn't allowed at your place?" I joke, knowing last night was a rare exception for him.

He turns his face towards me, his sharp edges illuminated by the moonlight. "That was before," He sends me an achingly beautiful, dimpled grin. "When I thought you were safer without me."

TWENTY-TWO

There's no grand moment when I wake up in Foster's bed; no enormous weight lifted from me whatsoever. Instead, a swirling mess of emotions courses through my veins. Relief mixed with equal parts fear.

Everything has changed.

In one night, my world has turned upside down.

No, right side up.

Foster walks out of his bathroom, steam flowing around his muscled body and a towel hanging dangerously low on his defined hips.

I bite my lip, feeling like I'm doing something wrong by laying lazily in bed on a Sunday morning in a guy's room. I, Skyler Johnson, never do things like this. But the new me apparently does.

I'm not sure how I feel about it.

The one thing I'm absolutely certain of is the

adorable way he looks when he throws his head to the side to get the water from his ears, the delicious way his dark hair is an unruly wet mess, and the way his midnight eyes still hold the sleepiness of the night before.

After we climbed back onto his bike at our spot last night, all of my adrenaline dissipated. I held onto him so tightly, not paying attention to the speed we were going or the many traffic laws he broke to get me home.

Aside from a few odd looks from his roommates at the idea of Foster having the same girl in his room, two nights in one week, on the way upstairs, we were finally alone and in a small but safe spot to unwind.

He held me, and although his grip was tight, I didn't care because I felt *safe*.

"Earth to Skyler," Foster sings, grinning. I tilt my head, having not realized I spaced out. "Sleep good?" he asks, opening up a drawer and pulling out a neatly folded black t-shirt. He grins and looks at me, then puts it on. I remember organizing his drawers the other night, and I'm glad it's being appreciated.

Now, to figure out the mess of my new, unorganized life.

I stretch my arms out. "Yeah," I mutter, my voice still hoarse from the constant stream of tears from the night before. I don't think another droplet could fall from my blue eyes.

"Good," He nods. "Get up. We're having a *you* day."

I laugh, flopping back onto the soft comforter. "A *me* day?" I ask. I turn my head on the pillow, watching with curious anticipation as his towel drops to the floor in a thud. I gulp seeing all of him. "Is umm ..." I don't know what to say now.

Foster grabs a pair of black jeans from the top of his dresser and slips them on after pulling on a pair of boxers. "Why are you blushing?" he asks, tilting his head in inquiry.

He knows exactly why I'm blushing, but I want to play with him. "I don't know." I shrug, looking slowly up and down his body. "I thought it would be bigger." I lie and burst into laughter when he lunges onto the bed to tickle me.

After a few minutes of out of breath laughing from Foster—carefully—tickling me, making sure to not touch one single bruise on my body, we collapse onto the bed together.

His eyes bore into mine. "I saw the drool. You don't have to lie." he teases, a crooked grin on his face.

I tilt my head. "Drool?"

His tattooed finger slides across my forehead, moving the unbrushed, messy hair from my face. "The surprised look on your face tells me you've never seen something so big before." Foster bites his lip.

My cheeks flush a deeper shade of crimson, and I want to tell him I've never seen one *ever*, but I refrain. "So, what are we doing exactly on my *me* day?" I ask, changing the subject.

Laying on his back with his arms folded under his head, I get a striking view of his long, muscular body. I try to keep my face straight, knowing this new sense of freedom is definitely going to get me into trouble when it comes to him. I've never in my life been around a man this much.

Besides Brett, but that's different. That's Brett, and this is Foster. A walking representation of temptation.

Foster screams *sex* with the way he walks, talks, and breathes. I've never felt this swept up in someone before. I mean, shit, my entire world is crumbling around me, and he sends one dimpled grin, making me melt. Making me forget troubles exist in this world.

When he casually places his large, warm hand on my bare thigh, a rush of nerves jolts my body. "We didn't get a lot of things from your house." he says.

I shake my head, the butterflies getting crushed by a large pit in my stomach. "I don't want to go back there." I whisper.

He sits up, his eyes squinted in anger. "You'll never fucking have to, okay? I'm never taking you anywhere near that fucked up neighborhood." I calm at his words, taking in a deep breath. "We're going shopping."

A ridiculous smile takes over my face. "So, you're going to stay at the mall for hours while I shop. Are you ready for that?" I giggle, trying to imagine him in American Eagle.

Foster throws me a funny face. "Do I get to see you in tight clothes?" he inquires. I nod with a blush, looking away. "Then I'm in."

I reach for my phone, going to text Kate, but there's nothing to reach for. "Dammit!" I cry.

Foster looks me over. "What is it?"

Flashbacks of the night before seep into my mind, with Foster shattering my phone on the marble floor being one of them. "Kate probably thinks I'm dead. I don't have a phone anymore." I groan, not annoyed with him but annoyed in general.

Foster shrugs, looking unfazed. "Already called her."

"Oh," I say, wide-eyed. "What did you say?"

"Your business isn't mine to tell, but friend to friend," I deflate at his words, and he kisses my forehead. "Sorry, weird way to phrase that. But you're going to have to let me ease into whatever this is, since it's all new to me." A beat of silence stretches between us. "You need to tell her. She won't judge you. No one would, Sky." His deep voice slips over me like a silk dress.

I shake my head. "I don't want to air it out."

"Okay," he replies simply.

I bend my head down, and he lifts it back up. "Is that okay?" I ask.

Foster looks at me intently. "Of course. You can do whatever you want, okay? This is your world, and you control every single aspect of it."

I knew he was special, I always did, but I never knew the extent of his heart. I breathe a little easier. "So, can I text her from your phone to make sure she's okay?"

"No,' He deadpans, sliding his phone away from me.

"Okay?" I raise a confused brow.

He opens his nightstand drawer, pulling out a rectangular box and grinning from ear to ear. "You don't need to because I got you your own."

My eyes gloss over at the gesture, but I shake my head. "No, I can't accept that."

"You need a phone, right?" Foster asks.

"Yeah," I admit, but I don't want him to pay for it.

He slides the box in my hand. "Okay, then you can and will accept it."

It's the best gift ever because it's from him. I open the brand-new iPhone, and guilt washes over me as my eyes pan to his older phone. "Why don't we switch?" I suggest.

"I don't need more than this. I went to the store before you woke up and got this. If I wanted a new one, I would have gotten it then. Please, don't be difficult and just accept it." Foster pleads.

I jump into his arms, knowing how lost I would be without him but also knowing how much power he makes me feel. "Thank you," I say with a small smile. "But you're not buying me one single thing today!" I gently demand, pointing a finger in his face. Foster laughs, nipping at it.

"And I did take the liberty of giving you a new number." he mumbles.

"Oh," I look at the phone, shrugging. "That's fine. But why?"

"I didn't want them contacting you. So, now you have that choice if you want to contact them, but they have no way to call you."

I nod, thankful. "This means a lot to me."

"Okay, now get up. We've got to pick up Kate."

I perk up. "Really? She's coming?" I squeal.

Although I'm not ready to tell her what's happened, I'm happy to see my best friend.

༺❦༻

After quickly getting ready, we hop into Foster's car. It feels weird not having a car of my own, but I know with the support system I have around me, I'll be okay.

We pull up in front of the dorms, and Kate jumps into the backseat, throwing her arms around the chair and me. "I was so worried. What happened to you? You practically ran out of the hospital!"

I give a nervous laugh, looking over to Foster. "I didn't eat yesterday." I shrug uneasily.

I look in the rearview mirror to see her shake her head a little. "So, that's why you passed out on the field like a ton of bricks? You skipped dinner?" I know she doesn't believe me, and I don't want to tell her the truth right now.

I look to Foster, my face coated with worry. He throws his arm over the seat. "Where to first, ladies?" he asks, his smooth tone demanding attention be put on him. I'm grateful and he knows it.

"Um, Merrick?" I suggest, knowing there's plenty of options there.

He nods, turning the stereo nob and blasting music through the open windows. Drowning out all room for uneasy conversation.

And for that, I'm thankful.

༺❦༻

In the first store we go to, I find a few outfits that

I love. Something that wouldn't be allowed in the posh dress code Mom requires. I grab them off the shelves with a sparkle in my eyes, knowing I can't be told what's okay to wear anymore.

Kate's off looking at heels, roaming through the shoe department and clueless as to what's going on. I don't want to worry her, and I don't want to admit I've been lying to her all this time either.

Foster grabs the clothes from my hands, sneakily trying to bring them to the counter. "No," I smile, walking with him. "You already got me a phone, so let me get this." I offer.

The woman scans and bags all the items, and I hand her my card. "You're going to look fucking delicious in that one." Foster gestures to a fiery red dress that I picked out. The middle-aged woman at the counter nearly scoffs at his words, but I just laugh.

"Do you want to grab something to eat before the next shop?" he asks.

My stomach growls. "Ugh, ye—"

"Declined." the cashier states, and my eyes pan up to the realization.

"Um," I dig through my wallet. "Try this one?" I offer, handing it to her.

I wait in silence while Foster rolls circles on my back with his fingers. "I can pay," he whispers.

I shake my head, not believing until my third and final card gets declined.

"Here," He hands her his card. I don't speak, and we walk out of the store with him holding my bags. I didn't want him to spend more money on me.

I didn't want that at all.

Standing in front of the store, Foster places his palm on my face. "Breathe, Skyler."

With a wave of sudden nausea, I realize I have nothing.

My breathing picks up at a rapid pace. "I don't know what I was thinking! I have nothing now. My life is over." I cry.

"Hey, calm down, okay?" Foster coos, his voice growing a little stern the more frantic I become.

Kate walks up, worry coating her features when she sees me. She places her hand on my shoulder, but I can't think. Her phone rings, drowning out my ability to think clearly, but she doesn't answer it.

I pace in front of the store, checking all of my bank accounts on my new phone. "They really cut me off. Completely wiped me out." A worry I've never felt seeps through me. "They were right; I'm nothing without them!" I exclaim in desperation, knowing what this means.

My education, gone in the blink of an eye.

Foster grabs my shoulders, holding me tightly. "Fuck that. You're more than they'll ever be. They treated you like garbage."

"No, Foster. I can—"

Kate's phone rings again, and she quietly answers it. Her eyes growing wider with every word from the other end of the line. She stumbles a bit on her words. "Uh huh," She gulps, appearing frantic. Then, she taps her heels, anger wrinkling her nose. "Oh, he did, did he?" She sneers.

Her eyes pan to Foster. Mine do as well because I have no idea what's going on.

Foster sheepishly rubs the back of his neck, and I feel completely out of the loop.

Kate hangs up and shoves the phone in her pocket. "What in the actual fuck were you thinking, Foster?" she snaps, pointing an accusatory finger at him.

Instead of answering her, his midnight gaze searches me. He gives me puppy dog eyes but anger still courses through me at his answer. "I mean, I may or may not have had Brett arrested."

TWENTY-THREE

Grabbing Kate's hand in mine, we rush past Foster and out of the mall into the parking lot to head for the Miami police station. I sigh when I realize I have no car. I'm fuming knowing that our only ride is Foster, who put my best friend in jail.

Foster doesn't speak as he walks out. He slides into his car and cranks it up. I weigh my options, knowing this is the fastest way.

"What did he say?" I ask Kate, sliding into the backseat with her and leaving Foster alone in the front.

Her face scrunches in disgust. "They picked him up last night, and he was too worried to call his parents. He tried dialing your number, but he didn't know you got a new one!"

"What the fuck were you thinking, Foster?" I croak, throwing my head back. "This could ruin everything for him."

He looks in the rearview mirror, and his eyes roam my chest, then Kate's. I scoff, wondering why he felt that to be necessary. But two seconds later, when the car comes to a screeching halt on the side of the road, I realize he was checking to make sure we had on our seatbelts.

"Get out." he orders, twisting his body to look in my direction.

I shake my head, furiously. "No, you're taking me to the police station now!" I demand, and he rips open his door and walks around to open mine.

"Step out of the car, now." he gently demands, and with a huff, I peel my seatbelt off and step out.

Leaning against his car, I cross my arms. "What?" I ask, frustrated.

He places his hands on my shoulders. "I need you to calm down."

"Why should I?"

"Because," Foster runs a hand over his face. "I did what I had to for you, Sky. I thought he was hurting you. Can you understand what that was like for me? What did you want me to do? Kill him?" he questions. He talks quietly, and when I peek back, Kate's tapping away on her phone.

I shake my head, knowing he's right. "No," I respond, but I stomp my foot onto the pavement. "I'm still mad at you!"

"You're so damn cute." He smirks, a dimple raising on his face.

I shove my head into my hands, "Foster, I'm serious!"

I hear Kate laugh at me through the open window, and she leans out, gesturing for us to get back in. The tension has dissipated, but I still feel mad. Mad at the world, mad at my parents, and mad at Foster but thankful he was so quick to protect me. "You're too tiny to be this angry. You look like a mad kitten." Foster grins. "Kitten," He nods to himself, clearly pleased. "I like it."

I groan, not able to handle either of them. He bends down to whisper in my ear, "For real, Freckles. Please don't be mad."

"I'm not," I grit my teeth. "I just want to go get him out, but I have no money!"

"I'll get him." Foster offers, but I shake my head.

Kate pops her head back out the window, "I can get him! But why don't you have any money?" she asks, eavesdropping, but it's hard not to with the window down.

"Um," I look to Foster. "I lost my card." I lie.

"Oh, well you can use mine." She dangles the plastic between her fingers, but Foster rejects the gesture when I go to grab it. She slices her eyes to him, asking, "Why did you call the cops?"

"It was a huge misunderstanding, but I'm going to take care of it," he promises, and Kate turns her attention to me.

"Are we still mad at him?" she asks, and when I tell her no, she smiles.

Foster angles my body away from the window, bringing me to the back of his car. The air from the roaring muffler is hot against my leg. "You can't go in the station." he tells me quietly.

I throw my hands in the air. "Why?"

"Your parents put out a missing person's report on you."

I walk away and open the passenger door, sliding in without a word. Kate leans up in the seat, and I politely raise my hand when she goes to speak. "Nope," I tell her.

Foster gets back in and peels down the road. He places a hand on my leg, which calms me slightly. "What do—"

"Nope," I tell him, not wanting to speak to a soul right now. All I want is to handle the missing person's report, get Brett out of jail, and go to sleep.

"I don't want to bring you stress, Sky." Foster breathes deep, bringing his tattooed fingers over to graze my cheek. "It's all going to be okay, baby girl."

Kate taps on my shoulder, peeking her head around the headrest. "What's happening, Sky?" she inquires.

I look to Foster and shake my head, grabbing her hand that's resting on my shoulder. "I'll explain later, all right?" I suggest, trying to not say anything hateful. I'm just having a really, really bad day.

She nods, patiently leaning back against her seat.

When we pull up to the station, I grab Kate's card, my ID, and head inside. Foster follows, unwilling to let me go alone. But with the news of my parents placing a missing person's report out, I'm glad he'll be there with me.

A woman sits at the desk, greeting us when we walk inside. "What can I help you with?" she asks.

I look at her nameplate. "Hello, Ruby. I would like

to get my friend out of jail."

The woman nods, pulling up something on the computer. "Name?"

"Brett Miller," I reply with a waning breath, hoping he's okay.

"Okay," She nods, rolling through the information. "Miss, it looks like his hearing won't be until tomorrow, so bail hasn't been set yet."

"So, he's stuck here another night?"

She nods. "That's correct. The judge won't be in until Monday morning."

I quietly seethe. "He doesn't need a hearing." I reply.

"Have you seen his charges?" she asks, raising a brow.

I nod. "Yes, because the allegations of assault were about me."

Her brows lift, and she steps around the counter to walk up to a nearby sheriff. They exchange a few tentative words, and he looks over me. "Ms. Wells," He nods, then he turns his attention to Foster. "Nice to see you again, Jennings."

I don't ponder long on why these two know each other when Foster grits his teeth. "We need your help." he strains to say this.

The sheriff looks amused, crossing his arms. "Normally, you're running away from us. Now, you want our help?" He laughs. He's plump, with rosy cheeks that remind me of Santa.

Foster runs a long hand down his face. "Someone

used my name to make false allegations against one of your inmates, Brett Miller."

"Oh, the Miller boy!" The sheriff chuckled, adding, "He's being processed for release now."

"The clerk said it would be Monday before the judge would set bail." I state, furrowing my brows.

"She was mistaken. His dad came by about an hour ago." He nods his head towards Brett's father who is sitting against the wall, his eyes stuck in a magazine. I blanket my face with my hair, not wanting him to see me. My heart sinks; his dad knows. And I know why he's getting let go, because money controls everything.

I'm happy that advantage is going to Brett, who doesn't deserve to spend another second here.

We walk past the clerk, and she waves me down. "Anything else I can help you with, dear?"

I groan. "Yes, I need to un-file a missing person's report?" I question the way I word it, giving her a nervous look.

She lets out a low whistle. "Busy day for you, isn't it?" She laughs, trying to break the tension on my face. I can't help but smile a little.

"Name?"

"Skyler Johnson," I tell her, then I realize this is the first time I've ever had to deal with anything like this. I've never even gotten a ticket before.

"License?" she asks, and I hand it to her.

A few moments of clicking later, the clerk dust her hands. "Okay, all clear." she announces.

"Just like that?" My eyes widen in surprise.

"Yes, ma'am. You're an adult, so you could go to Siberia and no one could say anything. It looks like your parents filed the report, and you of course are entitled to not contact them. But as a mother, maybe let them know you're okay." Her words bring me calm. Even though my parents are still trying to control me with this report, all it has shown me is how free I actually am.

Knowing Brett is safe, we drop Kate off at the dorms. She does a little wave, but I can tell she knows something is majorly wrong. Foster squeezes my thigh, letting me know it's going to be alright when a tear runs down my cheek.

I would stay the night with her, but between Envy living there and my fear of telling the truth, I'm going to wait a little longer.

As we pull into Foster's place, I internally scream from the number of cars the driveway and yard are riddled with. I just want a quiet moment of peace, but these are the cards I'm dealt right now, and I want to be anywhere he is.

We walk inside, and everyone cheers, coming to greet Foster. A lot of the guys, including Ryder, address me by name, making me feel special that Foster undoubtedly brought me up in conversation. I see Callum taking a shot in the corner of the room, and he smiles at me.

Foster bends to my ear, saying, "Welcome to the house. You're part of an elite group of rejects now, Freckles." He grins, planting a kiss on my cheek.

It's like the bad boy version of a frat house. Everyone has something about them here that says they've been through some stuff together and that they're a family.

I'm starting to understand it a bit more.

We go to his room, ignoring the protests from the guys who beg us to stay and party.

The bed comes into view, inviting me to collapse onto it. Not bothering to change, I spring my tired body against the soft comforter, stretching myself out. Foster throws his shirt on the ground, and I can't help but stare at his sculptured chest.

He sends me a look, pulling his bottom lip between his white teeth while he walks over to me. Slowly, he climbs on top of me. His silver chain dangles from his neck, and the cold links touch my chin. "Want me to help you relax?" he asks, tilting his head.

I give a small nod, nervous but aching for him. I'm so ready to take my mind off of my reality and just get lost in him. No looming threat of if I'll be a student tomorrow or if I'll have money to eat. Just me, him, and a blissful moment.

I bring my nails across his back gently, watching as his jaw clenches from the contact. His lips are devouring my neck when a loud noise catches our attention. There's some music and chatting downstairs but nothing insane tonight.

The commotion stops, and Foster's obsidian eyes bore into me. "Where were we?" he asks, licking his lips.

It starts again just as I feel him hardening against my leg. "Get the fucking door!" Foster booms, but no one hears or cares about the persistent banging.

With a groan, he kisses my forehead and hastily removes himself from me. He paces the carpet for a moment to calm himself down before exiting the room.

My phone dings, an influx of texts chiming through.

Kate: "*That Bitch!*"

Attached to the message is a picture of her bed soaked in neon green paint. More pictures come through. The comforter, mattress, pillows, and her rug are completely doused in the ugly green slime.

Oh my God.

Me: "What happened?"

Foster comes trudging back to the room, and I see a blip of lime hair bouncing close behind him. I groan when he gives me a pouting look.

Ding.

Kate: "It was Envy."

I scoff, raising from the bed with a heated fury coursing through my veins. "What is she doing here?" I bark.

"It's Ghost's house, not yours." she chimes, pulling a piece of gum from her teeth and twisting it around her finger. Gross.

We both cross our arms, looking at him. Foster walks over to me, placing his hand on my arm. "She has nowhere else to go." he pleads.

"And that's her own damn fault!" I shout.

He shakes his head, cutting his eyes to her, and she retreats from his doorway to give us privacy.

"If she's living here, then I'm gone!" I threaten, seething with fury from what she's done to not only me but my best friend.

Foster looks away, his sharp jaw tensing. "Look, Sky. She's broken like us. She's one of us, and you're one of us now too. I can't just leave her on the street."

"Who will it be?" I ask, tapping my foot impatiently on the floor.

He shakes his head, "Don't make me choose." he pleads.

"It shouldn't be a choice, Foster. She's been awful to me, and Kate!" I cry, trying not to sound like an immature child, but it's unbearable to be in the same house with her. I turn my phone to face him, showing him exactly why she's not in her dorm anymore.

"Look," Foster says, taking my hand. "I know you don't get it, but she has nowhere to go."

"You don't think I fucking get that, Foster?"

"That's not what I mean." He slides a hand across his face in frustration, "She's a foster kid. No family, nothing. She's at school on a scholarship. She has to stay, but please don't go."

"So, she's staying here?" I ask again, ignoring the other things he said. I can't see past my anger for her right now. Not with what she did to Kate tonight.

"Yes," Foster replies, his shoulders slumping.

I hand him my phone, not wanting it anymore. "Then I'm out."

TWENTY-FOUR

A knock sounds on the door, and I groan from the pestering noise. When I peel my eyes open, I feel something stuck on my forehead.

It's a post-it note from Kate.

'Hey roomie. Didn't want to wake you up too early. Love you.'

I laugh a little at her sticking it on my face. Another knock sounds. "What?" I shout, my throat dry. What time is it?

"Sky?" Foster's voice travels from the other side of the door.

Shit. I don't respond.

"Sky, please open the door," he begs. When I don't reply, he curses under his breath. "I'll kick it off the hinges." he threatens, but I hear the soft thud of his forehead hitting the wood in defeat.

A long beat of silence passes between us. Then, he

slides something underneath the gap of the door. It's the phone he got me. "Listen, hate me all you want, but at least keep this phone. I just … I want you to have a way to call me …if you want too."

After another moment, I see the shadow of his boots disappear, but then they return not a second later.

"Why aren't you in class?" Foster inquires.

Why doesn't he just go? There's no point in going to school for one semester. I've been cut off.

Again, I don't respond.

"Alright, beautiful. I'll take the hint. I hope you're okay. I won't bother you if you don't want me too." He pauses. "Is that what you want?" His voice cracks.

My heart cries no, but I don't reply.

"If you need me, text me, okay? I never wanted to hurt you."

"But you did," I croak quietly, refusing to be a choice.

His boots scuff against the floor as he walks away.

When I feel like enough time has passed, I grab the phone. When I unlock it, there's a picture of Foster staring back at me. He changed the background, and it almost makes me text him … almost.

―――

I stay in bed for most of the day, sulking and trying to find out what I'm going to do with my life. I'm going insane in this tiny dorm.

I need a place to think. Somewhere quiet.

Kate comes back when the sun sets, dangling a set

of keys in her hand, surprised to still find me in bed.

She pushes about what's going on with me, but I tell her I'm fine. I'm going to talk to her soon—I am. I just don't want to right now. It doesn't take much convincing until she hands me her mom's keys and I climb into the car for a long drive to clear my head.

But I don't get far. I find myself pulling over on the side of a desolate road, a familiar tree my destination.

I step out and breathe in the salty air for a moment to clear my mind.

When I walk to the tree, our tree, I hear the mellow strumming of guitar strings.

I'm surprised to find Foster already sitting there on one of the branches. His feet dangle while an acoustic guitar sits in his lap. His body is facing the tree, away from me. I nearly turn around, but I don't. I can't.

Foster doesn't turn when I walk up. He simply says, "Hey, Freckles."

"I didn't know you would be here." I reply quietly. The more I close the gap between us, the more butterflies flap around in my stomach.

I sit on the ground, leaning my back against the wide trunk. He follows, turning to rest his back as well. I look at his face. The sliver of moonlight illuminates his features, casting long streaks down his angled cheeks.

He's been crying.

Breathlessly, I cup his chin in my hands and turn him to face me. "I'm so fucking sorry." he whispers, his voice taut with regret.

I don't know what to say, and I can't take much

more of the broken look on his face, but I at least deserve an explanation. The distant sounds of waves calm me, giving me a little strength to not dive into his arms. "Why was it even a choice, Foster?"

He looks at me so intently that I flush crimson under his gaze. "Skyler, it was never a choice. Ever. I truly had no other option, I swear to you."

"I don't understand."

"It's the crew," He shrugs. "Our rules are simple but absolute."

"Like a motorcycle gang?" I ask, and he laughs.

"It's not like the cheesy gangs you see in movies. We're a family, and once you're in you can't be turned away. We ride together, race together, and go through life together. Envy was a part of that."

"Was?" I ask, trying to hide my happiness when he smirks.

"Yeah, she's out. The house voted to remove her. Between drugging me and what she did to Kate—and you, and her bullshit antics, she won't be coming back."

"Oh," I respond, feeling a hint of guilt. But it's immediately gone when I remember she put herself in that situation.

Foster frowns. "I know it's dumb, but it's how we run as a family. It's also why Callum is still there after he pulled that shit with you." He balls his fist but calms when I place my hand over his.

"Why didn't you just tell me?" I ask.

"I didn't have a chance. You bolted." He looks at me intently. "You never have to run from me. Ever."

"I just don't want to be the second choice." I say quietly.

A dimpled smirk spreads over his face. "There is no fucking choice when it comes to you, Sky."

I flush scarlett when he interlaces his fingers with mine, and in a breathless moment, all is right in the world.

I wrap my fingers around one of the roots of the tree, always mesmerized by how beautiful it is. "What kind of tree is this?"

"A Banyan. They're native to India." Foster replies, looking up at the massive structure.

I grow curious. "Did you come here to think of me?"

His fingertips run up the rough surface of the tree, trailing over the jagged bark that meets soft wood. "You, racing, and my parents."

He's never talked about his family with me. "What are they like?"

Foster tucks his bottom lip between his teeth, resting his elbows on his propped-up knees. "They, um ... they rode too." he replies, averting his gaze.

"Rode?" I ask, wondering about the past tense.

He nods, looking at me with glossy eyes. "Yeah ... there was a crash." My stomach turns in knots. "No survivors." Foster gestures to the tree, and in his eyes, I know what he's saying.

This is why he brought me here.
Why he was crying.
Facing the trunk and playing his guitar.
It's his last connection to his parents.

The last place they were alive.

"Foster, I'm so sorry." My voice breaks.

He shakes his head, shrugging. "It's okay."

I feel the tears welling in my eyes. "No, it's not. You saw how I treated my parents. That's why you were so upset with me at the burger place. I'm so sorry, Foster."

"No, fuck your parents. If I would have known then what I know now," worry lines crease his forehead. "we need to communicate better." he jokes, but the weight of his loss is still heavy in the air.

I catch a tear as it trickles down his cheek. He flinches from the emotional gesture, not sure how to take it. "You don't have to fake it around me, okay?" I tell him.

He nods once, quickly brushing his sleeve over his face to rid away any sign of emotion. "Anyways," He smiles a smile that doesn't reach his eyes. "I've never really talked to anyone about that."

My face softens. "You can talk to me anytime about anything."

The heavy moment is drowned out by our smiles at each other. "Oh shit!" he exclaims, jumping up from where we sit.

Foster brushes off his pants, extending his hand to me. "I want to show you something." he offers, slinging his guitar strap over his shoulder. When I stand, I dust off my dress. "Wait right here." He points to the ground, and I listen. He rushes to his car, which I realize now is neatly tucked into the side of the road. The black of night gave no hint to it being there at all.

He leans inside and rummages around, pulling out

a smashed white box from the passenger window.

When he walks back to me, I ask, "What's that?" But he simply shakes his head and takes my hand in his.

In the darkness, he navigates us through palm trees and bushes. He walks in front, shielding me from their pokey leaves. His guitar is in front of my head, and I walk carefully so my face doesn't slam into the strings.

"It's really dark, Foster." I whisper, worried about the wildlife at this time of night.

"Almost there," he tells me, squeezing my hand.

We arrive at a small alcove, one created by sweeping vines and tousled Floridian ivy. I walk through, and the moonlight glimmers against the sea, exposing an intimate private beach. "I've lived here my entire life, but I never knew about this." I admit, breathless at the view.

His grin stretches wide as we take off our shoes and step onto the sugary sands.

Foster sits on a weathered piece of driftwood and slings his guitar around, putting it in front of him. I sit beside him.

His fingers strum the chords, creating a simple yet beautiful sound. The setting is so intimate; no one's around, no lights, no people. It's me, him, and his guitar. "The night you were drunk, you said butterflies."

"Hmm?" I ask, pulling my lips together in embarrassment. Then, I give an awkward nod.

"What did it mean?"

"You," I say, blushing furiously. "You give me butterflies. I always heard about them in books and movies, but I never really experienced them before you."

Foster breathes a sigh of relief. "Good, because if it was something else, I would look really stupid."

"Why?" I ask, arching a brow.

He strums the strings, a gentle melody playing through them. "It's not much, and it's not very good ... So, don't laugh, okay?"

I nearly squeal, sliding a little closer to him. "Go!" I encourage, clapping my hands.

Foster rocks his head to the beat, and I admire the way he looks. Nervous, and beautifully broken as the moonlight glitters against his tan skin. His jawline tightens when his lips open to sing.

His voice is deep and rich like expensive chocolate. Soft like silk as his words wrap around and hug every inch of my body.

The song is so sweet, and he laughs while he sings the cheesy parts. I can tell he's never done this, and that makes it so much more special.

I hang onto every word of his song, but one lyric in particular catches my attention, 'She's drawn to the broken. A reflection of herself. She hides her scars behind designer clothes, refusing anyone's help. While I hide mine behind ink and grease, surrounded by walls I've built. One look at her, and I was done.'

He pauses for a moment.

'I knew I had to release the butterfly from her cage.' Foster murmurs.

When he stops, I can't help the tears that stream like a waterfall down my cheeks.

He throws his head back, groaning, "No, no, no. I

don't know how to deal with you crying." Foster jokes, poking me in the side. He's excruciatingly beautiful right now. So vulnerable as he peers at me from under his thick lashes.

I put my hands to my face. "That was the cutest thing I've ever heard."

He rolls his eyes, but I can tell he appreciates the compliment by the dimples in his cheeks. "I know it's cheesy, and I'm still working on the last part. I wrote it for your birthday."

"No! It's perfect. Absolutely perfect," I chime.

He places the guitar on the sand. I can't take the stupid grin off my face, and it's beginning to hurt.

Foster grabs the white box and places it on my lap. "I threw it in the floorboard of my car when you wouldn't talk to me at the dorm earlier." he admits.

My fingers trail along the cardboard. I love the scrunched-up box and the smooshed, pink cupcake that sits inside of it.

Foster grabs the long, glittery candle that's rolling around inside the box and places it in the icing. He takes the cupcake out and sets the box to the side, pulling a lighter from the pocket of his jeans.

The tiny flame flickers, a little golden light dancing between us as he holds it between our faces.

"Happy Birthday, Freckles." Foster tells me, and I close my eyes. I wish that time would slow down so I could stay in this moment. I wish that my entire life didn't turn upside down like it did. But knowing that how it was, was never the right way to live.

Finally, I wish for him to know how special he is ... and to stop doing dumb things.

I pucker my lips outward and blow the candle out. The small warmth disappears, replaced by the scorching heat of Foster's body against mine and his soft lips pressing against me.

His hands are everywhere and on every inch of me as he eases or bodies onto the sand that's still warm from being scorched by the sun all day.

My chest rises steadily as I attempt to control my breathing.

"I want you, Skyler." Foster whispers, his lips on my neck.

TWENTY-FIVE

The rushing sound of the tide crashing against the waves doesn't match the smooth rhythm in which Foster kisses me, holds me, grabs me...

I would try to control my breathing, but it would be impossible with how perfect he looks on top of me. He draws back, ripping off his shirt and laying it down beside me.

Toned, golden muscles arch when he swoops his hand under my back and throws me on top of the shirt, protecting the lower part of my body from the tiny grains of sand beneath us. His leg sits between my knees, pushing up ever so slightly to create an ache deep in my core.

I run my hands along Foster's back, watching as he nibbles his lip. A cooling sensation peppers my skin as his silver chain touches my nose.

His lush mouth slides down my body, a cool sensation following quickly behind it.

Underneath the shirt, the soft sand conforms to my curves.

Everything is perfect underneath the midnight sky that's speckled with bright stars. The moonlight casts a glow on Foster's back, showcasing the sheer stretch of his muscles as he dots kisses down my stomach. He stops right above my pants, gripping the edge between his strikingly white teeth.

I lift myself off the ground slightly, to give him permission. A groan escapes him when he slips my pants off. Taking it slow, he trails his fingertips from the tops of my feet to my inner thigh, making me shudder from the touch.

"You're so fucking beautiful." Foster tells me, his obsidian eyes washing over me while the night sky washes over us both.

Nervous and unsure what to say or do, I look up at the stars. The moment I do, his warm finger slides over the slit of my panties, eliciting a pleasurable gasp from me.

He does this for endless moments, teasing and enjoying the way my body writhes for him.

Foster's hand dips down further as he slides one finger inside of me. "Fuck," he hisses. "You're so damn tight."

"I ... Foster," I moan, dipping my head back into the sand. My body twitches when he slides a second finger inside, slowly pushing it in and out. The feeling is so pleasurable, so perfect.

He bends down, and I can feel his hair between my legs. "Can I taste you?" He licks his lips, continuing to rub his finger up and down.

I look at him, finding a dash of want hidden behind his dark eyes. I nod, biting my own lip at the sight of him in this position.

Foster smiles and rings his fingers around the fabric of my panties, pulling them to the side. I moan as his mouth dives between my slit, filling me with warmth. Every smooth flick of his tongue sends me further into the galaxy.

I jolt forward at the same time as the waves do, diving headfirst into the first orgasm that someone else has given me.

"Fuck me." I say in an unfamiliar, breathy voice. I'm surprised by my tone and what I said. When Foster looks at me, his unruly hair lays wildly atop his head as he studies me.

"I'm not like your preppy boyfriends, Sky." His tongue darts out and brushes my inner thigh. "I'm not just going to leave you disappointed and wanting. I'm going to take your body and make it mine." He assumes, but he's right.

His large, inked hand constricts around me, grabbing my ass with a lustful squeeze.

Foster's thumb runs across my throbbing clit. "I'm going to devour every fucking inch of you." he promises, bringing his fingers up to gently pinch my hard nipples. Then, he rips off his pants, his throbbing cock bursting out from his boxers, bouncing from the freedom of the fabric being gone. I gulp as he whispers into the night air, "You'll be getting into bed with the devil."

From both my lack of experience and fear that he'll notice, I blurt out, "I'm a virgin." My words make him groan. A wild look grows in his eyes.

"And you want to give it to me?" Foster asks in a rough, gritty tone.

When I nod, he sits up, stroking his impressive length in his hands. The sight makes chills grow over every inch of my heated skin.

His finger trails the top of my clit, and I do everything I can to not cry out in pleasure. "You want me to be the first and only man inside of you?" he asks, a sultry look in his eyes.

The way he said first and *only* makes my knees shake. I nod my head, sliding my hands down his sides, wanting to feel his warm, tattooed skin against mine.

"Yes," I tell him softly.

He leans forward to plant a kiss on my forehead, and his tattooed knuckles brush my cheek when he pulls away slightly. "I'll be careful with you," he promises, dipping his head down to kiss my lips. "This time."

Foster pulls something from his wallet and cuts the wrapper open with his teeth. A condom. He looks down, rolling it onto his throbbing length before returning to me.

His thumb rolls over my cheek, and he brings his lips to mine.

Gently, he slides inside of me, and I moan into his mouth. A pang of pressure builds, shooting sensory overload to every nerve ending in my body as he gently rocks back and forth. The look of pleasure on his face excites me more, along with the throbbing of his cock inside of me and the way it twitches when I scrape my nails across his back so I can transfer a little of the pain to him.

"Is this okay?" he asks with a moan, clearly holding himself back from the size of the bulging veins in his neck.

My eyes are wild when I reply, "Mhmm,"

The more into the motions we get, the more the grainy sand makes its way over our perspiring skin. Thankfully, it never reaches me there.

I grow accustomed to him, his movements, and the way he feels inside of me. Well, besides the unmistakable feeling of being filled with him. The pressure doesn't subside, but the unusual feeling grows more comfortable.

I allow myself to roll with the pleasure, allowing the waves beside us to teach me how to crash against him.

Foster's breathing is heavy as he slides his tongue along my neck, sucking and nibbling on my skin, creating a hickey. His eyes meet mine, and I can tell he's on the edge, ready to cum.

He tilts his head, studying me as his body travels up and down with every held back thrust that he gives me. "I'm not the good guy, Sky." His dark eyes rake over my arching body as he slides in and out, warning me when it's too late.

But doesn't he know that he's perfect?

"I don't care, Foster." I tell him, moaning his name.

"You should," He uses one hand to pin both of mine above my head, stretching my body out before him. "Fuck!"

I would collapse if I wasn't lying down, both from

the way he looks and from the way his body rocks back and forth as he maintains his tight hold around my wrists. It's like I can let go; like I can breathe for the first time in my life.

At the same moment that a wave crashes upon the shore, Foster mimics it. Diving his body into mine with a passionate kiss and a groan from his full lips.

He catches his breath against me, and I look to the stars. I couldn't have imagined a better way to lose my virginity than like this ... and with him.

I giggle when he passionately sweeps his hand through my hair, filling it with sand.

"Let's go rinse off." Foster suggests, rising from where we lay on the ground. In his absence, a cool brush of wind rolls over my naked body. I shake my head, pulling his sand-covered shirt to cover myself. He bends down and rips it from my hands. "Come on," he says, extending his hand out.

"I'm scared," I admit, looking out at the dark waters.

"What do you have to be afraid of? Nothing is scarier than not living, Skyler," Foster helps me up. "Nothing."

All it takes is one dimpled smirk from him and I find myself running to the water, not away from it.

Foster chases after me, his long legs allowing an advantage to gain momentum easily. He slings his arm around my hips, careful to not touch the bruises that are barely there anymore.

It's a faint reminder of my life before as we plunge

into the after... together.

TWENTY-SIX

We wake to the sunrise. My head is buried into Foster's chest. I peek up with squinted eyes to find him already looking at me.

"What time is it." I croak, leaning up and placing my palms against the sand. "I can't believe we fell asleep here." I smile, looking out to the ocean that's being blanketed by the sunrise, a gorgeous pink and orange hue slowly awakening the beach.

Foster laughs, planting a kiss on my cheek. "It's six in the morning, and we have to get to school."

I groan, throwing my head back. "We have two hours, and you need to get to school, not me."

"Why wouldn't you be coming with me?"

I stand up, dusting a thin layer of sand off of my disheveled clothes and stretching my sore muscles. Remembering why they're stiff from our perfect moment last night. The memory makes me let out a weird noise from my chest, I cover it with a cough. "There really is no reason for me to go for one semester." I shrug.

Foster nods, taking it in and standing up. "We'll figure something out," he promises with furrowed brows.

I place my hand on his shoulder, saying, "It's not your problem to worry about. Please don't let this drive you crazy."

The moment we turn to walk back to the street, he yells out, "You're rich!"

An odd expression lays on my face. "Not anymore."

"No, I mean ... your parents probably paid for the entirety of your schooling."

"Oh, that's a good point." I reply quietly, running my fingers through my salt drenched hair. I desperately need to deep condition.

Foster tilts his head, fixing his guitar strap. "And why don't you look happy?" he asks, grabbing my hand as we walk towards the little jungle between the slice of paradise that we're in and the street.

"I am," I say, letting out a dark chuckle. "But I'm locked in on three more years of Accounting. But it's better than nothing." I grin, thankful I have a plan, even if it is the one my parents made for me. It's four years of college, and that's better than nothing.

Hand in hand, we pass by our tree, and Foster frowns. The tree that took his parents' lives. Every layer that he gives me makes me understand him more.

I squeeze his hand as he walks me to Kate's mom's car.

"I'm so sorry I took the car all night!" I tell Kate while she rustles in her sheets.

She turns, gripping her phone and being blinded by the bright light of the screen. "It's six-thirty in the morning, you psycho bitch. Go to sleep." She croaks, still not fully awake.

I jump into her bed, and my stiff hair doesn't bounce. Instead, it lets off a dusting of sand onto her.

"Sky!" she shouts, laughing when I shake my head. "Did you stay at the beach last night?" Kate curiously gives me a look-over after rubbing her eyes and dusting herself off.

I bite my lip, nodding. "Maybe."

"And did you happen to stay with a certain tattooed, muscular guy who's obsessed with cars and bikes?" she asks, grinning.

"I did," I reply.

"And did you ... possibly ... get laid?"

I roll my eyes. "I may have." I say with a smile.

"Yes!" Kate cheers, pushing me off of her bed and onto the floor. "Go take a shower. You didn't have to bring the beach home."

I look at my new home on the right side of her dorm room. The dark side of the space, with the scattered remains of Envy left behind. "You don't mind if I stay?"

She nods, getting up from the bed to shake off the sheets. "No, as long as you tell me why you need to stay here."

I get up from the floor and tiptoe back to the door, "Soon. I promise."

Freshly showered and in a comfy sweater and shorts, I head to Biology. Foster sits at our table looking hauntingly handsome, with a soft black t-shirt that looks so good against his honey skin.

I sink into my seat, and he slides a cup to me. I bring the warm liquid to my lips and sip the delicious latte. "Thank you." I grin.

Professor Dyer walks in and immediately starts handing out presentation grades. My hand flies up to my forehead. From the events of the past week and my ignoring school, I completely forgot about our presentation. There go my perfect grades, but I don't have to have perfect grades, right?

But I like to.

He makes his way to us, and I'm about to shoot out a plethora of excuses, but I stop when he sets a paper down in front of us that has a big red 'A' scribbled on it. "Good job, you two." Mr. Dyer looks at me with a remorseful frown. "I'm so sorry to hear about your father, Skyler."

I nod slowly, not knowing what to say. When he walks to the next table, Foster leans over to me and whispers, "I told him he died." He laughs.

I let out a massive breath of relief. "Wait, so you presented by yourself?" I smile, looking at the paper. "And you got an A?"

"Yeah. Don't make a big deal of it." Foster bumps into me playfully.

"Thank you."

Class ends, and we head to the hallway. I turn right, but Foster's hand tugs me left.

"Come on," he says.

"Where are we going?"

Foster looks over at me, grinning with deep dimples. "You don't look happy, so we're going to change your major."

TWENTY-SEVEN

The warm wind envelops me when we step outside, nearly thawing out my frozen mind as Foster guides us towards the administration office.

It seems like things are happening in slow motion, and my chest feels as if it's going to shatter from the weight of it all.

We stop walking, and Foster touches my face. "Hey, beautiful," He grins.

"Hey," I reply in a short breath.

A gentle breeze flows between us. "I know you're probably freaking out right now, but I want you to know it's okay."

"I just ... I have no idea what I want to do." I admit.

"I know, babe. You've never been allowed the right to decide your life for yourself, but trust me, don't waste your college tuition. What classes do you want to drop?"

"I'm not sure. Anything to do with accounting, I

guess, but I really like Mrs. Parks." I groan, knowing it's the class I'm doing best in and that I've grown fond of her. I wish I had someone to ask for advice. My mind travels to Mrs. Rita. I need to go visit her soon. I know she quit the day I left, and I hope she's doing okay financially.

"Sky?"

"Huh?"

Foster gives me a comforting hug before pulling back and saying, "You don't have to change your major if you don't want to. I guess I just wanted you to know you had the choice."

I look at the students buzzing on the green, at Foster, and finally at my reflection in the windows of the administration office. With a deep breath and a foggy sense of clarity, I decide my own future.

"Fuck Accounting," I snicker, opening the door and bursting inside. I'm embarrassed to find no one on the other side of the desk when I bravely stomp to it.

Foster laughs before pulling me in to ruffle my hair. He cups his hands around his lips and shouts, "Hey! My girl needs some assistance." My cheeks flush a deep pink.

A stocky old man walks out, the last of his stringy hair holding desperately to his shiny head. "How may I help you?"

"I'm looking for an academic advisor." I say in a quiet voice. I'm not sure why I'm talking in such a low tone. Maybe out of fear that I'm doing something wrong. From the feeling of my stomach erupting with a million nervous butterflies, I can tell that's exactly what it is.

He smiles a little, standing up straighter. "That's

me."

"Great! I need to change my major."

"Certainly. Come to my office." He gestures out down the hallway and we follow. The man turns to me and extends his hand. "I'm Danny Duncan." he states, and his glasses slide ever so slightly down his nose.

"I'm Skyler Johnson." I reply, returning his handshake.

We walk into his office, and I take a seat beside Foster. Mr. Duncan heads around and sits at his desk. "So, Ms. Johnson," He begins typing on his computer. "You're wanting to change your major from Accounting to …" He peers his eyes in my direction.

"Um. So, the thing is, I actually don't know what I want to do."

He gives me a dumbfounded expression before fixing his glasses. "So, you're wanting to switch your major from Accounting to undecided? Nothing?" A slight shake of his head makes me rethink. "Looking at your credits, especially from your previous school, you're heavily into your degree. I highly advise against—"

Foster raises his hand with a polite grin. "With all due respect, she's got a shit ton of base credits from her prior school and once she figures it out, she'll be ahead of most no matter what she chooses."

"It's your decision." Mr. Duncan looks at me warily. I mean, to be fair, this *is* a super weird thing to do. Besides, he doesn't understand my reasons for changing. I nod, and he continues, "You want to just keep all your classes for this semester but take off the major?"

"Yes, well, no ... I'd like to drop Accounting, actually. My second period."

"Alright. What would you like to replace it with?"

"Something artsy?" I reply, hoping he'll choose something for me. Right now, I just want easy. I have a lot of things to focus on right now, and a class that doesn't require me getting a one hundred as my final grade would be a huge weight off my shoulders.

"Oh, you're an artist?" he asks, raising an eyebrow.

I shake my head, trying not to sound like an idiot. "No. Honestly, I just want something calming and creative ... Artsy, you know?"

He laughs outright. "Artsy, okay." Mr. Duncan scrolls through an expansive list, and I can't help but chuckle at the awkward silence in the room, especially when Foster picks up a cat-shaped paperweight from the desk and pretends it's alive by patting its head.

Mr. Duncan gives him a look before turning his attention to me.

"Art Theory and Practice?" he suggests.

With a shrug, I give him my answer. Next semester, when I've figured out what I want to do with my life, I'll return to this seat right here and I won't need to shrug.

He exits and returns with my new schedule freshly printed on a crisp piece of paper. "Anything else I can do for you, Ms. Johnson?"

"That's all—"

Foster cuts me off, "Take her off the cheer team." My stomach twist in knots at his words. He looks to my stunned face and adds, "Please." But that's not why my jaw is open.

A small gasp escapes my parted lips. I lean into him, whispering, "Can I do that?"

He does the same, not whispering. "You can do absolutely whatever the fuck you want, Freckles."

I can tell we're eating at Mr. Duncan's nerves when he sighs. "That's something your coach will need to do. I assume you have practice today. Talk to them."

"Will do," I stand up, and I can't contain the smile on my face.

"These new changes will take effect Friday, so you'll need to resume your current classes as usual."

⁓

I show up towards the end of Accounting, but luckily everyone is working on their laptops. When the bell rings, I walk over to Mrs. Park's desk. "I just wanted to let you know that Friday will be my last day."

"Oh!" She sounds surprised but continues to thumb through her paperwork. "What school are you transferring to?"

"I'm not transferring, just dropping this class." I cringe. That came out harsher than I intended it, but Mrs. Parks sends me a smile when she sees my scrunched face.

She leans in close, a small frown taking over her face as students begin to shuffle out. "I saw the notification this morning of you not being on my roll after Friday and assumed you were leaving the school. I'm sad; you're the only student who pays attention in here. Everyone else is on YouTube all day. You get good grades. Are you struggling in any way? I can help, if that's the case."

"It was never what I wanted," I respond, surprised by my honesty.

"That's a shame, but I understand. You get one college experience, so don't waste it on a career you don't want." Mrs. Parks smiles.

Foster slinks his head around the doorway, hurrying me along to lunch. "I'll see you later Mrs. Parks." I say quickly.

She smiles and returns to grading her papers while we head down the hall.

"How'd that go?" he asks, slinking his arm around me.

I ponder it for a moment. "Good, I guess ... I'm just nervous about the change. Accounting is all I've ever thought I would do. It's what's been drilled into me."

As he looks up to the ceiling, his jawline tightens. "I really hope I didn't make you feel like you had to change your major."

"Not at all! I truly never thought of it." My whole life has been thoroughly planned out for me. Go to college, marry their choice of spouse, die unhappy but rich with money.

"Promise?" Foster prods, a scrunched look of worry making his hard edges look adorable.

"Pinky promise." I reply with a small smile.

He bites his lip. "What about Cheer?"

"No, Cheer is worse than Accounting. You know I don't like cheering." I'm so happy that Friday will be my last day. I'm just worried that the coach will rip me apart when I quit on such short notice.

"Friday will be my last day." I wring my hands nervously, standing before the coach.

"Okay."

"Okay?" I ask, dumbfounded by how hard I thought this was going to be.

"Yeah, just make sure you're at Saturday's game so I can prepare a new lineup for next week."

I've never felt so ... disposable.

I love it.

But I can't help the pang of sadness that rises in me when I walk away from the girls. I didn't connect with any of them, and that's probably my own fault, but cheering from elementary to high school has been such an integral part of who I am.

The comradery of it, the late nights practicing cheers with your friends, the lights.

Not the forced smiles, the lack of depth in the art of dance, the routine.

I find myself walking to the mechanical department to find Foster leaned under a hood, his white shirt embellished with fingertips of black from where he's been wiping his hands on it.

He sees me and immediately brings me in for a kiss, careful to not smudge oil all over me. Foster grabs a red rag and wipes his hands off. "Want to stay with me tonight?" he asks, his puppy dog eyes beaming down at me.

"I need to talk to Kate about everything."

The obsidian in his eyes hold a twinkle. "I know, but I need you tonight. There's a big race coming this weekend."

I raise a brow. "Oh?"

"It's worth a lot, and I need you to keep me level."

"Is it on Saturday? That's my last game." I respond, feeling a little nostalgic about my career of cheerleading but looking forward to finding a hobby or sport that I'm happy with.

He brings me in for another kiss. "I wouldn't miss your ridiculous football game for anything. The race is on Sunday, anyway."

"Can we swing by the dorm so I can grab some clothes?"

The dorm room is empty when I enter. Kate had mentioned during gym that she and Ryder were going to dinner, so I guess staying here would have been pointless.

While I pack a small bag, Foster claps his hands together. "Okay, now that you're a free woman with four years of college under her belt, what else do you want to change?"

My eyes flit towards Envy's side of the dorm room. Torn posters lay half hung and half scattered on the ground. Her clothes still linger, and the scent of apple perfume weighs heavy in the air.

"I want to change this." I gesture around. "Pink?" I guess?

Foster nods, smiling. "Okay, Kate may be a better

option for redecorating than me. Anything else?"

I run my hands through my hair, grabbing a loose strand. "Bright pink." I tell him, feeling a sense of empowerment washing over me.

"I like that. All of it?"

"No, like maybe a little bit underneath."

He sends me a boyish grin, one that almost makes me melt right into the poster riddled floor. "Alright, Freckles. Let's get started then."

TWENTY-EIGHT

And so, my wish is granted, and Foster drives us on the bike to a local drug store. He bends down and grabs a box with a pink-haired girl smiling on the front. "This?" he asks.

A little knot appears in my stomach out of excitement. "Yes!"

"Lift," Foster says, grinning, and I raise my hands high above my head. His fingers curl around the fabric of my shirt. He slowly peels every piece of clothing from my body, leaving only a pair of black boy shorts and my bra.

Foster exhales, his warm breath floating against my chest as he rips off his t-shirt and puts it on me. The scent is intoxicating, and the moment is intimate and quiet. Although, downstairs there's a rumbling of music traveling through the closed bedroom door.

We don't care, though; we're paying very close attention to what we're doing.

"I hope I don't fuck this up." he admits, gripping my hand to lead me to his bathroom.

―◯―

With gloved hands, Foster sets me on his counter while he reads the directions from the paper inside the box.

"Okay, it's a good thing you're already blonde because if I bleached your hair it would probably fall out." he jokes, leaning against the wall to very tediously check each step. His tan skin glistens, and I can't take my eyes from his hard body.

Every edge and curve is sharp and refined.

He shakes the plastic bottle and squeezes it, pouring out a small dollop of the pink liquid onto his gloved hand. I turn my body to look at myself in the mirror and pull out the section I want to be done: a thick piece underneath on the right side.

I turn back towards Foster with a mischievous grin, feeling like I'm doing something incredibly dangerous, although it's only pink hair dye. "Ready?" he asks.

It takes no more than two seconds for him to saturate the strand. He wraps it in a little plastic wrap so it doesn't go anywhere. "So, thirty minutes..." He crooks his finger under my chin. "What could we possibly do in thirty minutes?"

I nibble on my lip. The little butterflies that have taken residence in my stomach every single time he's near flutter about, making me blush. "I can think of a few things," I whisper against his lips when he moves in closer.

I wait with bated breath as his fingertips trail up my bare legs, landing on my inner thighs.

His hands slide up the outline of my curves, and his palms travel to either side of my face, pulling me in for a heated, passionate kiss.

I feel his length hardening as he stands close, between my open legs. He grips me everywhere, a low growl resonating deep within his rising chest. "Property of Ghost?" Not a statement, but a question.

I nod, raking my nails through his thick hair. "Of Foster," I remind him.

He reaches down to unzip his pants. "Oh shit!" he shouts, looking down at his hands. They're covered in blood.

His eyes roam over me to check for any injuries, but I already know what happened. I turn towards the mirror, laughing when I see red in my hair in lieu of bright pink. At some point during our tangled exchange, the plastic wrap fell from my hair. "Why did it turn red?" I laugh nervously.

"I don't know. The girl on the front is pink," he says, looking confused. I cringe when I look at his hair. When my hands went through it, I left behind a streak

I grab the box on the counter beside me and look to the back. There are three small pictures. The first one shows blonde hair like mine showcasing what it will turn into with this color. A dark, wine red.

I turn it to Foster, and he groans, "I looked at the paper, not the back of the box. I'm sorry, Freckles." He steps back and examines me, curling his knuckles under his chin like a statue. "Looks hot though." I blush at his words.

"Have you, um ... seen your hair?" I ask, pointing up. His eyes dart to the mirror, and a sigh of relief escapes him. It's not noticeable, except to us. Which makes it pretty funny.

"We've got to rinse this off of me ... right now." he says, a chuckle escaping him as he turns on the shower to warm the water. "Fuck ... Is this going to turn pink? Give me that box, babe." His eyes roam over the third picture with the darkest hair, and lucky for him, it's a very faint bit of color. "Looks like I'll be wearing a hat for a while."

I can't help the rolling laughter that escapes my lips, and neither can Foster. It's one of those laughs that warms your soul and clears your mind; the kind where you can't control yourself.

He comes in between my legs again, this time lifting me. "Foster! We still have clothes on." I yell out as he steps under the steaming stream of water.

He looks at me, winking. "Yeah, and now I get to peel them off you."

My bare feet hit the ground, and although the warm water overtakes my skin, goosebumps rise over me when Foster does, in fact, peel my clothes off me.

His lips gently press against mine while the warm water trickles between our faces. With a soft shove, he gently pins me against the tile. The cool sensation of the stones against my naked body makes me shiver in the most incredible way. Foster's warm hands slink underneath my arms, and ever so slowly, he slides them up above me. His tongue dives against my neck, and his stubble scratches me in a heavenly way.

"Your pants are still on." I tell him between parted, swollen lips.

He grins against me, taking my hand in his to grip it around his throbbing length that threatens to rip them apart. "Take them off then."

I gulp, hoping what I'm about to do will be good for him. I look into his eyes and keep that contact as I slide my back down the cool stones until I'm level with his zipper.

I undo it, having a hard time peeling his black pants to the ground from how soaked they are. He helps, kicking them off quickly to get them out of the way.

He places a palm against the tile to hold himself up when I wrap my hands around his thick, throbbing cock. Water splashes in my face as it rolls off of his shoulders. I make sure to keep my eyes directed at him, even though I'm nervous. So nervous that it won't feel as good as he makes me feel.

His other hand slinks through my hair and gently he brings me to him. I roll my tongue along his length, taking it fully. Feeling him slide down my throat.

"Fuck, Skyler," Foster moans, gripping my hair. "You ... fuck."

I look up innocently. "I don't have a gag reflex." I say, bringing my tongue back to play with him. This new me, this free me, wants to play. I want to do everything with him. I want us to explore each other.

"I don't want ..." He can barely speak. "To know

how you know that."

His jealousy makes me work harder, lapping him and using my hand to help with his pleasure. I try to talk, but it's impossible with him filling up my mouth.

"You speaking incoherent words with my dick in your mouth is going to make me cum in two seconds."

I pull back, grinning wide. "I said, I got dared at cheer camp to put a cucumber down my throat. That's how I know."

"Good girl." Foster nods, bringing me back to him and putting light pressure against the back of my head to guide me up and down his shaft. I watch as he comes completely undone by me. His muscles constrict when he nears his climax. "Do you want my cum down your throat or on your face." he asks, looking down at me with a dangerous, sexy glint to his eyes.

I don't pull away; I continue sucking. To be honest, I'm curious how it will taste. His entire body trembles as he pours himself into my mouth and down my throat. It's salty and thick. But it's him, and the warm liquid dribbles down my chin when I pull away to swallow.

I slide back up to him, and his fingers dip down to touch me. I moan his name. He covers my mouth, but we both know with the volume of the music downstairs that no one can hear my noises.

Foster gets on his knees, returning the favor in the most incredible way. The hot water streams across my bare breasts as he reaches up to cup them, to pinch my hard nipples. I feel powerful, grown, and in control while my hands slink through his thick hair.

I nearly collapse in pleasure when I reach my peak. Afterward, Foster stands, licking my taste off his lips.

His dark hair is slicked by the water when he looks at me, a small, washed-out string of red in his hair. I look into his obsidian eyes and see my past, present, and future laid out before me.

The way my body reacts to him. The way my heart reacts to him. Unexplainable.

My first love, perhaps?

I know it's fast. It must be lust ... not love.

But I don't care.

I want to drown in everything he is.

TWENTY-NINE

Friday.

It's the last day of Accounting, and tomorrow will be the last time I step foot on the field.

It's bittersweet, really, but I didn't enjoy cheering.

"Are you trying to burn a hole through it?" Foster asks, eyeing me curiously with a grin.

"I don't want to wear it." I groan, holding up my uniform.

He shrugs. "Then don't."

I hop onto the bed and plant a sweet kiss on his full lips. "It's Friday, so I have to."

Foster's fingers run through my hair. "What are they going to do? Kick you off the team?"

"Good point." I say with a smile.

I really can't believe how quickly this week has flown by. I guess it's the frenzy of preparing for my dramatic change of classes. Well, just no more Accounting.

I step into Mrs. Park's classroom, and she sends me a funny look when I take my seat.

Luckily, she doesn't hand out a test. Instead, we quietly study our books until the bell rings. I focus primarily on doodling my name next to Foster's.

"Skyler," She gestures to her desk when everyone rushes out of the room at the chime of the bell.

I approach her with a smile, not wanting to make the last day of her class awkward. I truly like her, and if she taught another class, I would have signed up for it, but I can't stay on the path my parents laid for me. "Hey, Mrs. Parks."

"I couldn't help but notice your lack of uniform. You quit Accounting and Cheer?"

I nod. "Yeah, I just didn't care for the whole organized structure of it all." I'm surprised by the honesty that spews from my lips.

She digs in her purse, pulling out a business card. "If you're ever interested in dancing again, I own a studio over in Liberty. Swing by sometime."

My eyes roam over the rectangular paper. It's pink with a cursive 'Grace Studios' embellished the front. I inwardly groan, unsure what to tell her. I mean, would that be something I would enjoy? I love dancing, but I loathe cheerleading.

But Liberty is not a good part of town. I was never

allowed there.

But I'm allowed anywhere I want now.

I'm torn trying to find myself. Every single day it's something new.

Who am I?
What do you like, Sky?
Who are you, Sky?

"It's no pressure, Skyler, but if you ever miss dancing, come over." Mrs. Parks suggests. The subtle tilt in her smile tells me she knows I was contemplating it when I zoned out.

"Thanks. I'll see you later, Ms. Parks." I wave as I retreat to the door.

"Call me Grace. I'm not your teacher anymore." She chuckles.

At the end of the day, I quickly rush to the shop class around the back of the school to see Foster.

Loud rock music blares through the speakers when I near the bay doors. Guys are covered in oil and grease while they tinker under the hoods of cars.

I spot Foster's leather boots as he lays underneath a black charger. He's on a rolling mat, and I place the point of my heel between his legs and move him a few inches. "What the fuck!" he yells, and I peek down to meet his grease-coated face. "Oh, hey baby!"

A few whistles sound from around the garage when he zips out from under the car and wraps me into a hug, covering my white crop top in a ridiculous amount of grime. "Foster!" I playfully slap him, but my palm lingers on his bare arm. The heat from the Miami summer has made his tan skin glisten with sweat; he makes grease look good.

"This is my way of marking you." He sends me a crooked grin, planting a kiss on my cheek that I'm sure has left a stain.

But I love it.

"How was your day?" Foster asks, taking a rag to wipe his hands while he leans against the car.

I shrug. "It was good. I'm just excited for my last practice to be over."

He stands tall, towering over me as usual. "It'll be fun. Just enjoy the last time you'll have to do it. And then tomorrow after your game, we'll celebrate."

I lower my voice, trying to ignore the eavesdropping mechanics that have quieted down since we began to talk. "What do you have in mind?" I tease.

"Well, I was thinking tonight we could—"

"No can do! She's busy tonight." Another pair of heels tap against the concrete, rushing towards Foster to dare him to stop her. Kate puts her elbow on my shoulder. She's so freaking tall.

"Busy with what?" Foster smirks, crossing his arms. I love the playfulness between him and my best friend when they fight over me. It's adorable.

Kate looks me up and down, giving my dirty appearance a once-over. "Well, after her much-needed shower, we're going to binge horror movies and eat our weight in Mongolian beef." She touches the faded lock of hair. "Red?" she asks, looking confused.

Me and Foster share a look, remembering the fun, passionate night we shared. "It was supposed to be pink." I giggle.

"I like it." Kate says with a grin.

"I'm so excited about our sleepover!" I nearly squeal. I need this. But I also know that I'm going to come clean about everything to her. Tonight.

Ryder walks over, and I know Kate saw him when she walked in. She's being shy around him for some reason, which means she really ... *really* likes him. "Hey, beautiful." he greets her. I watch as a blush raises over her fair skin, making her red freckles more pronounced.

"Hey, Ryder." The two of them look at each other for a beat, and seeing that look in her eyes makes me smile. She gets on her tiptoes to kiss him, which should tell you something about the crew; they're all freakishly tall. Whenever I'm near them, I feel protected.

"Y'all coming over tonight?" Ryder's southern draw mimics his calm demeanor.

"Girls sleepover," Foster answers for us, and I hear Kate make a small sound at his response.

"Call you later?" I suggest, looking up into his deep, dark eyes.

Foster grips my chin with his fingers and pulls me in for a long, passionate kiss before Kate pulls me away. "You two ladies have fun." he tells us, his eyes following my every move.

When we walk away, Kate and I can hear the chatter of grown men teasing both Ryder and Foster, and it makes us giggle.

"Do you have to go to practice? I mean, tomorrow is your last game, and you already know the routine."

I contemplate this for a moment. "I don't want to, but I need to, right?"

She shakes her head. "It's up to you. What did your coach say?"

"Just to be there for Saturday's game."

She skips a little. "Then you're all set! Let's start our sleepover early!"

With a fresh shower and the grease scrubbed from my face, I sit beside Kate with an entire gallon of strawberry ice cream to myself. "Did you know this is the first Friday night during a school year that I haven't been to a practice?"

"Yes, which is why you missed so much fun shit with me!" She giggles, bumping her shoulder into mine. "What'll it be? Horror or thriller?"

"Aren't they the same?" I ponder out loud.

Kate scoffs, grinning. "I guess so."

"I needed this!" She moans into her gallon of Chocolate Bunny Tracks.

"Yes! Girls night!" I giggle, using one hand to whack her with a pillow.

A knock sounds on the door, and she rushes to turn the knob.

Brett walks in with a few plastic bags and a tray filled with coffee mugs. "Brett!" I exclaim, setting down my dessert to run up and hug him, nearly knocking everything out of his hands. "I didn't know you were coming."

Kate looks nervous, pushing her feet together. "I was scared if you knew he was coming you wouldn't come."

"Why would you think that?" I ask, but sadly, I already know.

"Because of your controlling ass boyfriend." Brett answers with a raised brow.

"I'm sorry about Foster," I murmur.

"Don't apologize for Ghost, Skyler." Brett's nostrils flare. "He is who he is, and he'll never change."

"I know. He can just be a little protective," I reply quietly, making my way to sit back on the bed.

Brett hands me a warm latte. "A little protective?" He laughs. "I didn't want you getting caught up in his bullshit. Trust me, he's no good."

I look to Kate, about to go on the defense. She throws her hands up. "I like him. I think he's a dick for punching Brett, but the reason why was a bit confusing."

An awkward silence settles over the room, and they both look at me. "Oh! Is that Mongolian beef?" I squeal, leaning over to peek into the bag and ignoring their worried stares. They ask because they care and because I've been radio silent towards both of them for much too long.

"Quit deflecting," Brett snaps. His all-American smile is gone, now replaced with the taut line of his lips.

"As you said, he's protective."

Brett rolls his eyes. "Yeah, well, he's going to have

to get over that. You're my best friend, and I've known you way longer than he has."

"Chill!" Kate yells out. "She's my best friend."

We pile onto Kate's bed, me in the middle and my two best friends on either side. We're squished onto the small twin mattress, but I'm comfortable, at ease, and at peace ... besides the secret that I'm keeping from them.

With our respective tubs of ice cream, blankets, and Chinese food, we hit play on the movie.

My phone chimes, and when I see the name a rush of frenzied butterflies takes over. It's him.

Foster: 'What's up, beautiful?'
Me: 'Hanging out with Kate and Brett.'
Foster: 'Oh.'
Me: 'What's wrong?'
Foster: 'Nothing, I just thought you were having a girls' night.'
Me: 'You can trust me.'
Foster: 'Yeah, baby. I know I can trust you ...'

Brett breaks the silence in the room. "I'm just wondering why he thought I would hit you." He's staring at his hands, and I set my phone aside.

I'm going to talk to them. I am. But I just wanted a normal moment before it's out there forever. "Brett—"

"What's been going on with you lately?" he cuts me off, nervously drumming his thumb along his knee cap.

I bite my lip and open my mouth to say something, but I need to do this action three times before the words drip from my lips. "There are things you don't know." I whisper, and they both lean in to hear me better.

"Whatever it is, we're here for you." Brett provides a comforting hand on my shoulder, and Kate follows.

"Seriously, Sky. You know you can come to us," she assures me.

And I can. I always knew I could, but I didn't want to be a burden. But now I'm free, and I can share the weight of my crushing world between them.

"I'll start," Brett says, running a hand through his bleach blond hair. "Why are you letting him keep you from us?"

"He's not keeping me from you." I reply uneasily.

"Then what is?" he asks, pausing the cheesy horror flick.

"Me," I breathe. "I didn't want to tell anyone the truth. I didn't want either of you to feel guilty." A single tear trickles down my face. The two of them move from their backs resting on the headboard to being at the bottom, sitting crossed legged and facing me.

"What truth?" he pleads with me for answers that I don't know how to say. I've kept them hidden for so long, buried underneath long sleeve shirts and concealer.

"My dad ..." It's now or never. "He hurt me."

"Skyler," Kate whispers as she places her hand on my leg. Brett follows suit with his hand on my other leg. And there they are. Grounding me from falling. "Are you injured?" she asks.

"Healing," I reply with a nervous smile.

Brett pinches the bridge of his nose. "So, that's why Foster hit me. He thought it was me when it was your dad." He snarls at my father's name, the muscles in his jawline tightening.

"Yeah,"

"Has this been a new thing?" His words are hesitant, as if he's scared to know the answer.

I shake my head. "Years," I reply, hearing an audible gasp escape from their lips simultaneously. It's the only thing you can hear in this quiet room. "I've been suffering for a long time."

"Why didn't you tell us?" Kate demands, her voice cracking from obvious heartbreak. For me.

I was trying to protect you. "It's hard to explain. I would try to rationalize it." I look to the ceiling to try and stop the flow of tears. I'm so fucking sick of crying over my parents.

"Does this have anything to do with quitting cheer?" Brett asks.

I nod, and the tears flow freely. They sweep down my cheeks and onto both of my friends when they lean forward to wrap me in their arms. The emotional release of having them know is freeing and exhilarating and heartbreaking all at the same time. They don't let me go until my tears are gone.

Brett whispers into my hair, "Don't shut me out again, no matter what it is. I'm here."

Kate brushes the palm of her hand along my hair, adding, "Ditto."

He hands me a tissue. "I'm sorry I didn't know."

"Me too." she agrees.

"That was the point—a perfect home from the

outside. A nightmare inside. You were never supposed to know." I assure them.

Brett lowers his head. "Yeah, but Ghost knew you for five minutes and figured it out."

"Right place, right time," I state. I knew this would be their worry; that they didn't stop the monster from hurting me.

But they didn't know there was a monster in the first place.

All they saw was all my parents let them see.

Just my dad, who hosted football games in our backyard and smiled while grilling hot dogs for us on summer nights.

Just my mom, who put band-aids on our knees when we scraped them on our bicycles but would turn her head at the sight of my bruises for the sake of luxury.

Just the princess in her castle, with her grand staircase and pearls.

With her long blonde hair that was always curled to perfection.

Screaming to escape, but only in her head.

When all along, one call to my best friends would have given me a different life.

THIRTY

"Make it stop!" I scream into the cramped, dark room. Terror rakes through my body when the shadowy figure grows closer.

I retreat from the danger only to find a wall that foils my escape plans. A monster stalks towards me, and there's no escape.

A stream of light enters the room, similar to morning sunlight bursting through the glass panes of my bedroom window when I was a little girl. At the center of the brightness stands a tall, handsome man.

His dark hair is a tousled mess, and his eyes are as deep as a midnight sky that can't possibly compete with the light that surrounds him. Tattoos wrap around him like vines, illuminated by the glittering gleam. The monster is beside me now with his hands raised in a dangerous position.

He steps forward, his hand slashing through the

darkness like a valiant sword.

I reach my hands towards him, and at that moment the dark, lurking shadow monster evaporates before my eyes, creating a cracking sound as the smoke trails on the ground.

"What the fuck, Ghost?" Brett yells out.

My eyes shoot open, and when I lean up, I can't tell if I'm still dreaming or not. The bedroom door is ripped from the hinges, lying on the floor.

And Foster is bolting right for me.

He dips down beside me while I lay in the bed with Kate who is tossing to wake. "What happened?" Foster stammers, his voice a rugged octave in the morning.

I look to my hands, to Kate's fiery hair, and to Brett on the other bed, trying to figure out what happened. "What do you mean?"

"I came by to bring you this." He holds up a couple of bags and two drinks which I'm surprised he didn't spill. "But I heard you screaming from the hallway."

I sit up, recalling my nightmare. "Bad dream," I shrug, trying to hide my mortified face from his so he doesn't get a whiff of my morning breath. All we did last night was watch movies and eat ridiculous amounts of food, but it was a much-needed sleepover.

"Did you bring me anything?" Kate mumbles, her sleepy eyes trying to stay open as she leans up.

Foster smiles, handing her a small bag. "Chicken minis and hash browns." He looks back to Brett, a devilish sneer taking over his features. "I didn't bring you anything."

Brett laughs bitterly, annoyed and huffing about the broken door. "I'm jumping in the shower." he states, gathering his duffel bag and stepping over the splintered wood on the floor.

I fall back onto my soft mattress. "Did you kick it down?" I ask, trying to wrap my head around everything that's just happened.

He shrugs, placing his warm, inked hand on my thigh. "I thought you were in trouble."

With a shake of my head, I open the box and begin to eat. "Just a really bad dream." I say simply.

"You know, I'm going to kill you for fucking up my door." Kate threatens while she chews her food. She smiles, adding, "But thank you for breakfast."

"I'll fix it." Foster promises, catching his breath. After a moment, he plants a kiss on my forehead while I'm enjoying the delicious crunch of hash browns.

"Did you ..." Kate begins, nervously biting her lip. "Did you see Ryder last night?"

"Yeah, what's up?" he asks.

She shrugs, taking a sip of her drink. "He didn't text me back all night."

Foster smiles, knowing she's worrying for nothing. I can tell by the way Ryder looks at her that he's all about her. "He's preparing."

"For what?" I wonder.

"The race tomorrow."

"Have you checked the weather?" I ask. "A tropical storm is coming in."

Foster shrugs, unfazed. "It'll be fine. Probably

won't even rain long."

I doubt that; it's definitely going to rain. But they can postpone, I'm sure.

Kate retreats to the restroom, and I follow her to brush my teeth. When I return alone to the room, Foster's measuring the door frame. "Do you just carry that around with you?" I inquire about the measuring tape.

"Had one in my car," he says with a grin, then his hard edges stiffen. "I didn't know guys could stay in the dorms."

"He's not a guy, he's Brett." I joke, but the sentiment seems to annoy him.

Foster leans his broad shoulder against the door frame and wraps his hands around my waist to bring me in for a minty, fresh kiss. "Does he have a dick?"

"Wouldn't know," I say with a smile. "Seriously, he's my best friend."

"A pain in my ass." he mutters.

I sigh. "I know you don't get along, but maybe you could try? I mean, what happened was an accident."

"Him running over my bike?" Foster sneers. "Hardly an accident. He was drinking and decided to drive." He grips me a little tighter, and it makes my body tingle. "I beat his ass for that, but if I ever catch you in a car with him when he's had even just one sip of alcohol, the past will repeat itself. Only way worse."

I shake my head. "So, it's not a jealousy thing?"

"What the fuck do I have to be jealous of?" he lies. I can tell when he's lying because his scarred brow tilts upward above his left eye.

I slide closer to him, trying to ease his mind. "I promise you don't have to worry about him; he's just a friend. You're my ..." I trail off, unsure what to say.

"Man," Foster responds swiftly, cutting off any room for negotiation. "I'm your man."

His words give me butterflies, as per usual, but is he worried to put a label on what we have? I don't have much time to respond before Kate comes back into the room, her red curls bouncing with her happy steps. "Need me to do your hair for tonight?"

Foster kisses my cheek. "It's your last big game. Are you excited?"

I look to Kate and nod with a grin. "Big curls, high pony!" I decide. "I'm excited, nervous, and nostalgic." I reply to Foster.

"You'll do great." He plants another tantalizing kiss on my lips. "I'm running to the hardware store. Don't worry; the door will be fixed by tonight." Before he walks out, he turns to Kate, "I'm stealing her tonight."

"No!"

"Yes. You had her last night." Foster teases.

"Ugh," she snaps with a pout. "I'll think about it."

I run a hand through my hair, adding, "I'm right here guys."

Foster leans down to give me a peck on my neck. "I'll see you tonight, sweetheart."

The whizzing electricity from the stadium lights bursting on sends a familiar shockwave through me.

The tropical, warm wind rustles my hair when we rush out onto the field, pom poms waving and fake smiles blaring. But my smile isn't fake; if this is my last night ever cheering, I'll do it happily.

Kate, Ryder, and Foster are in the stands. Kate has her hair curled and pulled into a high pony like mine, and our faces are painted to match the school colors.

The crowds adorned in Miami Hurricanes attire as they cheer on our boys. A blast of light shines on the green as the guys break through the barricade and march in long, running strides towards mid-field.

Brett, in honor of it being my last game—or in an effort to infuriate Foster—runs up and swoops me into his arms, taking me further into the field while the grass swarms with helmets. "You're going to piss him off." I state, holding down my skirt.

He sets me down and grips the metal guard to tip his helmet. "All in a day's work, darling." His boyish grin can't keep me mad, but as my eyes pan to Foster when I walk back to formation, Brett's all-American smile doesn't have that same effect on him.

When I'm looking at Foster and running through my first routine, my eyes pan to the right. I didn't ask them to move in that direction, but they gravitated into the stands. The third row up to be exact, and they land on her.

Perfectly curled hair, a light pink blush swept across her cheeks to match her rose colored lips. As our eyes connect, she looks away and steps off the metal seat to retreat into the crowd.

I shake it off, writing it off as hysterics from

261

everything I've been through recently. She wasn't here ... My mom wouldn't be here.

⁂

In a glorious night of staged dances, bright smiles, and hard work we end the night in a massive loss. But who cares? I had fun. Though I don't fit in with the girls and I haven't made any friends in the squad, I still had fun.

Foster rushes onto the field as soon as the game ends. Everyone else is tuckered out and sad they lost, but his crooked smile brightens the dark mood. "You looked so fucking good out there, babe." He picks me up and wraps my legs around him, planting a kiss on my neck and turning his body towards the field so Brett can see. I playfully slap his shoulder; he has nothing to worry about.

When I exit the field, I meet up with Kate, hoping she's okay with me staying with Foster tonight. But Ryder is next to her, twirling her hair and whispering something in her ear that makes her smile.

"I'm coming with you." she grins.

A drop of rain falls onto my forehead. "Can we get out of here before the dam breaks?" I look to my best friend. "See you soon!" I promise her.

Hand in hand, we head towards the parking lot. Foster's inked hand is tangled with mine. I look back to see Callum coming our way, but Foster seems to ignore him.

"Don't you want to talk to him?" I ask.

He looks up to the gray cloud's overhead, a heavy gust of wind swirls dangerously around us.

I'm worried this will turn into a hurricane by

tomorrow.

Foster says, "Nah, I want to get you home." He tickles my sides, making me rush forward and giggle. My skirt flies up, and I along with Foster attempt to hold it down.

When I peek my head back, Callum's climbing into Ryder's car. "The wind is freaking awful!" I shout over the howling gusts.

Foster nods, looking around the dark parking lot. "Let's get you home." he yells back. *Home.*

I slide into his passenger seat. I love the smell of his car. It smells like him. Grease, leather, and spices. The rain begins to patter down against the windshield, fogging up the car.

A moment of silence stretches between us, and his fingertips brush against my cheek. My chest rises heavily, matching the quick rhythm of my heart as the parking lot clears and we're left all alone.

He places a toothpick in between his teeth and studies me. I blush under his wandering gaze.

Trying to get some fresh air, I barely roll open the window. "Are you happy?" Foster finally asks, leaning his long frame towards me.

Slowly, I slide in between him and the steering wheel, straddling him. "Of course I am. I have you."

A sideways grin as crooked and delectable as anything I've ever seen adorns his face. "You're sweet, baby, but besides me ... besides my presence bringing you happiness ... are you happy?"

"Yes," I whisper without hesitating. It's all thanks

to him, though. "Why are you asking this?" I wonder, running my hand through his damp hair. For a moment, he looks like he's going to say something, but instead, he pulls me in for a kiss. "Foster," I breathe between his lips, going into a trance with his hands gripping me in every perfect place.

"Yes, Freckles?"

Deep breath. Don't pass out. "I... I lo—"

Foster cuts me off, flipping my body to rest against the long leather seat while he hovers above me. His chain tickles my nose, and his damp hair drips cool water against my flushed skin. "What was that?" he asks, dipping his head down to nibble my ear.

THIRTY-ONE

"I ..." shit. I can't think or breathe. His inked hands cup my breasts, then they move down to push my skirt up.

"I can't get enough of you in that skirt." Foster admits, grinning seductively.

Playfully, in a torturing tease, he grips my hips and bucks his hard length between my legs. I want to rip his pants off, to throw myself onto him and lose myself with him inside of me.

His hand dips between my legs, and his finger slides slowly across my clit. "Fuck me, Foster." I moan, biting my lip to keep from screaming into the night air as it seeps in through the barely cracked window.

"Gladly," he growls lowly. Before taking his pants off, he slides down and plants his lips along my exposed thighs, his tongue landing between my legs. I grip his hair in my fingers when he kisses me over my panties before pulling them off.

"Foster ..." I gasp out.

"Yes, Freckles?" He chuckles, his warm breath against my clit sending a pleasurable shiver through me.

I buck my hips towards him, not wanting this feeling to go away. "Don't ... stop." I plead.

His hands cover my breasts again, and he squeezes them tightly when I come undone, my thighs coming together, keeping his face between them. Heavy breathing overtakes me as he slides up. The rip of a condom wrapper and the exhilarating rush of him entering me, filling me ... It makes me feel like I'm floating on air.

He runs his thumb slowly along my bottom lip, and his tongue dives into my mouth mimicking the way his cock dips inside of me. Thunder shakes the car as lighting cracks around, the shining electricity showcasing Foster's sharp-as-a-knife jawline when he opens his full lips to let out a delicious groan.

My fingertips slide across the fogged window like Rose on the Titanic, heated and passionate.

I moan into the air, able to look up and see the clouded sky from my position. I never want this to end—I never want this night to end.

Our hands are tangled together when he moves faster, harder. It's a fiery passionate moment shared between only us and the falling rain as we both climax to the sound of ground-quaking thunder.

With him still nestled on top of me, I slide my index finger along his jawline. "I want to do this all day tomorrow since you won't be racing."

"I'm still racing." He pants, zipping his pants back up.

I point upward. "Have you seen the storm? This is just the beginning."

"Still racing," Foster shrugs, dipping his body down to kiss me.

I scurry from underneath him, pulling my skirt up. "During a tropical storm? A possible hurricane?" I ask, dumbfounded.

Frustrated and heated, he gets back into the driver's seat. "Look, it's just ... the bets are higher when there's more at stake."

"Like your fucking life?" I shout, my body jumping involuntarily.

"Freckles, listen—"

"What do you need the money for so badly that you'd risk your life?" I gasp. "Is that why you were asking if I was happy?"

When he doesn't respond, I furiously pull the door handle and step out into the blistering rain.

"Skyler!" he shouts, hopping out and running after me.

I whip around, pissed. "You are so stupid! You know that right? I mean holy shit, Foster ... It's dangerous! Does Ryder do this?"

He nods. "When he wants the big bets, yeah. We all do."

I can't help the sarcastic laugh that escapes me as raindrops pelt my arm. "You freak out about an imaginary situation where I could get in the car with Brett drinking, but you'll risk crashing during a tropical storm?" I don't let him reply. Instead, I allow the raging storm to fuel the anger inside of me. "Better yet, you of all people should not be riding in the rain. You know what took your parents from you, so why would you risk being taken from me?"

My words changed something inside of him, and his hard edges stiffen. A vein in his neck tells me I crossed a line. "Don't fucking bring my parents into this!" Foster yells, shaking his head to sweep the dripping tousled hair off his face.

"I knew you were reckless, but I didn't know you had a death wish." I throw my hands up. The delicate flutter of butterfly wings inside me has turned into a swarm of murder hornets trying to saw their way through my stomach lining. "If you do this, lose my number." I threaten.

"You can't be fucking serious, Skyler." He sneers, his voice booming over the cracking lightning and echoing roar of angry thunder.

"Deadly." I snap. I'd do anything to keep him safe. He kept me safe.

Why can't I do the same for him?

He rethinks his anger momentarily, and his sharp edges soften for a brief, fleeting moment. "What were you going to say in the car, Sky?" he asks, and I know exactly what he's referring to.

I clench my lips tight.

"I love you more, Skyler!" he hollers against the sound of thunder.

My heart skips a monstrous, glorious beat. "Then

love me enough to not do this."

He looks up at the sky, and his marble-like appearance being barely illuminated by the covered moon brings me a moment of peace in the storm. "I ... I can't," he finally admits.

I walk closer to Foster until I'm directly in front of his perfectly haunted, handsome face. "Then you don't love me." I sneer. My fear for his safety overrides the warm, gushy feelings inside of my chest.

His white t-shirt is soaked by the rain, and his hair is drenched. "Fuck this shit." His face goes stoic, his black irises matching the swirling storm brewing around and between us. "Fucking leave then, Skyler. Go!" he shouts.

I turn to walk away, and a groan of relief escapes me when I notice the taillights of a familiar Jeep. I rush over and knock on the plastic window with tears masked by the falling rain. "Brett," I cry, climbing into his seat. "I can't stand him!" I lie, knowing I'm just upset.

He leans back in his seat, and the roaring sound of Foster peeling out in the rain shatters my heart. I hope he's careful, but what do I care if he doesn't even care about himself? A lot. That's how much.

A strand of my hair is moved, and Brett wipes away the tears. A desperate laugh mixed with a cry shakes my chest. "He's so fucking stupid!" I shout.

Brett nods in agreement. "I warned you. And since when do you cuss?" He looks amused but concerned. "What happened? What do I need to do? Knock his face in?"

I laugh at the thought of them fighting. Clashing

like night and day, but it's happened before. "He's racing tomorrow." My eyes have cleared slightly; enough to take in Brett's features. He looks upset. "You okay?" I ask, and he laughs, wondering why the crying girl with dripping streaks of war paint is asking if he's okay.

"Is he seriously racing during a storm?" A look of worry crashes over his face. "You're not going, right? You don't ride with him in the rain. So help me God if he puts you in danger—" I cut him off with a shake of my head. Apparently, neither of these guys wants me to be in a vehicle with the other.

"Can we just go back to the dorm? I'm freezing." I shiver. He leans back and grabs his letterman from the backseat. It's warm and dry, and I hug it around my shaking body.

"Do you want me to stay the night?" he asks.

I shake my head, frowning. "No, I know you've got your party."

"Parties are after every game; I can miss one. Besides, Kate left with Ryder. You'll be alone." Brett counters.

"I'll be okay." I lie as he drives out of the lot.

The black war paint bleeds down my cheeks when I walk from Brett's Jeep to the dark, lonely dorm.

I don't want to fight anymore; I don't want to battle.

I'm done.

THIRTY-TWO

The halls of the dorm are quiet. There's no chatter of girls gossiping or the tapping of fingertips against keyboards, which would make for a relaxing midnight shower, if only I could relax.

I step in to let the warm water cascade across my shaking body. To let it wash away the running paint and tears. I run my fingers through my hair, hastily shampooing it to distract myself from the fact that Foster is being an idiot and risking his life racing tomorrow.

"I wish I had someone to talk to …" I mumble to myself. Kate's with Ryder, and I don't want to bother her. I feel like everything is always collapsing around me, within me … I don't want to bring that stress to anyone.

I touch my fading red streak, the fierce reminder that Foster is real and that I'm not imagining my feelings for him. The deep, real feelings I'm experiencing for the first time in my life.

I ring my hair with a towel while I walk back to the room with every intention of studying and catching up on some homework, but it isn't long before I collapse onto Kate's bed. Since we haven't made my side *my side* yet, I feel more comfortable here.

I've heard my phone buzzing for hours; I've tried my best to ignore it. But now, in the still silence of the night with only the thunder to bring me company, I need a distraction.

Mrs. Rita: 'Niña Dulce! (Sweet girl.) Why haven't you come to see me?'

My heart warms. I do need to go visit her. That's what I'm going to do right when I wake up tomorrow. Ignore the reality that Foster will be racing tomorrow during a tropical storm. Scrolling further ...

Foster: 'You really are ridiculous, Freckles.'

Foster: 'Did you get home okay?'

Is he seriously acting like nothing's wrong? I can't help the flutter in my chest.

Kate: 'What happened? Foster just came in heated. He broke like everything. Why aren't you with him?'

Kate: 'Talked to Brett. He told me he took you home.'

I don't reply. Kate knows I'm safe, and I'm sure she informed dickhead ... I mean Foster.

Before falling asleep, my phone dings one last time.

Foster: 'If you have another nightmare, just call me.'

I would allow the sunshine to wash over me as I head towards Mrs. Rita's apartment building, but it's ten in the morning and still dark out due to the storms rolling in.

Which reminds me—although I don't need any reminders—that Foster is going to be on a motorcycle in this shit.

And while I'm pissed at him, he's still consuming my every thought. I can't help but plug my phone into the AUX to pull up his playlist. I'm so happy Kate let me borrow her mom's car again. I really need to get some sort of income.

I strum my fingers to the rhythmic beat as I drive down the street, and my eyes wander around the area. They land on a building with a familiar name: Grace Studios.

I laugh to myself, imagining how it would look if I joined. Mom would get a kick out of that. Just what she wished for. Though her dream for me was cheer, I'm simply going to say any form of dance is something I want to stay far, far away from. Just out of spite.

The GPS alerts me to turn right. A small stream of rain patters against the windshield, mocking me. Pushing the shifter into park, I take in a deep breath. Only, it isn't a full one. The sting of panic brings my anxiety back in full force.

A quick, sharp knock sounds against my window, making me jump. "Skyler!" Mrs. Rita sings, opening my door for me.

I can't help but smile. I've missed her so much.

The parking lot is swarming with children as they run in circles to catch little drops of rain on their tongues. A few of them stay glued to Rita's hip.

I wrap my arms around her when I get out of the car, "I missed you so much!" I nearly cry into her arms.

She looks up at the graying sky, saying, "Come on. Let's get inside before it starts raining more."

I can't help but notice the four little ones who are trailing behind us like ducklings while we walk through the doorway. Rita's apartment floor is adorned with toys, blankets, and books. "Are these your grandchildren?" I wonder, looking around at the four zooming children.

"No, dear. I opened up a small daycare to keep myself busy while Mario is at work," she replies with a grin. Mario, her husband of forty years, owns a small business near her home.

She guides me to a loveseat, and when I sit, my mind rolls back to all the times Mrs. Rita helped me at home and how much more unbearable that glass castle would have been without her guidance. "How did my parents take it when you left?" I wonder.

Her shoulders move up and down as she laughs to herself. "I'm not sure. I just never came back."

I can't help the snort that escapes me. She gets up, returning with two mugs of steaming hot coffee. Her playful, rosy cheeks don't match the serious look on her face.

"How has it been for you?"

I shrug. "I never went back either."

"Good for you," she says with a nod. "I saw your

new car, so at least they left you something."

I take a long sip of the hot coffee. "It's Kate's mom's car. They cut me off."

"I'm sorry, dear." She frowns. A little girl with curly brown hair climbs onto her lap.

"It's better this way," I tell her. "I'll get a job soon and save up for my own car. At least my school is paid for."

Her eyes widen. "Well, I could always use your help here! You can earn a little extra cash and help me manage these rugrats." She tickles the girl on her lap, making her giggle.

I look around the room seeing two girls and two boys. "That actually sounds really nice, Mrs. Rita. Thank you!" That would really be perfect. I can see Mrs. Rita and earn some extra cash while still attending my classes.

Mrs. Rita's face lights up. "Let's get you acquainted then! The red-headed boy, there." She gestures to the one reading, his face crammed between the open pages of his book. "That's Bobby." She then points to a little girl with long blonde hair, saying, "That's Lucia. She's always sleeping. The other boy, Alejandro." She lowers her voice. "He's the troublemaker." This makes the girl in her lap giggle.

"And who might you be?" I ask.

"Sophie," she replies quietly, twirling her fingers through her hair.

"Say hello to Ms. Skyler, children!"

They all turn to wave, and Lucia picks up her head and smiles with tired eyes. Mrs. Rita watches me for a moment. "It's no pressure, dear. You can come on random days to help, and you'll be paid in cash."

"Thank you." I reply with a grin.

Her eyes roam my body, and she gently lifts Sophie to set her on the floor with the other kids. "Are you hungry dear? I can whip up your favorite!" she offers, but I politely decline, not wanting to be a bother.

"Tea?" she insists.

"That would be lovely."

"Oh, goodness! We've sat here for hours!" Mrs. Rita laughs, looking at the time. "Get home, dear. You need to race the clouds before the storm rolls in." She pats my shoulder. "I love you."

I can't help but cringe at the irony of her words. "I love you too, Mrs. Rita."

She wraps me into a much needed, smothering hug. Her weathered palms grip my face, holding my gaze. "I'm so proud of you, Skyler. So proud." I nearly fall into tears from the beaming light that shines in her brown eyes, but I allow only one to fall, and she wipes it away.

With my fingers white-knuckled around the steering wheel, my mind tirelessly wonders how I'm going to sleep tonight with Foster out racing. Maybe I should go to make sure he'll be okay.

Maybe not. I can't just support this ridiculous stunt.

My tires roll to a stop in the parking lot of Grace

Studios. I pulled in without thinking, and I can't explain why I'm walking inside the front door. "Hello?" I call out, but there's no response. The lights are off, and only a few windows let the darkening sky seep in.

My hands trail along the clean, white walls as I tiptoe down a narrow, dimly lit hallway.

"Mrs. Parks?"

I go further until I step into a large room. It's empty besides the smooth, light hardwoods and floor-to-ceiling mirrors. A string of windows sits along the high side of the far wall, allowing for a sliver of light to seep in.

I walk up to one of the mirrors to study my reflection.

Perfection.
Sadness.
Pity.
Beauty.
Ugly.

Overwhelming emotions cause me to collapse within myself and onto the cold wooden floor. It may be dramatic, but I can't explain what it's like to see yourself from every angle in the mirrored room.

I try to regain my composure and turn my head; there's no escape. But it's endless, not claustrophobic.

You can see every demon looking back at you, every fear and consequence.

I could lose myself here.

I could dance.

My phone ... the bittersweet songs I've compiled from Foster's playlist.

It was always cheering that Mom wanted me to do, even though I wanted more, even though I wanted expression ... maybe this could be my thing.

But again, wouldn't this make her happy?

Stop, Skyler.

Flipping on a sweet song, I attempt to match the rhythm of dancers I've seen during nationals, where every form of dance came together for competition. I've learned dances for grand galas and for over-the-top parties. Dances 'every young lady should know,' as my mother would say.

But ballerinas are so graceful; the way they can pirouette with ease, how their bodies move like the rolling tide.

Calm, dangerous, and inviting.

I twirl my body, keeping my arms fluid yet stiff. I look to myself and through myself as I lose myself for countless minutes.

A string of dangling stars flicker above me, no ... the lights are on.

A clap sounds behind me, and Mrs. Parks walks into the middle of the room. "You've got wonderful structure," She leans against one of the mirrors while I catch my breath. "Give me a few months, and I'll help you find yourself."

"Find myself?" I ask, wondering if she could hear my thoughts through the dance or if I've lost my mind and was talking out loud to myself.

She nods, adding, "Yes, find your rhythm." She walks over to the bar and stretches her leg upward, gracefully pointing her toe out. "I can help you, Skyler."

"No one can." I reply quietly, unsure what I'm actually doing here.

Why I walked inside.

Why I feel like home in the never-ending walls of this mirrored room that makes me see myself in ways I've never imagined.

"*I* can't." I finally say, turning to walk away from it all.

She looks at me through her reflection, her back facing me. "Why?"

"My mom ... she wanted me to cheer, and this would just be ..." I stop talking, turning to walk away.

She nods, bending down to stretch. "Go on. You can talk to me about anything."

I wring my hands nervously. "She forced me into cheer. I can't be her porcelain doll of dreams anymore." I admit.

"What you were doing just now?" Mrs. Parks begins. "That wasn't cheer, darling. It was you. You wanted to be here. I can tell."

She paces a bit, her stride is different here in her studio. The way she walks like a swan, the simple way her footsteps seem effortless and difficult all at once.

I wrap my fingers around the metal door frame. Turning my head back towards Grace, I say, "When do I need to come back?"

THIRTY-THREE

I lie in bed beside Kate, nervously strumming my fingers against the comforter. "I'm so worried about him."

Kate nods, painting her pinky nail a faint blue hue. "I would be too."

I sit up slowly, turning my head to look at her. "Wait, so Ryder isn't racing?"

"No," she replies quietly while a constant stream of heavy rain on the roof drowns the room in a deafening sound.

My heart flutters. "So, Foster isn't?"

She looks out the rain-pelted window, avoiding my eyes. "No, he is."

I lay back down slowly, the weight of it all pressing against my ribs. "How did you get Ryder to not go?" A crack of monstrous lightning follows my curiosity, sending chills down my spine.

"I just ... asked him." she replies, trying to hold back the relief in her worried, tilted smile.

"Oh," I wish it were that easy for me.

Kate looks over at me hopefully. "So ... you like the ballet studio? I miss dancing with you." she asks. I told her about it earlier.

My heart bursts to life a little. Just a little. "Grace said to come back Tuesday. Do you want to go with me?"

"Absolutely!" she says in a sing-song voice.

The thought makes me smile, but it's going to be a long night full of worry.

"Kate?" I whisper, shaking her shoulder.

"Hm?" she mumbles, drooling from her open mouth, still out cold. I sneak out of the bed and grab the keys off the tray.

A heavy, constant gust of wind nearly tackles me when I climb into her mom's car, but the storms are settling down now. Only wind and a little residual rainfall are left in its wake. Foster was right; the tropical storm didn't turn into a hurricane. But still, it could have.

A pained sigh of relief escapes me as I pull into his driveway. The garage doors are open, and his bike is sitting inside.

There's a party, of course. It's two in the morning, but I couldn't sleep without knowing if he was okay. Especially since I have an excuse to swing by.

Music bumps as I walk in and bypass all of the partygoers, trying to silently slip through the crowd. My eyes scan for Foster, but he's not down here.

I tip-toe to his room, and I soon find my fingertips hovering above the knob of his closed door. Over the music that trickles down the hallway, I can't hear what he's doing on the other side. He may be asleep ... or he may not be.

Gathering my courage, I twist the handle and step in to find him sitting on his bed in gray sweatpants and no t-shirt. He's freshly showered with wet hair. Shit. He looks good.

"I knew you missed me." A devilishly handsome smirk adorns his face while he organizes the massive amount of cash scattered on his bed.

"Don't get too excited. I'm just getting my charger." I lie, walking around to the other side of the bed to rip it from the wall. Only his lamp is on, creating a golden hue along his tanned skin.

"So, that's why you didn't text me back?" he wonders aloud, tilting his hard-edged face towards me.

I shake my head. "No, I didn't text you back because I'm mad at you."

A chuckle escapes him. It's small and deep, and it sends warm, fuzzy feelings down my spine. I love that sound, the sweet sound of his laughter. "Okay, so you drove here at ..." His eyes pan to the clock on the nightstand. "Two in the morning to get a charger for a phone that isn't dead?"

I cross my arms. "Yes."

"And you couldn't have used Kate's charger?" Foster asks with a boyish, cocky grin. He knows we have the same phone.

I roll my eyes, trying not to crack a smile. No matter how adorable he may be, I can't live in constant fear that he's going to die.

My fingers linger against the wall slowly while I make my way back out. When Foster stands, the piles of money slide off of his comforter. "Would you believe me if I told you the money is for something good?"

I bite my lip nervously, shaking my head. "I just don't get it. It's not worth your life."

He shrugs, saying, "You'll either have to take me how I am or walk out of my life, Skyler. I can't do the ultimatums." He crosses his arms, but the look of fear on his face tells me he doesn't mean what he says.

His words make me freeze in place. That's what my parents have always done to me. "I'm not trying to control you. All I'm trying to do is keep you safe."

Foster walks closer to me, towering over my small frame and looking down through thick, dark lashes. "I know that, but you can't have a tantrum when I tell you no."

I slide against the wall to get away from his magnetic gaze. "I want to enjoy life with you, not worry about your every move."

"Look," He climbs back onto the bed and crosses his legs, gripping a large stack of bills in his inked hands. "We can enjoy life with this. I made enough to get you a car tonight. It won't be fancy or anything, but it will be yours, Sky. And if you want, you can have mine, and I'll get something else."

This sweet, stupid, thoughtful man almost brings me to my knees. I climb onto the bed and cup his face. "Foster, did you race to get me a freaking car?"

He looks away, his midnight eyes trailing to the impossibly dark sky outside the window. "Just let me take care of you."

"None of that matters to me." I shove more cash onto the hardwood floor. "I just want you safe. That's what's important to me."

His hands wrap around my waist, fervently and possessively. "You're used to so much more, though ... and I have so little."

I can't believe he's saying this. "Look at me," I plead. "Don't do this anymore. If I would have known this is why you wanted to race during a storm ... Just don't do this again."

"I have to."

"Please," I whine, hating myself for begging him, but I have to keep him safe. I don't have many people left.

"I promise you it's for the best. I need this money."

"But not for me." I repeat, making sure he knows this is not what I want.

"For me," Foster admits. "I need to create a life for myself. It's not so easy being from where I'm from. There are no advantages, so I take what I can. I do what I can."

"You're wrong." I tell him.

"What do you mean?"

I shake my head, sliding my hand to cup his hard bicep. "I mean ... you're talented, you are getting a degree and you are going to make something of yourself."

"There's more to it," he says, sighing.

An idea pops into my tired head. "Why not pick up a gig, like singing at a coffee shop or bar?"

"No way," He laughs. "That shit wouldn't earn me this type of money. Just trust me, okay? There's more to it."

"Just promise me you won't do this for my sake, please. I'm set now with money." I reply.

Curiously, he looks into my eyes. "You didn't ... go back? Right?"

A pained laugh escapes me. "To my parents? No way! I'm going to work with Mrs. Rita sometimes. It won't be enough yet for a car, but it's enough for everything else I need. Trust me; Kate's parents are going to get her whatever car she wants soon, and we can share. We always have."

Foster nods, laying his back onto the bed.

I gently lay beside him. "Why are the guys okay with this?"

The moonlight casts a glittering stream in front of us, and as Foster lifts his hands to explain, shadows dance along the ceiling. "We vote as a family. Depending on the severity of the storms, we talk. But as long as it's unanimous, we don't have to discuss it too much."

"So, it's a crew thing?"

Foster nods.

"So, Envy got to make decisions?" I wonder.

"Yes ..." He draws the word out.

"I want to be a part of your crew," I state.

He sends me a weird look. "You can't join just for

the sake of telling me no, Freckles."

"Scouts honor," I retort with a grin. "I'm not trying to control you, and I want to support you, but I also need to be able to have a say if we're going to be together. We're adults, Foster. This isn't some bullshit high school relationship. I'm serious about you. More serious than I've ever been about anything. And the thought of something happening to you? I can't ... I can't imagine it."

I take in a deep breath, trying to gather my thoughts.

"I know that's a lot to take in, and I'm sorry my feelings are happening so quickly," I ramble. "I would just rather tell you how I feel and tell the truth rather than hold myself back. If you want to slow do—"

I can't finish my sentence. His hands are cupping my cheeks firmly, his eyes drinking me in.

"Don't apologize for how you feel. Feel everything, Skyler. Breathe it all in. You don't have to hold back with me. Ever. I don't give a fuck if anyone thinks we're moving too quickly. We're different, you and I." Foster plants a kiss on my lips. "You mean a hell of a lot to me."

My heart happily matches the thundering outside as butterflies dance inside me, and I nearly squeal from his sweet, poetic words. "I'm so thankful for you." I tell him.

He flashes a smile that could break any girl's heart, and I hope that smile doesn't break mine. "You're sure about this?" he asks, gesturing around the room and pointing downstairs to the sound of roaring guys partying.

I nod. "Definitely."

His fingertips graze my chin. "Once you're in, you're in. The only way out is death."

"Holy shit," I gasp. "Seriously?"

Foster's shoulders shake as he laughs. "No, you'll just have an extra family." His expression grows more serious, and he adds, "You can't join just for the sole fact of opposing every single storm race, though."

"Okay. But like I said, I just want to be heard."

He agrees with a nod.

The room goes silent, with me laying on my back staring up at the shadow-flaked ceiling and him lying on his side admiring me. "If you're going to race during a storm, I'm going to go and make sure I get struck by lightning at the finish line." I tease.

"Mm, Barbeque." Foster teases.

"Ew! You're impossible." A strained breath escapes my lips. "Just be careful," I groan, not sure why I'm supporting this. But I support whatever he wants. Whatever makes him happy in this life.

His hand tangles in mine while his eyes sweep over me.

"So, is that it? Am I in?" I ask, raising a brow.

He slides the rest of the money on the floor, turning off the bedside lamp. "Not even close. Let's go to bed, okay?" Foster suggests, pulling me into his arms. My anxious muscles turn to jelly the moment he touches me.

I need to get back to the dorm, but maybe I'll just lay here until he falls asleep.

He holds me from behind, dipping his head down to whisper in my ear, "How was your last practice? We never got to talk about it since you were pissed at me."

"I skipped it."

"Rebel." He replies.

"But I may be doing something else." I turn to face him, thankful for the sliver of moonlight that illuminates his face.

"Do you still hate me?" he asks, his puppy dog eyes making my heart skip a beat.

I roll my eyes. "I never hated you."

Our hands touch, twining together naturally. "So, what are you doing today?"

I laugh at how he used 'today' at two in the morning. "Well, after I get some sleep and go to class, me and Kate are redecorating my side of the dorm."

"You missed the email. There's wind damage to the north side of school. Classes are done until Wednesday."

"Oh," Nice.

"Hm," Foster gently runs his fingers through my hair. "Would you maybe want to go on a date with me after you and Kate redecorate? I'll make everything up to you."

"Maybe," I tease.

THIRTY-FOUR

The summer sun has warmed Miami all morning, leaving behind no trace that it even rained. Apart from the fallen palm branches and debris that lie on the road.

A call comes through the car phone. It's Kate. "You better be happy Ryder let me know you were over there! You could have texted me, ass head!

"I wasn't going to stay, but we fell asleep. I'm sorry!" I groan.

"Well, get your ass back here. School's out, bitch!" she sings the words.

"I heard! Time to decorate!"

"So, what are you thinking?" Kate asks, holding her elbow with her other hand like she's admiring an art piece.

I stare at the space, remembering my old room.

Pink, pink, and more pink. "Let's do something different than my usual. Maybe creams, lace, and greenery?"

"I love that." She nods.

Hours later, with command hooks, vinyl wallpaper, and all things dorm friendly, the space has been transformed from a neon green and black hole into a calming, lively space.

We both fall back onto the cream comforter, throwing the soft, lacey throw blanket over us. "I'm so thankful your mom had all of this stuff." I look around at my favorite part, a hanging potted plant. "You swear she wasn't sad letting that go?" I point to it.

Kate chuckles. "Are you kidding? She has too many plants. You just helped the water bill."

I look at my best friend, smiling. "Thank you for today."

"Of course," She tosses a chunk of red hair out of her face. It's always everywhere. Wild and untamed, just like her. "So, movie night on your side of the room tonight?"

"Actually, Foster's taking me on a date."

A cheesy, too-wide grin takes over her face when she says, "Oh, fun! Where are you going?"

I shrug, acting nonchalant. But inside, I'm so nervous. "He won't tell me. He just said to wear something nice."

"Hm, let's get you ready for your date then!"

"Hair, perfect. Makeup, flawless." Kate sings.

"Now, for something to wear."

I thumb through my clothes. "I don't have anything fancy," A worried croak escapes me. I want tonight to go perfectly.

"I do!" Kate says quickly, running over to her dresser. "This! This will be perfect."

She holds the floor-length gown against me, a deep crimson shade that matches her hair. When I slip into the silky material, I notice a seductive slit that slices up the left side of the dress.

"Okay, Miss Legs." Kate chuckles, clapping at my transformation.

I run my hand along the glossy fabric. "You don't think it's too much?" I ask, but as I look at myself in the mirror, I don't feel like too much. I feel beautiful.

"Psh," She waves me off, picking out a sultry shade of red from her lipstick drawer. "You look perfect."

I swipe the romantic hue across my lips, loving the way it looks with my makeup. A swoosh of darkness surrounds my eyes, a subtle smoky look.

A knock sounds on the door, and I rush to open it. Foster looks ridiculously handsome with his hair slicked back. He's wearing dark jeans and a crisp white shirt with a fitted black blazer.

"Wow." I mouth, then bite my lip, taking him in.

His fingertips touch my chin, forcing me to look into his eyes. "Wow what? Have you seen yourself?" Foster's words make me blush. "Are you ready? I can't wait to show you off." He smirks, taking my hand in his to send me into a movie-like twirl in the tiny dorm.

"I'm ready," I say with a grin.

For the first time, he looks past me. "The room looks great, babe."

"Have her back by eleven, Mister!" Kate jokes.

Foster winks at her. "I'll have her in the backseat of the car at eleven."

"And that's our cue," I add with a laugh, bowing as I push Foster out the door. I swat his arm playfully while we head down the hall. "Where are we going?"

"I made reservations at The Canary Grille," he replies, taking my hand when we head towards the parking lot.

I nearly stop dead in my tracks. "Foster, it's like fifty dollars per plate. I don't have any money."

"I didn't ask if you had money. I asked if you wanted to go on a date."

"Okay," I smile, not wanting him to think I'm not appreciative. "I just feel bad because I'm broke."

We stop in front of a blue Corolla, and he walks me to the driver's side, leaning me against the door to steal a kiss. "Foster!" I look around. "This isn't your car."

He kisses my neck. "I know. It's yours." A crooked grin lays on his face as he hands me a set of keys. "You're driving us to dinner."

"Wha—" I nearly pass out. "I can't. This … this is too much." Internally, I'm screaming out of excitement, but guilt eats at me. "I told you not to buy me a car, Foster."

"I didn't."

I tilt my head, wondering what extravagant excuse

he has. "I don't understand."

"I promised you I wouldn't buy one, but we had this at the shop." He taps the hood. "And it needed a new motor. I bought you a motor, and the owner gave me the motor casing for free."

I snort. "Motor casing? You mean … he gave you the car for free?"

"Yeah, we're close. Anyways, congratulations on your new ride!"

"I'm going to pay you back," I promise, and I am. I was going to call Mrs. Rita about helping her with the kids, so this gives me more motivation to do so. Plus, it's near the studio where I'm sure I'll be spending plenty of time.

"No, you're not." Foster opens the passenger door. "Just say thank you, babe."

I lean on my tip toes to kiss him. "Thank you! Thank you! Thank you!" I squeal, feeling a massive sense of freedom at my feet when I crawl inside.

Foster makes his way to the passenger seat. He slides in and starts pointing at the dash. I drown out half the things he says; I'm just too excited.

"This is the nicest thing anyone's ever done for me." I cry.

"Freckles, don't ruin your pretty makeup." He gently wipes my cheek. "It's no Range Rover, but it's safe and will get you where you need to go."

My mind rolls back to the memory of how I obtained the Range Rover when I was sixteen. Dad didn't like my grades, and he took it out on my jaw. Typically, the bruises were never where anyone could see, but he bribed me to stay home for a month without being seen by giving me a Range Rover. I was young and naïve and wanted to fit in with the snotty girls at Crestview, so I obeyed. Mom doesn't even know about that; she was out of the country on a two-month long girls' trip.

"This is better." I tell him. "Way better."

THIRTY-FIVE

"Pull here." Foster gestures to an empty parking spot. "But the restaurant's the next block over?"

With a shrug, I turn the wheel and park my beautiful, amazing new car in the spot.

He walks over and opens my door, then pays at the meter. "I know, but the best part of the city at night is the walking."

Arm in arm, we cross the street, making our way past tall buildings and couples roaming the city. Couples like us. "I needed this so much," I tell him.

"I did too," He smiles, and that perfect grin nearly makes me trip over the uneven walkway. Foster straightens me up, as usual. "Careful, baby. Lift that dress. I want a better look at those heels."

I blush nervously. "They're a bit tall," I show him.

His teeth graze his lip, and he pulls me in for a hug, dipping down to whisper in my ear, "Those are going to look great when I have your legs lifted in the air tonight."

"Foster!" I playfully slap him. "Don't be so cocky," I tease. "I may just let you take me on a date, then straight home."

Playfully and sweetly, he squeezes my side. No bruises, no soreness. Just the delectable feeling of his inked hands on me. Safe and secure. Again, he leans into my ear as we stroll down the darkening city streets. "I'll bet you five hundred dollars that I'll have those red lips wrapped around my cock by midnight."

Everything he says shocks me every single time. I wish I had his confidence. "Oh, there's the restaurant!" I point to the lush ivy that hugs the brick building.

He chuckles. "You may change the subject, but you won't deny it."

"You're in rare form tonight." I smile as he opens the door for me.

As we wait for the hostess to seat us, his hand slinks around my side. "How could I not be? I nearly didn't take you to eat; I just wanted to take you." A low growl resides in his chest.

I bat my black lashes at him. "So, good choice on the dress?"

"Fucking excellent choice."

Foster pulls out my chair for me after we're escorted to our table, and I take a seat. I shouldn't be surprised by his kindness. The way his obsidian eyes flicker against the golden candlelight as his piercing gaze slices through me makes me feel like I'm the only girl in the world.

The table is set with a thick white tablecloth. In the center, a candle flame dances between us. Red roses in a crystal vase match my dress.

I notice a few people who gaze our way, their narrowed eyes directed at Foster a little too long. I want to rip off my heels and throw them, but I refrain. He doesn't seem to notice. Well, maybe he does, but his only concern is me.

We both roam over the menu, and I can tell Foster is confused on what to order. He looks uncomfortable as he mouths different dishes quietly. "What do you want?" he asks. "I want to order for you."

"Um, fish?" I suggest.

A waitress wearing a sleek black dress arrives at the table, greeting us thoughtfully. "What would you like this evening?"

Foster's eyes come up from the menu. "She will have the Pan-Seared Sea Bass with Miso butter, and I'll have the same." he states, working to keep his voice level. He closes the much too large menu, handing it back to the woman before she steps away.

Him ordering for me, although he was nervous, was adorable.

Small, sweet conversation flows between us. Stolen moments inside this much too fancy restaurant.

"So, tell me about this new thing you've got going for you?" Foster reaches his hand across the table to clamp around mine.

My fingers trail along the overly fancy wine glass filled with ice water. "Ballet," I reply with an excited smile.

"I can't wait to watch you." he tells me, his tone implying something more. Something we can't talk about in the quiet restaurant.

The mirrors at the studio felt like a new beginning for me, one endless and all-consuming. A graceful way for me to outrun my own fate. Not tied down to the life my parents so possessively laid out for me.

College for the status.

Cheer for family tradition.

Marriage to Warren for money.

A planned life. Signed, sealed, and delivered before I could even make my own way. What a sad life that would be when there's so much more. I believe in choosing my own destiny now. Out here in the world, my life could be anything I want it to be.

I dash my gaze across Foster's full lips, allowing myself to get lost in the moment and not in the past. It's absolutely his fault that I only have one thing on my mind right now, and it's not food.

"Have you done ballet before?" he asks.

A delicate laugh escapes my rose-tinted lips. "No, but I think it may be my new thing. My first practice is—"

"Your dinner is served," the waitress announces, and a man in a white chef's hat lays out a carefully plated dish in front of both of us. A puff of smoke leaks out from the fully intact fish head.

"Oh my God," I whisper, unable to look at Foster as his eyes twinkle with laughter. I snort, and it's over. His deep laugh fills the space. The chef's nose crinkles in disgust at our outburst. But how could we not?

When they step away, Foster uses his fork to pick up the face of the fish from my plate. "I didn't know they brought that part."

"Neither did I," I look back at the eyes, feeling a swirling sense of nausea creeping into my stomach.

He shrugs. "Maybe it tastes good?"

I'm growing courageous because he looks so sweet. "Yeah!" I agree, digging my fork in and trying not to hurl. Simultaneously, we both take a bite, followed by a swift journey to our napkins to spit it out.

Foster contorts his face. "This shit sucks."

"It really does," I laugh. "Do you want to go?" I suggest.

"Yeah, but I want you to eat something," He takes one last look at our plates before swiftly throwing the thick napkin over the glaring fish head. "Somewhere else."

"How about that burger place in your hometown?"

His eyes light up. After he throws a hundred-dollar bill on the table, he walks around to pull my chair out. "Jack's sounds like a perfect date,"

We can't help but laugh while we walk away from the table, a fun carefree moment as we dash away. Foster opens the thick wooden door to exit the restaurant, and a group of people sweep through, nearly knocking me over.

"What the fuck, man? I was opening th—" Foster takes an intimidating step forward, then he cuts himself off. His fist is as clenched as his sharp jawline. I follow his line of sight and notice who he's talking to …

My father.

THIRTY-SIX

My surprised eyes roam to the other familiar faces of the group behind him. Mom, an angry looking Warren—my supposed future husband if I would have followed my parents' wishes—and lastly, his parents.

My father mutters the word 'slut' just as Warren looks away from me. His parents are already turning their backs before we can make it away.

Against all of my will, my father's words make my face fall. I tilt my head downward, only to feel Foster's fingers curling under my chin to lift me up.

I look back over my shoulder once more as Foster protectively guides my body outside, my eyes keeping a magnetic hold on my mother's. But just like at the football game, she disappears from sight.

The city streets, dazzling with lights and booming with the sounds of laughter and conversation, can't distract me from the racing, sick feeling in my heart.

"I'm so sorry," I say quietly, my voice rasped.

Foster doesn't speak; he continues to guide me until we're down the street and away from them, the stupid restaurant, and the fish heads. Carefully, he pulls me in for a tight, sweet hug that thaws my soul the moment his long, sturdy arms wrap around me.

"Don't apologize. It's them, Skyler," He looks down at me, his eyes wandering around my face. "You don't have to apologize for them. They are nothing. *Nothing*. I don't want this to ruin your night, Sky. This night is about you."

I nod, taking in a few matched breathes with him to calm myself. I can't believe how worked up I got just from seeing them. That sense of control I've gained since I left them now feels like a complete and total lie.

"Let's go." I feign a smile, gripping his hand.

Foster leans down. "I would race you to the car, but you're in heels." Then, his hand slides around my side to tickle me, and when I let out a snort that bounces off the tall, brick walls surrounding us, I blush.

"So fucking cute," He laughs.

My hand tugs his towards the alley we came from, but he gently pulls me to keep walking straight. "We're taking the next block down to get to the car."

Walking hand in hand down the darkening street is romantic, and when we turn down the next road, all I can see are dangling lights sparkling from overhead, tied to the buildings and drooping down to create a canopy of lights with rows upon rows of flowers spread out along the brick walls.

"I forgot this was here!" I exclaim, covering my mouth with my hand.

Miami's flower market. Mom used to take me here when I was little so she could get fresh flowers for the house. I think about seeing her, and my heart hurts a little.

"I didn't know which ones were your favorite or else I would have gotten you some when I picked you up, so I figured this was the next best thing." Foster admits. I love this sweet side of him.

"Any flower you bring me would be my favorite." I tell him. The smell is heavenly as we walk past the tulips, daisies, and daffodils. My gaze lingers around the roses.

"Get any bouquet you want," he whispers in my ear. I trail my fingers along the silky, delicate rose petals.

"Can we …" I turn to him. "Can we take a picture right here, so I remember this moment?" I know it's cheesy, but we've never taken a picture together.

He pulls his phone and turns it towards us. Before he can press the button, a young woman with long brown hair jumps in front of us. "Want me to take it?" she offers with a happy smile.

"I'd love that!" A cheesy grin spreads over my face as I hand the woman his phone. I angle Foster beside me. She snaps a few and hands it back over.

There's one with Foster's arms around me, one with a kiss on the cheek, then one with a kiss on the lips. The backdrop is a trolley of roses and a rustic brick building lit up by twinkling lights.

My favorite photo is that sweet, simple moment

before he plants his lips on mine. Where I'm looking up at him and he's looking at me. I set the frozen memory as his background.

"I can get one of you guys!" I offer, gesturing back to the small crowd that's waiting on her.

"Aiden! Eliana, Pat, Rose!" she calls out, wrangling her kids and pulling her husband close. "Say cheese!" the woman sings, and while everyone else is looking at the camera, her husband is looking at her, smiling with adoration.

She grabs her phone and thanks us, but before turning away she says, "Get a dozen yellow. Trust me!" With that, she winks, walking off with her husband and children.

Following her advice, I decide on the yellow roses that matched her dress. Plucking a deep red rose that's nearly black, I hand it to Foster. "You deserve a flower too!" I tell him, laughing when he playfully rolls his eyes at me.

༺༻

"This is so much better." I chew on my delicious, greasy burger, taking a swig of my sweet chocolate milkshake to wash it down. I'm sitting on the trunk of my new car, and Foster's standing in front of me, eating his food.

He nods, wiping a fallen drop of ketchup from my chin. "Seriously, remind me next time to skip the fancy date, and we'll come here."

"Deal," I reply with a smile. "But I do appreciate

it."

I'm at his height while sitting on the trunk, so he leans forward to plant a kiss on my cheek. His warm hand lingers on my thigh, diving under the slit of my red dress.

"Your place?" I suggest, biting my lip seductively.

Foster's gaze roams from my eyes directly to the slit in my dress. "Absolutely."

THIRTY-SEVEN

The moment we pull into Foster's driveway and he helps me out, our lips are locked, and the air around us swarms with passion. I wrap my legs around him when he picks me up, not caring about my dress opening for him.

He fumbles with his keys, but the doors are already opened. Thank God.

Foster reaches the first step and stops in his tracks, glancing past me. "No. Fuck no." he hisses.

I turn my head to find Ryder and Callum looking serious, their arms crossed against their broad chests.

Foster carefully sets me down. "We'll be back in a minute," he tells them.

Ryder shakes his head, a sinister sneer on his face. "Rules are rules, Ghost."

"Give me five minutes with her."

In Callum's hand is a potato sack, and when he lifts

his arms everything goes black.

I scream, kicking and punching past the darkness. Foster's angry voice overtakes everything in the room. A quick, thump sounds, then another.

Foster lifts the bag from my face, holding it in his hand. "I'm so sorry, baby." He frowns, then his eyes turn to a standing Ryder before resting on Callum's body as he lays on the ground, knocked out. "Like I said, I just needed five minutes to prepare her."

"For what?" I ask.

He takes my shaking hands in his, kissing my fingertips.

Ryder next hands me a pair of jeans and a t-shirt. "Put this on."

"Here?" My voice trembles.

Foster's icy gaze cuts to him. "Turn around." he demands.

And they do, so I change quickly behind the banister while Foster protects my body from wandering eyes. But they all respectfully keep turned until he says I'm done.

"Do you trust me?" Foster asks, and I reply with a nod. "Okay, good. You wanted this, Freckles, so I promise you're not in danger. We're going to put you—"

"No, no, no." Callum peels himself from the ground, brandishing a bloody smile. "She can't bypass shit. Grab her, Ryder." He orders.

Foster gives me an apologetic look before throwing me over his shoulder. "I've got her."

And for some reason, I'm not scared. I think I

know what this is: initiation.

After walking outside, he sets me down next to his bike. Ryder gets on a different one than usual, one classic and loud with thick tires, and Callum slides on his red bike.

"Don't be scared, okay?" Foster soothes me with a calm tone, pulling out a black t-shirt from his bag. Carefully, he wraps it around my face, tying it at the back.

"What about the bag?" Ryder asks. I can't see anything, but I can tell it's him from his voice.

Foster places the helmet over me, fixing the blindfold. "No bag. This will do just fine."

"Why do I need anything over my eyes?" I question, trying not to chuckle at their very careful kidnapping scheme. He slinks his leather jacket over me.

Foster's presence disappears, and I hear the sound of his foot peg clipping in. He's on his bike. "I've got her." Ryder says, and moments later I'm being picked up and guided onto Foster's back seat.

"Hold on, okay?" Foster tells me. I wrap my arms around his waist, and my heart rate picks up from anticipation. His cool, earthy scent surrounds me, and I'm ready for anything. Riding without sight. This will be dangerous and interesting.

The bikes rev to life, and a rumbling current shoots through my body. We zip off before I can ask any more questions, and the feeling of not seeing but feeling everything is surreal. The wind, the vibrations of the bike, Foster's hand as it travels to my knee momentarily for comfort.

"This is ..." I shout, then grow momentarily

speechless.

"What?" he yells back. "Are you okay?"

I let out an excited breath. "This is amazing!"

Foster's shoulders shake from laughter as we go wherever it is we're going. I'm just along for the ride.

We eventually come to a stop.

"I hope you still think that in a minute." He says. I try to listen for sounds, but I hear nothing besides empty Miami streets. We're on a backroad somewhere. "Pick a number between one and twenty."

"Um, fifteen?" I decide.

The guys yell out, excited. "Fuck," Foster sighs.

"What? Did I do something wrong?"

"Hold on," he replies, gripping the throttle and pulling it back. The front tire lifts off the ground momentarily before we go flying down the road. I hold onto him for dear life, unable to lift my shield and move the shirt that's stolen my vision away.

Intense wind is all I can feel for what seems like a long time until we finally come to a stop. The bike exhaust is puffing out hot smoke; I can feel the hot air traveling near my legs.

"Did we break down?" I ask.

Guided off the bike, I remove my helmet and blindfold. "Congratulations, Blue. You survived." Callum cheers, getting off his own ride.

My feet feel a little wobbly, so Foster holds me steady. "You okay? Sorry about that. Just stupid rules."

"Rules you made up!" Ryder laughs, throwing a punch into Foster's arm and hitting his leather jacket. But

I'm wearing it?

My eyes pan down to the jacket which I notice now doesn't devour me. It's a perfect fit, and it's mine. "You got this for me?"

The guys crowd around us. "*We* got it for you." They all say together.

I pull it off to get a better look; it's all black with a few pointed black studs. No patches except one on the left arm that's blue, matching the accents on Foster's bike. It reads, "Ghost."

"I love it! I really like the patch." My face breaks out into a cheesy grin.

Foster cups my cheek. "I'll get a matching one on mine with your name."

I look around. "Where are the rest of the guys?" I ask, thinking about the large number of bikers at the parties.

Callum rolls his eyes. "Foster's request was that it was just us since you were familiar. Besides, we're the main men in the house, so we're all you need," He winks, and Foster rolls his eyes.

"I'm all you need." Foster tells me.

"Oh, chill out, Ghost. She's yours now. You know I can't touch her … again." Callum holds back a chortle.

"She's always been mine," Foster grits his teeth, cutting his sharp jaw to him. "Are you trying to get fucking knocked out again?" Quickly, they're on the ground. Not really fighting, just wrestling like brothers. Foster twists Callum's arm. "Tell her you're sorry."

"Sorry, Blue!"

"It's Skyler." Foster snaps. "Don't call her pet names."

They stand, a little out of breath and laughing. Callum walks over to me, casually slinking his elbow on my shoulder. For once, Foster doesn't look mad or worried.

"You know she needs a nickname. You don't have to go all caveman. She's family now. Untouchable, Ghost." He looks down to me. "I'm partial to Blue because of your eyes, but we can call you Freckles like he does."

"No. Fuck no." Foster waves his hands in the air, huffing out angrily. "Blue is just fine."

"So, what are we doing here?" I wonder, my gaze panning around the empty parking lot.

Foster pats the leather seat of his motorcycle. "Teaching you to ride, baby girl."

THIRTY-EIGHT

"Okay, that's it. Just ease off the clutch." Foster tells me.

I'm straddling his bike, the purring making my entire body shake from the sheer power of the motor. "Can't you just climb on?"

I groan when he shakes his head. "Trust me, you can do it."

"Is this even legal?" I ask, raising a curious brow.

Foster laughs, patting my helmet. "You're in a parking lot. We're not going on the street."

Callum walks up, putting his hand on the gas tank. "Just don't get whiskey throttle." he warns.

"What's that?"

Ryder grins. "It's when you turn the throttle and keep holding it even when you want it to stop."

"Why would I ever do that?"

They step back a little. "It happens. Just ease into it. We showed you the clutch system, and all you need to do is ride in a straight line, slowly braking when you stop." Foster's terrified, but there's an undeniable glimmer of excitement twinkling in his obsidian eyes.

I slowly let off the clutch, and the bike dies.

"See? I suck. I can't do this." Frustration takes over me. Everything I've tried before I usually master. But this? It's too dangerous to even learn.

"Breathe, Freckles." Foster reminds me. "You can do this,"

I nod, determined to try even if I'm scared.

I try again, and the bike dies. A cranking metal sound follows my failure. Their faces all cringe, including Foster who is being incredibly patient. "I'm sorry."

He crosses his inked arms over his chest. "Again."

This time, the third time, I ease off the clutch and roll forward. I only make it about five feet before I carefully push in the break, but you would think I just won a race with how proud they seem. Foster's at my side in an instant, helping to steady the bike because my feet don't touch the ground.

"Again," they encourage.

The boys disperse, going to different ends of the area. I make it to the end of the parking lot, realizing that going slow only makes me feel unsteady. Speeding up here and there allows for more momentum, thus less wobble. I turn, going left and then making a circle. Foster again grabs ahold of the bike once I stop.

"Okay, now put your right leg down so you can

kick out the peg on the left side." he orders with a victorious smile.

I plant my bright pink Vans shoe against the concrete, using the other foot to push out the rod of metal. "Are you sure that I'm not going tip it?"

He shakes his head, letting his hands hover over the handlebars. I'm glad he trusts me because I have no idea what I'm doing.

But it's so much fun.

They all wrap me into a big, tight hug with me still on the bike. "We're all here for you. Anything you need at any time is only a call away." Ryder tells me, and Callum nods.

The awkwardness from mine and Callum's kiss has worn off, thankfully. But Foster still watches him like a hawk.

"We've all got you. We're family." Foster whispers through the helmet.

When Callum slides on his bike and waves goodbye, Ryder gestures to me. "Alright," Ryder smiles, "I need to get back to Kate." He helps me off Foster's bike and climbs on himself.

"Why aren't we taking your bike home?" I ask, gesturing to Ryder as he rides away, leaving the classic, thick tired bike behind.

He slides on the seat, patting the back. "Because our date's not over."

⁓

Foster places his feet on the ground to steady us

when we pull up to our tree. I grab his muscled back to step off, but he twists his body to look at me. "We're going to go through the alcove and onto the sand, so just hold onto me."

A tinge of panic rises in my chest. "No way. How can we ride on the sand?" I question, my voice pitching slightly from my nerves.

"See the tires?" he says, nodding towards them. "This is like a street legal dirt bike. Totally safe, I promise."

One large circular headlight brightens the path, and I dip my head down to deflect creeping branches.

This will never get old, going through our alcove. Whether on foot or tire, the magical moment of seeing where the vines meet the sand and the sand meets the ocean will always make me have butterflies.

Foster doesn't stop. He doesn't waste time explaining anything either. We simply ride. When he dips the tire into the rising tide every so often, water splashes against us. I laugh, throwing my head back as Foster revs the throttle, making us jump up and down a little.

We're playing around, young and carefree. Like it should be.

I raise my hands, allowing the mist of saltwater to sprinkle over my body.
This is what freedom feels like.

Foster stops the bike and picks me up, placing my body in front of his and wrapping my legs around him with his boots embedded in the sand.
"I love you," he says softly.

THIRTY-NINE

Last night was magical and everything I could have ever wished for. Kate bumps into me as we walk down the parking lot. "So, you're in a gang now?"

I roll my eyes. "For the hundredth time, it's not a gang."

She looks at me, giggling. "So dangerous! My best friend's a bad ass. Look at this!" Kate exclaims, touching the leather jacket Foster and the guys gave to me last night. "And you know how to ride a motorcycle! How was that?"

I recall the parking lot we were in and the basic gist of things they taught me. I went in a straight line, I turned, and I nearly fell over. I also killed the bike a few times. "I wouldn't say I know how, but it was fun." A mischievous twinkle sparks in my eyes, mirroring the way Foster looked as he watched me last night.

Soft, classical music dances down the narrow hall

when we step into Grace Studios. It's coming from the mirrored room. Kate and I walk side by side, a little nervous but packed full of excitement.

"Girls!" Grace grins as we walk in, a little sweat coating her forehead. "You didn't have to show up so early."

I shrug, saying, "We're so far behind already, so we wanted to see if there's anything we could help with."

"Just stretch. You'll need it." She gestures for us to join her.

I walk over to the balance bar and pull my leg up, discovering I'm incredibly sore from riding yesterday. Who would have thought riding a motorcycle would make your legs this sore? But I loved it; the adrenaline rush was just what I needed.

Minutes later, four other girls walk in.

"Okay, ladies," Grace calls out. "We have two new girls in the group, Kate and Skyler!"

They wave, and smiling faces look between me and my best friend. They each come up and hug us.

A small girl with bleach blonde hair and a quiet voice says, "I'm Natalia, but everyone calls me Nat."

Another girl, one tall with thick black hair, rests her arm around my shoulder. "I'm Charlotte. It's nice to meet y'all!" Her thick southern drawl matches her cool demeanor.

"I'm Marie!" the next one says, a girl with honey brown hair who's curvy and beautiful.

The last girl steps forward. "and I'm Mackenzie, but everyone calls me Mac."

Charlotte snickers. "Like the truck."

Mac playfully slaps Charlotte, and they burst into a fit of giggles. Grace gathers us in the center of the room. "Today, we're running through the basics to get the girls acquainted.

"I don't want to hold you guys back," I protest.

Everyone smiles. "You're not holding us back at all," Marie shakes her head. "A break from the routine will be ah-mazing! Grace here is more like a drill instructor than a ballet teacher," she teases.

Holding my ballet slippers in my hands and totally clueless to anything we're doing, the girls crowd around me and Kate. They show us how to lace and warn us about the blood we'll see after practice.

―――

They weren't lying. My shoes are stiff and flat at the ends, and my toenails feel like they're going to break off after the hour of rehearsals. I've never been in so much pain.

But it was pain that I chose for myself and pain I worked for.

There are a million positions. Positions for your arms, hands, knees, and feet. Pretty much every limb needs to be accounted for and thought of.

"Perfect rehearsal, girls. And thank you for welcoming our new ladies, Kate and Skyler. For now, practice will consist of learning for you two, and you can be a part of the next program." she explains.

"Why can't they do this one?" Marie wonders, her

eyes pouting.

"Because it's in three weeks, and they just aren't ready." Grace frowns. Three weeks. School will be done soon, and I'll have ample time to practice.

"I'll train. I'll be ready." I promise, wanting this so badly.

She shakes her head. "These girls have all worked for months. It wouldn't be fair."

"I understand," I don't want to take anything away from them. Kate nervously wrings her hands, and I know she wants it too.

Every single girl in the room shakes their head. "It's fair! They can do it!"

"Yeah, I'll stay after and help." Marie, the girl with the honey brown hair, offers.

"And we can record the routine so y'all can watch it!" Charlotte sings.

A tear falls down my cheek, and I turn to smile at Kate. We've found our people.

With a sigh that contains pearly white teeth, Grace surrenders, handing us a roll of blue fabric that was tucked into a shelf along with a drawing of the style dress we'll need. "Here's our colors. The usual tailor is booked up, so if you can find a seamstress, we would love to have the whole team together for the performance."

I don't need to think for more than a second. "Mrs. Rita." I say, looking at Kate.

"Oh, and you'll both need to find a partner." Grace adds.

"We can be each other's!" Kate cheers.

The room burst into a fit of giggles. "No, you'll need a male partner."

Before we exit to the locker room Grace pulls us aside, "You two fit right in." she says with a grin, then she gives me a thoughtful look. "Thank you for coming."

"Thank you for having us!"

"One more thing. If you'd like to have a special dance with your partner at the end, it's freestyle. Anything you want. The program will follow as such: We will have our choreographed dance, which is around eight minutes. Then, we will break off for our solos. Wear whatever you want for that dance, and you can choose any dance style, song, and hairstyle. Okay?"

The thought of having the freedom to dance to whatever I want intrigues me. "I'd love that." I reply, the corners of my mouth turning up. I just hope Foster is prepared for what I'm going to ask him.

As I grab my bags from the locker room, I send a text to him.

Me: 'You're so handsome.'

His response is almost immediate.

Foster: 'You're so beautiful.'

I sit down on the bench, smiling and wondering how I'm going to talk him into this.

Me: 'I mean seriously. Like, you're the best person I've ever met.'

Foster: 'What do you want? Lol.'

Me: 'Are you busy? I want to come over.'

Foster: 'Never too busy for you. See you soon, baby girl.'

"So," I wring my hands, standing in Foster's room. "Do you know how to dance?"

"My grandma taught me a few moves," he admits, sliding in front of me and capturing my hand in his.

We dance for a moment, and I can imagine a small Foster dancing with his grandmother as a child. The thought warms my heart. "Were you two close?"

"Yeah," he says with a small smile, his mind lingering on a memory.

I worry for him, for the loss of family. "I wish I could have met her."

Foster stills for a moment. "You still can."

With a wide twirl, I come back to his marble chest with happiness in my eyes. "She's alive? I want to meet her!"

Shyly, he looks towards the door. "Maybe soon. She's busy a lot." he tells me. "So, you need my help practicing?"

I'm going to let him change the subject. Based on the look in his eyes, it seems like he wants to. "I actually need a dance partner." I say quietly, biting my lip.

"Oh," His eyes go wide. "I don't know if I'm good enough for all that. She taught me fifties dances, nothing fancy."

I plaster on a hopeful grin. "I have to learn the dance too, so we can do it together." I suggest, and he cringes a little. "Kate's going to ask Ryder." I assure him. "You won't be alone."

A laugh escapes his perfect lips. "That's not going to work. He can't dance at all."

I'm sure they'll figure it out. "So, will you? I really want this." I beg with a subtle pout of my lower lip.

"It'll make you happy?" Foster asks. I reply with a nod. "Will it be in front of a bunch of people?"

"A few," I lie. It's a simple lie, but a lie all the same. We're going to be performing at a fancy theatre downtown. If he doesn't feel comfortable after the first practice together, then no worries. I can ask Brett if need be.

His hand slides through his thick black hair. "Okay, I've got your back, but I'm not wearing fucking leggings or anything."

I'm not sure what the guys will be wearing. "I promise if they make you wear leggings, I'm out." I chuckle. "So, it's one dance with the group and an optional solo after. I figured if you wanted to, we could do that." An idea pops into my head, so I quickly add, "You could teach me one of the dances your grandma taught you!" He grows quiet, and I grow nervous. "But I'm so thankful for the one dance we're doing. A solo isn't necessary."

Foster's tattooed hand lands on the nape of my neck gently. "I would be honored if you would dance with me."

FORTY

Classes will be coming to a close soon, and by the way the teachers are being lax, you can tell. After a relaxing day at school—which I never thought I would say—me and Kate are headed out to Mrs. Rita's.

The Miami sun beats down heavily, allowing warm salty wind to flow through the open windows of my new Corolla. "I still can't believe he got you a car," Kate admires the interior, patting her hand on the glove compartment.

"I know. I told him not too. I still feel guilty about it." I admit.

She turns up the radio a little, chiding, "Just enjoy it; he's a car guy. This probably makes him happier than you know."

"We're here!" I sing, pulling into Rita's apartment building.

Kate jumps out when we stop. "I feel like it's been

years since I've seen her!"

I grip the roll of fabric and head to her door, knocking once before she rips it open with a huge smile on her face. "Girls! I'm so happy you called. Come in, come in!"

The usual children are floating around, Lucia is asleep, of course. Sophie runs up to hug my leg, hiding shyly from Kate.

She pulls on my pants and I bend down. "Your friend looks like Princess Merida," she whispers.

Kate, who hasn't spoken a word yet, leans down. In a terrible Irish accent, she loudly says, "Hello! It's so nice to meet you."

Sophie instantly releases my pants leg, traveling to Kate. "Are you ... are you ..." She takes in a deep breath. "Lucia! Merida is here!" she screams.

Lucia gets up, walking over and wiping her eyes. The boys pay us no mind; they're too busy working with their Legos to build a fortress around G.I. Joe. "You're beautiful!" Lucia sings in a sleepy tone.

"We need to go watch Brave," Sophie decides, trying to drag us towards the television. I notice she looks just as sleepy as Lucia.

I bend down. "Why don't you go lay down on the couch. Me and Merida need to get dresses made, so go enjoy the movie."

"Dresses for a ball?" Lucia asks, her eyes going wide.

Kate, in her ridiculous Irish accent sings, "Yes, a ball!"

Rita can't contain her laughter when we step away from the kids, ones who are now all occupied. "So, you need dresses made?"

"Yes," I sigh. "I'm sorry it's such short notice. Three weeks from now."

I hand her the blue, silky fabric and the drawing of the dress.

Mrs. Rita smiles wide. "Three weeks is plenty of time, girls. I'll get your measurements before you leave."

FORTY-ONE

The next day at practice, we've roped both Foster and Ryder into attending rehearsal with us.

We pull into the parking lot to find our guys standing by their motorcycles. Foster is wearing all black, a cigarette tucked between his tattooed fingers. He takes a long drag, blowing it out into the warm air before stomping the butt out under his boot.

He walks over, looking every bit as mysterious and dangerous as a bad boy from a novel. "Ready for this?" He gestures between him and Ryder.

I let out a light laugh, "You're going to do just fine, I promise."

He looks around the room. "So, what are we wearing?" Foster asks Grace, a hint of worry in his midnight eyes.

"Black suits, black shoes." A sigh of relief escapes him. He turns to me, leaning down so only I can hear him.

"Then I'd love to see you back in that red dress from our date."

I smile up at him. "That can be arranged." But I may go buy a louder dress, one with a little more frill so when he twirls me it shimmers under the stage light.

I've traded stadium lights for stage lights.

What is my life? I love it.

Once rehearsal starts, we stand to the side watching the rest of our group and mimicking their movements. I don't know what's funnier, Ryder stepping on Kate's toes or Foster nervously looking around to make sure he's getting the steps right.

"If you're not comfortable, it's okay, Foster. I promise." I tell him.

"I just want to get this right for you," he replies with a nervous ring to his typically cool tone.

"You're doing great! Even if you make me trip, I'll still be the happiest girl in the world. Are you sure you're okay?"

"Yeah," He stands straighter, nodding his head in Ryder's direction. "But I'm not sure how he's going to do. The man has two left feet." he whispers, but the room is small, and Ryder glares at him.

I blush a little bit. "Thank you for this."

"It's nothing I've ever done before, but I'm happy to be here with you."

"Fuck!" Ryder yells out, quickly apologizing to everyone who stopped dancing. "I'm sorry." He bows his head, "I can't do this. I can't dance."

Grace, walking like a swan, dances to him. "That's

okay. No worries! This isn't for everyone." Her eyes pan to Foster, and he gives her a thumbs up.

'I'm good.' he mouths.

"I'm sorry," Ryder tells Kate.

Grace places her hand on Ryder's shoulder. "Look, you can try longer if you want. I bet you could get it down. It's up to you."

"I'd rather her have a better chance with someone who can dance," he admits, looking at Kate who kisses his cheek.

"I'm just so happy you tried!" she says, beaming.

"I've got a cousin who can dance with you!" Charlotte offers.

Kate shakes her head. "No, it's okay. I'm fine. I can watch."

Ryder seems to deflate at her words more than Kate does. "What about your fancy friend ... the football guy?"

"Brett?" she asks, placing her hand under her chin. "Yeah, he knows how to dance. But will it bother you?"

He leans in close to her. "I'm not worried about some jock. You're my girl."

She blushes, swooning over his charm. "Thank you!" She squeals. "I'll call him!"

I turn to Foster and quietly tease, "You wouldn't let me dance with Brett."

His fingers wrap around my waist. "That's because the thought of someone else's hands on you makes me want to kill people. I'm doing this so I don't end up in prison." Foster jokes. I think.

FORTY-TWO

Class, practice, Bike Night, class, practice, Bike Night. Three weeks of this. It's been busy and exciting. Foster stayed with me in the dorm last night, I love when he stays over.

But tonight is the ballet recital, and I feel completely confident in myself to pull it off.

The fun break we've had in between all of our regular duties is Foster taking me for burgers on Friday nights and letting me ride his bike in the parking lot. I'm getting pretty good. Or I'm not, and he's been lying to me saying I've done a good job. Either way, the bonding has been fun.

Thankfully, Brett has nailed the dance with Kate.

Foster is doing great too, but he's insecure. He doesn't feel like he's got the moves down. His nerves are making him miss a few steps.

But my only worry right now is the open laptop

sitting in front of me which is loading up my final grades for the semester. Our last day of class was yesterday, and I'm not sure how I did with finals. I need to get this out of my head so I can focus on our dance. I still have to swing by Rita's tonight, and the dance is at seven, so I need to be there at five.

"You know not looking won't change the outcome, right?" Foster tells me, watering the flowing greenery above the bed.

Kate squeals, clapping her hands. "Yes! I passed."

"Ugh," I groan, not wanting to look. "But yay, Kate!"

Foster dips down, stealing the laptop to stop me from torturing myself. He clicks a button, and the color drains from his face. "You failed everything," he whispers in shock.

"What?" I jump up, ready to smash the computer against the wall. I peek at the screen and a blast of sweet relief travels through me as I see all A's and one B. I playfully slap Foster's chest. "You jerk!"

He shrugs. "See? Now that B doesn't look so bad," he teases. "Celebration burgers at Jack's?"

"Yes!" I glance over at Kate. "You and Ryder want to come?"

"No can do. We're practicing our solo dance in a little bit." she replies with a grin. Since he couldn't get the choreographed routine down, Ryder absolutely wanted to do a solo with her. Simple and no fluff. I can't wait to see them on the stage.

I think that's what I'm most excited for. The solo.

I picked the most perfect song for me and Foster, but I won't tell him what it is. He's taught me one of his grandma's favorite dances, and we've practiced without any music on the beach with his headlights illuminating the sand. It's been beautiful. With only the sounds of the tide and our feet moving the warm sand around as we twirled.

"I need to throw some makeup on before we go," I tell him.

He shakes his head. "No, you don't. You're perfect, and I'm starving."

The wind is picking up outside as we head to eat. Even in Foster's classic, sturdy car the blows attempt to move us along the parking lot.

"There's a storm coming," I say quietly, hoping with everything I won't be left on that stage alone tonight.

He parks at the restaurant. "I'm not going anywhere, I promise."

Hand in hand, we walk inside Jack's. The delicious scent of freshly made fries lingers in the air, making my stomach growl. "I'm *so* hungry." I admit with a laugh.

Walking to the counter, a flash of neon green blurs my vision. Envy.

Like she knows we're behind her, she whips her head around. "Hey, Ghost." She smiles at him, ignoring my existence. He treats her with the same respect, ignoring her.

"Order up!" the man behind the counter yells out. Envy turns to grab her food and places a French fry in her mouth, eying me up and down. Then, her eyes soften when she turns back to Foster. "I need to talk to you … alone."

"You can talk to me right here." He stands firm.

Envy tosses her hair. "Whatever, I'll just come by when she's not home." She winks, then walks away. *Home.*

A sick feeling rises in my stomach, "What was that about?"

"Nothing, she's just a bitch." He sneers.

"Does she go over there?" My stomach's not growling out of hunger anymore, but instead it's churning from anger. "Why did she say home?"

He barely shakes his head, adding quickly, "She's just trying to upset you. Don't worry about her."

We sit and eat, but a terrible feeling lays on my stomach the entire time. "Are we hanging out until the dance?" I wonder, throwing the remainder of my food in the trash.

He shakes his head. "I've got some things to do." He looks nervous as we step outside.

"Okay ..." I frown, walking with him to the parking lot. "Are you going to meet up with her?" I finally ask when I slide into the passenger seat to escape the howling wind.

"Envy?" Foster laughs. "No, babe."

"Promise?"

"Yes, I just have something I need to take care of."

The ride is quiet on the way back to the dorm. When we park, a sheet of rain falls against the windshield. "Are you going to race?" I wonder. My emotions are on hyperdrive.

"No, babe. Everything's fine. I'll call you later, okay? Need me to walk you up?" he asks, planting a kiss on my lips.

I shake my head. "Am I going to see you before the dance?"

"I'll meet you there. I have to get my suit from the tailor. You and Kate take her Mom's car tonight. It's bigger and safer." He gestures around the darkening sky.

"Sounds good," But something feels off. Wrong.

"I'll see you tonight, baby girl." Foster calls out from the car.

But something is definitely off. I can feel it as I wave goodbye.

FORTY-THREE

FOSTER POV

I had things that I needed to take care of, and I hated her face being so sad when I drove away.

Most of all, I hate lying to her.

I don't want to stress her out. Her big dance is tonight, and I fucking hate what I'm about to do, but it is what it is.

I pull out my phone and make the call. "Dude, I'm sorry, but are you busy? I need your help. You know I wouldn't be asking if I wasn't desperate."

Ten minutes later, Brett's Jeep pulls into Grace Studios beside me. I just need to get one last minute practice in, but I don't want Freckles to know about it.

Rushing past the rain, we head inside. "Alright, boys," Grace smiles at us both. "I'm heading home to get ready, so just lock up before you leave—and for God's sake, don't be late."

Brett looks confused. I called her earlier, but I haven't explained to him why he's here.

We both nod, and Grace waves goodbye. "I'll see you two in a bit!" she shouts. I'm so thankful for her presence in Skyler's life; she needed someone like her.

We step into the mirrored room that Skyler loves so much. I don't understand it, but I'll support her in whatever she needs. Never in a million years did I think I would be practicing for a fucking dance recital, but here I am.

Brett has his hands in his pockets, wearing that stupid grin he usually does, along with his letterman. "So, what do you need, Ghost?"

"I don't want to fuck up the dance. It looks like you know the shit pretty well, so teach me."

Brett crosses his arms, his eyes slightly rolling. "You called me out here, needing my help, but you have an attitude."

"Fuck this," I spit, turning to leave.

He groans, grabbing my arm. "Wait, dude. It's for Skyler. You don't have to go; I can dance with her. Ryder's okay enough for Kate." he states, his square chin showcasing annoyance.

Over my dead fucking body will he dance with my girl. It's fucks like him that I don't like. On their fucking high horses, rich and mighty. He's probably had dance lessons his entire life.

"Please," I attempt to not sneer so hard my face hurts. "Would you please help me? I know you hate me, and I wouldn't be asking for your help if I didn't need it. It's just, you're dancing with Kate, and no matter how much I fucking try I can't get the steps down. Just do it for her."

"For her," he repeats, standing in front of me and putting his hand out.

My phone rings. It's Callum. "Hold up," I tell Brett.

"Dude we don't have time for this shit."

I slide my finger to answer the call, "What's up?"

"Race tonight." Callum replies.

"No can do."

"You sure? It's twenty grand."

Shit. "What time?"

"Seven. That's when the eye will be closest. It's going to be a wild fucking race."

Hurricane coming. "Why is it so fucking early?"

"Just when the storm is falling in, but it'll be dark, so cops shouldn't see us too much."

Freckles's recital starts at seven. "Won't work."

"Twenty Grand, Ghost."

"I know." I hang up the phone before I do something stupid.

"What was that about?" Brett asks, his smirking grin nearly making me punch him in the face. He's waiting for me to fuck up with Skyler, I just know it.

"Let's just get this done." I sneer, annoyed that I'm even considering racing. I'm even more annoyed that I'm about to dance with the guy who I know wants my girl.

Twenty fucking grand, though.

BRETT POV

Why am I doing this to myself?

"Let's get started." I say with a tight smile.

Foster's hand intertwines with mine, and the breath nearly ceases to escape my lungs.

"Am I doing okay?" he asks, clearly uncomfortable with my movements.

"Your problem is leading. You have to take control of the steps. I know you're not a dancer, but the man takes the lead." I tell him.

"Trust me, she's used to letting me take the lead." An arrogant smirk rises on his face.

I internally cringe hearing him talk that way about Skyler. "Here, just follow me. I'll be what you need to be," I tell him, showing him the routine from the leads side.

And in twenty minutes, he's got the dance down perfectly. Of course he does.

"Thank you for doing this," he admits, flipping his dark hair to sit above his brow line.

I can't believe he called me tonight, but the words linger in my mind. *Desperate.* 'You know I wouldn't call you if I weren't desperate.'

The same moment that a bolt of powerful lightning cracks, Foster's phone rings again.

He takes another call, and this time, his face goes white. He sends me an apologetic look after hanging up.

"Don't you fucking dare do this to her." I threaten.

"I have ... I have to go."

"Foster!" I scream as he runs out of the room.

Leaving me to look at myself in the wall of mirrors wondering why in the fuck I'm so utterly in love with him.

I would say I came here for Sky, but I'd be lying, and I hate myself for that.

SKYLER POV

God, I hate that Foster's acting so weird. I hate it. Kate's going to meet me at the theatre and I'm trying to be careful as I battle the rain to pick up our dresses from Rita's apartment.

A confusing sigh of relief escapes me when I pass Grace Studios. Foster's car sits out front, and before my line of sight leaves the parking lot, Brett's Jeep pulls in behind him. Maybe he wanted to practice?

I knock on Rita's door with more confidence under my belt and more time to think. Knowing Foster, he was probably just worried about the dance and didn't want to admit it. Soon, I'll be dancing in his arms.

Nothing can ruin this night for us.

"Come in!" Mrs. Rita calls. I step inside and see our dresses laid out for us on the dining table.

"They're perfect!" I squeal.

She smiles as she walks in from the kitchen, "I'm so happy you like them, dear. I'm sorry I had to get them to you last minute. Things have been wild here."

"Is everything okay?" I ask, studying her glossy eyes.

She waves her hand. "It's okay, Skyler. Nothing for

you to worry about."

I'm so excited about the dance that my brain can barely register the sad look in her eyes. "Do you need anything?" I ask, my voice filling with concern.

"No, dear. Just head out. Enjoy your dance," A single tear rolls down her cheek.

I step closer to her, capturing her tear-stained face in my hands. "What's happening?" My first thoughts in times of distress are that my father did something.

The dam breaks, and tears flow down her face. "It's Sophie," she cries. "She's in the hospital."

A gasp escapes my lips. "What happened?"

"She's sick, Skyler."

Maybe the flu? "What can I do?"

"Nothing, sweet girl. Please go to your dance. It's in God's hands now." Rita looks to the ceiling, offering a pained smile. "She needs a heart transplant. We thought we'd have more time."

"Oh my God." I breathe. "Poor Sophie," My voice cracks.

"If you could, please place her box in my car for me while I go freshen up. I'd really appreciate it." She sniffles.

She dabs her eyes with a tissue, retreating into her room. Poor, sweet Sophie. I glance around the room and find a pink box with her name on in. Carefully, I pull out a small fuzzy brown bear that rests on top. It's well-loved with flattened fur and tattered fabric.

I hug it to my chest for a brief moment before extending my hand to place it back in the box, but I stop cold as my eyes travel to the bear's paw.

It can't be.

I clutch it against me, dropping everything but the matted bear and my keys as I race outside of the apartment.

FORTY-FOUR

On a terrifyingly dark evening, the eye of the storm would come crashing down on Miami, forcing the palm trees to sway, already broken hearts to break, and butterflies wings to stop flapping.

The young lover would remember everything from that terribly stormy night.

As they were driving alone, with storming clouds angrily rolling overhead, they swept through a familiar curvy road.

They remembered the way the wet road looked as another headlight swept through the opposite side.

How they were both going much too fast on the dark, shiny curve.

The crunching sound of twisting metal when the other person lost control of their motorcycle and how the scraping, sparking sound bled through their ears as they slammed on their breaks and threw the car into park.

The way their feet trekked quickly along the dark pavement following the long black line riddled with shredded motorcycle parts, a guttural scream escaping them when the bike stopped scraping and the body continued flying until it slammed into a tree. *Their tree.*

History repeating itself.

The way they raced to them, how they dived beside them.

There are millions of flashes of memories from that terrible, stormy night that will haunt their dreams forever.

The young lover will never forget running to the downed racer.

But most of all, for when the helmet was lifted, and a lock of silky blonde hair slipped out.

He knew the painful memory of her blood ridden hair would be etched into his memory forever. The way he couldn't find her faded red streak through all of the other never-ending red.

Along with the song that leaked through her headphones, *To Build a Home* by the Cinematic Orchestra. That must have been what they were going to dance to.

What they would have danced to if …

And as he carefully unzipped her jacket to check her delicate body for more blood, a familiar well-loved bear sat tucked neatly inside. *Sophie's bear.*

With his name etched on the foot.

'Love, your big bro Foster.'

How?

The already terrible night became much worse.

While waiting for Skyler at the theatre where they were going to dance, he received the call that Sophie had collapsed.

Foster knew that his little sisters' hourglass was running out, her life spilling out of the shattered glass in tiny grains of sand no matter how many treatments she went through.

She needed a transplant.

It was now or never and nothing was more important to Foster than his little sister. Until Skyler came into his life.

So, he planned to race and as he left the theatre to get his bike, he ignored Skyler's relentless phone calls, not wanting to hear the heartbreak in her voice when he told her he would need to race this storm.

He needed to race for Sophie, Freckles would have understood if he wasn't so stubborn.

He could have told Skyler, but he didn't want to admit his little sisters failing health to himself, much less anyone else.

Now, he would do anything to answer Skyler's relentless calls.

Money solves everything, and Foster couldn't sit by while Sophie's life withered into dust.

"Why would you do this?" He cried out with a quivering lip.

And as his world came crashing down on him, he knew why the love of his life was lying on the wet pavement clinging to life as he screamed for someone to help her.

She was racing to him, or for him.
For Sophie.
He wondered if he would ever find out which one it was.

EPILOGUE

"Bro, you've gotta get some rest," Brett told Foster, walking up beside him as Skyler lies on the hospital bed hooked to wires, tubes, and beeping machines.

"No I don't," he spat, wishing the world would quit telling him to walk out of the cold hospital room that contained everything he cared about.

Foster laid his hand along Skyler's arm, lightly touching her bruised body. He blamed himself for her scars, maybe if he hadn't been on the road that night she wouldn't have swerved and lost control. He hated to be the one to cause her pain when her young life had already been so filled with hurt.

"You've been here for a week, man." Brett attempted to curb Foster's resilience.

With every beep of the machine that monitored such precious life he would gasp for breath, wishing he could trade places, hoping he could be the one laying there. "I need to be here if they," he cursed himself for saying that word, "when they wake up."

Brett placed his hand on Foster's shoulder, wanting to comfort him. If only Foster had known how much it hurt when he jerked his body away, maybe he would have been more aware of his body language. "I know, but you don't have to Edward Cullen it staying awake, just go lay down and I'll come get you if they need you." Brett offered with glazed eyes.

Then, still at the hospital and in the same room as Sky, Foster walked over to Sophie's bed with the same worries.

"Take me, not them," he prayed, brushing Sophie's forehead. He did this back and forth every twenty minutes, not caring that Brett was seeing him in such a vulnerable state.

A racer unable to sit down, his instinct to dash back and forth between their beds until one of them showed signs of life.

But this isn't a race, and no one wins in a situation like this.

And so, they sat in the small fluorescent lit room listening to machines beep.

Brett watching Foster, and Foster observing Skyler and Sophie with no finish line in sight.

END OF BOOK ONE

Acknowledgments

My husband, you're the best thing that's ever happened to me.

⁂

Kristen, I don't think these books would be published if not for all of your endless help. Thank you for constantly being by my side and encouraging me when I begin to get in my head.

⁂

Neko, for always creating such beautiful artwork of my characters. You truly bring them to life! Along with my author photo, which I cherish so much! You can find her on Instagram at nekos_drawings

⁂

To my editor, Ashley Oliver. It's always a wonderful experience working with you!

⁂

To my family, I love y'all more than words.

⁂

To my readers, thank you for your never-ending support, you've made my dreams come true.

ALSO BY H.L. SWAN

AIDEN

EMILIA

EMILIA'S SWEET TREATS

GUARDED BY DEATH

HAVEN

Printed in Germany
by Amazon Distribution
GmbH, Leipzig